Acclaim for Francesca Marciano's

## *The End of Manners*

"A gem of a tale.... Under Marciano's pen, the current situation in Afghanistan comes vibrantly alive.... *The End of Manners* is one of those novels a reader never wants to finish reading, one that gets passed among friends."     —*The Roanoke Times*

"Marciano deftly portrays the gulf between cultures, the precariousness of life in war-ravaged Afghanistan, the fierceness of patriarchal culture and the isolation of tribal women.... [She] explores emotional nuances and moral choices that can in such extreme circumstances mean life and death. The inner landscape is as convincing as the lawless and unsympathetic countryside."
     —*Portsmouth Herald*

"*The End of Manners* weighs the relative powers of courage and fate.... Characters test limits of intention and will, discovering that people don't get to write their stories; they are all, finally, subjects ruled by fate."
     —*Women's Review of Books*

Francesca Marciano

## *The End of Manners*

Francesca Marciano is the author of two previous
novels and several screenplays, including *Don't
Tell*, which was nominated for an Academy Award
in the category of Best Foreign-Language Film.
She lives in Rome.

ALSO BY FRANCESCA MARCIANO

*Casa Rossa*
*Rules of the Wild*

# The End of Manners

# The End of Manners

*Francesca Marciano*

*Vintage Contemporaries*
VINTAGE BOOKS
A DIVISION OF RANDOM HOUSE, INC.
NEW YORK

FIRST VINTAGE CONTEMPORARIES EDITION, MAY 2009

The Library of Congress has cataloged the Pantheon edition as follows:
Marciano, Francesca.
The end of manners / Francesca Marciano.
p. cm.
1. Female friendship—Fiction.  2. Women—Afghanistan—Fiction.
3. Self-Actualization (Psychology)—Fiction.  4. Afghanistan—Fiction.
5. Italy—Fiction.  I. Title.
PR9120.9.M36E53  2008
823'.914—dc22  2007029571

Vintage ISBN: 978-0-307-38674-8

Book design by M. Kristen Bearse

www.vintagebooks.com

One

"THEY WON'T LET US INSIDE TILL the very last minute and it must be at least ten below out here . . ."

We were all standing perfectly still, under the flurries of snow. Out in the open, holding on to our luggage in front of the airport building, staring at the only being moving in this frozen scene. Imo Glass, of course. Measuring the parking lot in long strides, eyes to the ground. Shouting into her cell.

"What did you say? . . ."

She laughed and threw her head back to reveal her throat, drawing her Pakistani wool shawl tighter around her shoulders.

"Oh. No, I haven't got a clue. I guess it's because of car bombs, kamikaze, you tell me."

The Western passengers, stiffened by the cold despite their thick quilted jackets and woolen beanies, were staring at her, mesmerized, without much sympathy, at least it seemed to me. Perhaps they resented the way Imo was insisting on pacing back and forth in the snow shielded by only her thin shawl, jeans and a pair of flats despite the polar temperature. Or perhaps they were annoyed by the way she kept laughing at the jokes of the mysterious party on the other end, lacking entirely the same worried look as the rest of us.

The Afghan passengers—all men, and a minority among us—although covered just as lightly as she by their pattus were eyeing her with visible hostility as well. A woman yelling and laughing on the phone in front of everyone as if she were on a stage was not exactly their idea of modest behavior.

"The thing is, this morning I gave all my warmest clothes away . . . What? Can you hear me? . . . Yes, I gave them to the cleaning woman at the guesthouse and now I'm freezing to death. . . . Hello . . . can you hear me? CAN YOU HEAR ME?"

Hanif was eyeing her with concern. I looked at him as he did his little nod and smile thing; he did it in that automatic way of his, as if to reassure me that everything was okay, but I could tell he too was on edge.

". . . She only had this thin thin sweater on and plastic babouches, so I gave her my coat, my boots and my woolen socks too . . . What? . . . Demian? I'm losing you now . . . Demian? Can you hear me? Yeah, now I can hear you. What did you say? . . . No, I figured I wouldn't need them anymore, I had no clue they'd leave us standing in the freezing cold for three hours!"

The minute she was done with the call, Imo snapped her phone shut and her features at once reset into that serious, vaguely imperious expression she habitually wore. She joined me in the crowd of numb-with-cold passengers.

"Fuck, I'm freezing my ass. Where's Hanif?"

I pointed out Hanif a short distance away, busy greeting a tall man in a mud-colored uniform with a moustache à la Stalin. She tugged at his sleeve.

"Sorry, Hanif, but isn't there any way of getting us inside? I'm freezing without my coat."

Hanif nodded. He consulted with the uniformed moustache man in Dari with his most obsequious expression. The moustache nodded vigorously and yelled something to the soldiers manning the barrier, the one barring the way to the passengers still waiting to enter the building. There was a further exchange of pleasantries, introductions and hearty handshakes all round. The bar was raised and Imo Glass, Hanif and I, under the now openly hostile gaze of the fifty passengers sculpted in the freezing wind, were wheeled across the parking lot with our luggage in tow and marched inside the building. At the door there were more guards, fully armed. After a brief consultation and due recognition of Hanif, they let us enter.

Inside, the departure hall looked like the empty lobby of a spectral Soviet structure: no check-in counters, no airline signs, no heating. Just dark marble and lights switched off in the glacial chill. It felt more like a prison, or a gigantic empty freezer where you could hear the sound of your own footsteps.

"Excellent," said Imo, with a relieved smile. "Let's go upstairs to the restaurant. I read somewhere they do the most delicious pilau."

ONLY THREE WEEKS AGO, it was the middle of November, I was in the studio in Milan shooting a *soufflé di zucca* for the cover of *La Cucina Italiana*. The dish was beginning to look deflated and sad. Nori couldn't get it glossy enough, neither with sprayed-on olive oil nor with glycerin. Dario tried to move the lights around to get better highlights, but the thing was looking pretty dead, visibly losing volume by the second. It was almost eight and we all wanted to go home, but we had to wait for the kitchen to make another soufflé. By then we knew there was no way of reviving the one we had. Food comes undone quickly under the lights.

Nori and Dario went out for a smoke and I turned on my cell just to give myself something to do. The photography studio was on the outskirts of the city, in a drab industrial area where there wasn't even a decent café to hang out in. There were three messages from Pierre Le Clerc in London. The first said: "I'm looking for you, call me." Then: "Where are you? It's urgent." Third message: "Call me at home, I need to talk to you by tonight."

Pierre is my agent; he's a lanky, attractive man with a leonine head of prematurely white hair who still retains a slight French accent. He moved to London a few years back because he felt "Paris was slowly dying, culturally speaking." His agency, Focus101, soon attracted the best young photographers from different parts of the world. He offered to represent me when my picture of a ten-year-old Thai prostitute won a World Press Photo award in the Contemporary Issues category three years ago. With his handsome, angular face and the holes in his thick, worn-out sweaters that he sports with such casualness, he is a man I could've developed a crush on if only I'd given myself permission. I once had this childish fantasy of the two of us in a house in the south of France sipping a Châteauneuf-du-Pape in front of the fireplace with a couple of Labradors sprawled at our feet.

My name's Maria, I'm thirty-two years old. I'm a redhead with gray eyes, a pasty, freckled complexion that doesn't easily tan. I got my colors from my Irish mother. I'm thin, but not in the way models are thin. Clothes simply hang on me in a funny way, so I stick to the same outfit every day: black jeans and a long-sleeved T-shirt, a thick turtleneck in the winter and desert boots. I hold my hair up with chopsticks I steal from restaurants. I've been playing with the idea of getting a tattoo on my forearm of a black panther ready to pounce. I haven't had the guts to go ahead with this project yet, partly because a panther has very little to do with my personality, partly because I'm scared of the pain.

As a student photographer I wanted to do portraits. Arbus was my idol. But I lacked her perversity. I was too shy. I possessed neither the authority nor the ability to make my subjects feel at ease. So I started with reportage work, trying to capture things as they were happening without having to stage them. Ironically I think I chose photojournalism out of convenience. I was hoping I could move around my subjects like an invisible eye and that it would be easier to disguise my discomfort.

I did stories on Albanian immigrants, AIDS victims in Africa, transsexuals in India, angry factory workers on strike, but it was a string of sad stories that made me feel like a thief, intruding on people's grief, waiting like a vulture for the right second to click the shutter. I could never sleep the night before an assignment, I'd be so wound up.

Then, in the last couple of years, I started suffering from recurrent panic attacks and severe claustrophobia. It had to do more with personal issues than with stress from the shoots. A relationship had ended and a deep depression followed.

One day in the middle of a shoot—I was doing a story on the homeless people who lived inside the Milan railway station—I felt my throat tighten till I couldn't breathe anymore. My assistant ended up having to call an ambulance. That was my final exit: wheeled out on a stretcher, rushed through the congested streets with wailing sirens. After that I stopped working for four months.

Pierre was very supportive, he said it was just a matter of starting again, that I needed to work to get out of my own head, but eventually he realized this was no joke. I think he knew there was no way he could count on me for a big assignment. He was the one to suggest I start back with commercial photography. At first I recoiled, thinking of Arbus and Avedon and the ambitions they had inspired. But the minute I switched to studio work and shot my first food photo—an asparagus quiche for *Sale e Pepe*—I had a revelation. I felt comfortable and secure within a contained space. I could tell things were going to be under control again.

Now I've come to love food as an object of art. Its aesthetic speaks to me. Often I have intense food dreams. I dream of white porcelain tubs overflowing with cherries or red as blood-stains; candid cakes swathed in icing as smooth as freshly fallen snow, covered in violet mounds of petals. The other day I dreamt of a huge pyramid of shiny yellow potatoes that looked like they were made of pure gold. The images are so clear, the colors so stark, that they wake me up in the middle of the night.

Things are much better now: I stopped taking antidepressants and I've been working for the food sections of several magazines based in Milan and London. I recently did a book on a Neapolitan chef for an American publisher and may do his next one too. In Milan I have two young assistants who do the lighting, and a food stylist, Nori, who finds inventive ways to resuscitate wilting food by brushing it with clear nail polish or glycerin and can make any culinary creation stand at attention with complex toothpick arrangements. We spend days on end in front of pork roasts, orecchiette with broccoli, *panna cottas,* and we discuss texture, color, shape, ways to make something look crunchier, softer, crispier, moister. These are the kinds of problems I have to face. To solve them we have our tricks, which we keep to ourselves, like magicians.

Now all I do is point my lens at a risotto. The food does not talk back to me and it does not cry or yell, either. If I don't like the way it looks, I throw it out and get the kitchen to make me another.

After the shoot for *La Cucina Italiana* at the magazine's studio, I came home, ran a citrus-scented bath, lit a couple of candles and put on the Bach cello suites. I'm not sure where I borrowed this prefabricated idea of comfort—probably from some magazine—but it has become my ritual whenever I come home from a long shoot. There's a new list of rules I never would have dreamt of following before—like taking a cold shower in the morning, eating complex carbs and proteins for breakfast, sleeping in flannel sheets, to name just a few—that I religiously observe. It's like a script. It keeps me busy and I like the discipline.

I moved into this apartment on Via Settembrini only a year and half ago, after Carlo and I split up. It's in an old neighborhood behind the Stazione Centrale, which everyone says is on the brink of becoming fashionable. I fell in love with the turn-of-the-century building with a carpentry and a blacksmith workshop, where they bang and drill and saw all day in a beautiful inner courtyard covered in ivy.

The place where Carlo and I lived together for six years was in the center of the city. I could have carried on living there after he left but it held too many memories. I couldn't handle living in the same apartment minus his books, clothes, desk, sofa, paintings. It would be like living in a place filled with holes, empty walls and ghosts everywhere.

Actually it was my father who insisted it was time I bought my own place. I guess, having grown up during the war—and given his vivid literary imagination—he has an innate fear that I could end up homeless out on the streets like a poor orphan girl in a Victor Hugo novel.

It's only a one-bedroom with a large living room, but it has a terrace; minuscule, but it looks out onto the roofs of Milan. The apartment is furnished with a Scandinavian touch that comes from Leo, my younger brother, a dealer in Danish furniture from the sixties. He travels back and forth between Milan and Copenhagen, constantly loading and unloading blond tables and chairs from his van. He's convinced that Danish style is here to stay and is a good investment. In fact, he's done very well so far—much better than me. My father always trusted that my brother had a talent for living a maximum-quality life with minimum effort.

No, he's never projected his Victor Hugoesque fantasies on Leo.

• • •

I took the phone into the bath and dialed Pierre's number. It felt somewhat naughty to be speaking to him while steaming in that lemony vapor.

"Finally," said Pierre. "I've been looking for you all over. The photo editor of the *Observer*—the magazine—wants you for a job."

Behind the gravelly accent there was a certain anxiety in his voice, and I liked that.

"It's a fantastic assignment. The writer is Imo Glass."

"Imo Glass?" I had never heard the name. I wanted to ask Pierre if Imo was a man's or a woman's name, but decided against it.

Pierre said she was a very good writer based in London who also happened to be an old friend. He told me I had to leave right away, as soon as I got a visa and the vaccinations.

I didn't say anything. I wasn't sure what the word "vaccinations" actually involved.

"To Kabul. You have to go to Kabul."

A pause.

"What? Are you kidding me?" I laughed as I traced my finger through a bubble of water and soap. "I think you have the wrong number, Pierre."

Pierre cleared his throat, feigned a nonchalant tone. "No, I don't. This is for you."

"Pierre, are you out of your mind? Why are you even—"

"Wait, Maria—"

"No, listen. Why are you even calling me about this? This has nothing to do with me. Send someone else. One of those guys who go to war zones. They'll love an adventure."

"This is a story on Afghan women and arranged marriages, Maria. We can't have a guy shoot women in Muslim countries. And here's the thing—Imo told her editor how much she loves your work. She actually requested that we hire you."

"Which work?"

"Well, she has *seen* your work."

"You mean the Barbie doll picture?"

This was the shorthand Pierre and I used for the Thai child prostitute photo, which had done the rounds of the world, had been published in so many magazines and had made me famous for a year.

"I wish you hadn't done that," I said.

"Done what?"

"You know. Showed her the photo. Since you represent me— am I right?—you should've told her I no longer do reportage."

"I haven't *done* anything. The photo is on our Web site and anyone can look at your work. Imo knew the picture perfectly well. The photo editor is extremely excited to have you on board. And besides, I think it's time you did something like this. You're ready to start again and this is why I really insist that you say yes. Because I'm your agent and I represent you. That's why."

He paused. I didn't say anything.

"Maria? Are you there?"

"Yes."

"What's wrong?"

"Nothing. I just can't believe this is happening."

Three years ago, at a time when we were still trying to spend as little time apart as possible, I had followed Carlo to Bangkok, where he had to attend a conference on AIDS. He thought I might enjoy coming along. I had planned to see the Golden Buddha, a couple of good museums and the floating market by myself while he was at the conference, but I didn't feel comfortable on the streets—too much noise, pollution and traffic, too many gadgets and fake designer labels sold everywhere. I spent most of my time in our air-conditioned hotel room reading novels and waiting for Carlo to come back from his meetings.

Then one night, as we were heading to a restaurant, our taxi broke down and we had to pull to the side of the street. While

Carlo and the driver were fidgeting with the engine, I saw her. She must have been around ten. She was sitting on a low stool on the step of a dingy little house. Her face made up, her skinny body swathed in a glittering fabric, dirty feet and flip-flops. She was intent on braiding a broken Barbie doll's hair, with the serious look children have when they are imagining scenes and secret plots. The next minute I saw her step off the stool and barter with a client on a scooter, the Barbie doll abandoned on the chair. I searched for my digital Leica in my purse. I clicked.

The glitter, the red taillights of cars in the distance, her dark red lipstick, the face of the man on the scooter, the way she arched her back as she'd been taught to do. The broken Barbie lit by a neon light looked like a tiny naked corpse. It was perfect.

Only I wasn't that photographer anymore.

"I don't even like driving a car on the highway," I said. "As if I want to go to Afghanistan."

"Maria," Pierre begged. Then he said he was asking on bended knee.

"But why me? There must be a million photographers out there you could—"

"I tried. Everyone who I would trust to do this job right is on assignment somewhere. Margaret De Haas was supposed to go, okay? Yes, I did think of her first. But last night she fell—can you believe this?—from her *bicycle* and broke her foot."

"Then you should call that American woman. The one who moved to Baghdad for six months, what was her name?"

"I rang her. She's pregnant." I heard him sigh. He blew into the phone.

"Maria, I'm asking you as a personal favor."

"But there's a war—"

"What war?" he said, regaining strength, sensing a chink had opened up. He immediately wedged his foot in. "The war per se is over. There is *no* war as such in Afghanistan, Maria. Iraq, yes, there's a war. But in Kabul there's a proper parliament now. Don't you read the papers?"

"Yes, I do. And I also read about the Taliban, kidnapping and bombs going off still. Seriously, Pierre, I don't want to go."

"It's going to be a big feature. Besides, it'll put you back on the map, Maria."

"Oh, please. Which map? I don't care about the map."

"I do, as your agent and your friend. You know the way I feel about that. I think that by the time you're forty you will look back to this moment and regret not having—"

"Oh, God, Pierre, please, please, please. Don't start with me on this."

"We'd make sure you'd be traveling safely, taking all necessary precautions. It's a great assignment, Maria, it's material for another World Press Photo award. And it'll be an in-and-out kind of thing. No more than two weeks of your life, I promise."

"Pierre, I—"

"Sleep on it and call me in the morning. You owe me that much at least."

"All right. But the answer is no."


The next day I was sitting at the table in the small kitchen at my father's place. After my mother's death he had sold the apartment in Via S. Marco where we grew up—he said he didn't need the space anymore—and moved into a cheaper neighborhood now bustling with immigrants from North Africa, Sri Lanka, streets lined with Asian groceries, Chinese take-out joints. He liked the feeling of being surrounded by people from other countries, who spoke different languages and listened to their loud music all day. He said he had had enough of living next to *"sciurette e cummenda"* all his life, an untranslatable expression that describes uptight Milanese.

That day I watched my father as he was puttering in the kitchen and realized his getting older actually meant he seemed to be getting lighter and lighter. He made me a coffee with his single-cup coffeemaker. Aging is this too, I thought. One becomes cautious, economical. Everything begins to shrink, not just the horizon one has ahead, not just the time that's left, but one's needs as well. One is careful not to let anything go to waste. Extravagance becomes a thing of the past.

I had told him about Pierre's phone call and he had already put a folder aside for me with newspaper clippings and documents he had downloaded from the Internet.

"*Ecco, guarda,* here I put some background material for you to read. A brief history of the Soviet invasion; this one here is about the civil war, and this is a story on General Massoud's assassination, when two kamikaze pretended to be reporters wanting to interview him. You remember that, don't you?"

"Yeah, right . . . more or less." I nodded vaguely. I was in a hurry to go home and I didn't have time for a lesson.

"And all this material I got from an American Army site. It tells you about the movement of troops, contingents, et cetera. Good idea to keep an eye on it every now and again. It's interesting. Well . . ."

He flipped through his ordered pages, moistening his finger, his reading glasses perched on his nose. He had already highlighted the more relevant paragraphs in yellow. He smoothed the pages with his hand and lined them up, taking care that the margins all coincided perfectly.

He still used the same teacherly gestures even now that he had retired from school. But he no longer looked as well groomed as he used to be when he was a professor of Italian literature at the Liceo Parini.

He taught Italian literature for over forty years. He's had hundreds of students. Every now and again I happened to run into one of them.

"Maria Galante? I had a professor named Galante in school," they would say, and when I told them that he was my father, they wouldn't stop. The most passionate teacher I ever had, such an inspiration; he was the one who encouraged me to write; if it wasn't for him . . . And on and on and on.

Sometimes, when my brother and I were teenagers, at the dinner table he would mention their names, talk about the ones he thought were more gifted, or the ones who made him laugh, as if they were distant relatives, or people whose names we were supposed to remember. At times he would read some of their writing aloud to my mother. I'd watch my parents bend over the paper, laugh, discuss, make comments, with the same participation as if it were their own children's work. My brother and I would make a face and snicker.

Now, since my mother's been gone, a sweet Filipina named Teodora comes for two hours a week and takes care of ironing my father's shirts. He has, however, learned to do the laundry, and does his own shopping at the supermarket with the discount coupons. When my mother was alive I don't think he even knew how to cook himself an egg. I feel a sense of great tenderness whenever I think how much he has adjusted, without the faintest trace of bitterness, to this new life. How he's willing to look after himself as if housekeeping was just another skill he was eager to learn.

"The Bactrian Empire, where Alexander the Great treaded." He was smiling and musing. "The river Oxus. I'm so jealous."

He pulled out a book from the shelf. *The Road to Oxiana* by Robert Byron in an old-fashioned British edition.

"Your mother's. You should read this before you go. It's a masterpiece."

I smiled. The shirt cuff poking out under the sleeve of his sweater looked frayed. His hair too long.

"I found a little Dari dictionary online and I saw it's not a very hard language to learn. It sounds beautiful, like Farsi. I printed it for you. Look, I put it here at the back. I'm sure the people there would be very pleased if you said 'good morning, thank you' in their language. These things do make a difference."

I could see the child he once was float to the surface and reveal himself. It was this child—not the retired teacher, the scholar of *lingue romanze*—who was grinning at me, imagining himself in Kabul.

"It's a country that's suffered a great deal and is still suffering. An extraordinary people, I think."

He pushed his reading glasses halfway down his nose and looked at me, checking my sullen expression.

"When would you have to leave?"

"Hmmm. I'm not sure. It would have to be soon, I think."

"You accepted, didn't you?" he asked.

"I'm still thinking about it, Papà. It's not an easy decision."

I'd been awake much of the night, worried and anxious. It felt to me, as I stared into the blackness of my room, like when I was a kid standing on a diving board and everyone behind me was yelling, "Jump, jump!" So great was the shame of doing an about-face and going back that I closed my eyes and jumped. Better to get it over with right away than to face the humiliation. But a dive is only a leap—yippee, you instantly reemerge screaming with joy, amazed that you did it—and terror gives way to euphoria in half a second. A trip to Afghanistan felt more like a never-ending tunnel. A fear that would never subside till I reached the other side and the light.

The *metropolitana* was crowded and stuffy. I leafed quickly through the folder my father had put together. Too many names, too many dates to take in. Too many factions and wars. Too complicated the plot of this country for the last five hundred years. I almost immediately put the folder back in my satchel.

I realized that I never owned that particular character trait that had always defined my father: he had always retained his relentless curiosity, the desire to be engaged in other people's lives. The persistence in keeping track of what goes on in the world still seemed to concern him, as if crises, wars, famines, the tiny heartbreaking victories, the huge defeats of the planet were happening right on his own doorstep. Nothing was too remote for him, not a flood, not a dictatorship, not the conditions in a refugee camp of unknown minorities. In his solitude he was never alone. He was busy and engaged, participating in all the world's grievances.

That afternoon I had to shoot a slice of tofu blueberry cheesecake next to a mug of steaming coffee for a new yoga magazine. Dario was leaning over the set moving tiny blueberries around the frame with tweezers. Nori was busy blowing cigarette smoke on the surface of the brown liquid through several straws joined together. She had to avoid any airflow in order for it to curl up nicely from the cup, so once she had blown the smoke, she had to retrieve the straw very slowly; but we could never get it right, it kept looking like a cloud of cigarette smoke rather than steam. After a while Dario started complaining about a sharp pain in his back. Nori said she was going to be sick if she had to inhale any more nicotine. By five thirty we were all in a lousy mood and I felt we couldn't wait to get rid of one another.

I heard my phone ring at the other end of the studio. Dario ran to get it for me, but I saw I had one missed call and a message on the voice mail.

"Hallo, Maria, Pierre here." He sounded annoyed and detached, like a stranger. "It's after five and I still haven't heard from you, so I figured that means no thanks in your language. This is just to let you know that I've alerted Samantha Jordan, you know, the one from Cape Town, I think you met her once at the office. I'll call her to confirm tomorrow, so I think I'm covered."

He paused and then sighed.

"Just in case you were feeling guilty about letting me down."

Of course I remembered Sam Jordan. A slim thirtysomething blonde with piercing blue eyes and a very good body. I had checked her work online after we had met hoping it wouldn't be as good as her looks. But it was.

When I got home that night I googled Sam Jordan once more and went through her portfolio. Her portraits were stunning. The landscapes were like paintings, brushstrokes on a canvas, brilliant use of the light, splashes of vibrant color. The images were bold, ironic and poetic at the same time. She would be good in Afghanistan. The minute Imo Glass and the photo editor saw this portfolio, they would forget all about me.

I was exhausted and I had a long list of shots for the following day. Gelato, mousses and sherbets, which are particularly hard work as they tend to ooze and need to be shot very quickly. I dozed off in front of the TV. Fragmented images of the tofu blueberry cheesecake kept creeping back into my sleep like a song I couldn't get out of my head, but the vivid colors were those of Sam Jordan's photos. I sprang up from the sofa around midnight, possessed by an unusual fury, and dialed Pierre's number. I got his voice mail this time.

"Pierre, it's me. This is crazy, I can't believe you didn't get my earlier message. I rang this morning to tell you I was going to take the job. Now I get this message about Sam Jordan. What the hell is going on here?" The more I lied, the more confident I became.

"I even sent you a text three hours ago. Were you joking or what? Don't you dare alert anybody. This isn't funny anyway."

I hung up the phone without even saying good-bye.

A power move—I knew from when it had been done to me one time too many.

———

MY PARENTS MET in the early sixties, a time when an Irish girl was a rare and exotic thing for a young Italian to come across. They met in Rome in Babington's Tea Rooms at the feet of the Spanish Steps, the only place in Italy where one could get proper English tea and cucumber sandwiches. My father was staying with his uncle at the time, theoretically looking for a job after graduation, in actuality loafing around, toying with the idea of being a poet. Every afternoon he would pop in there because he loved anything foreign and because the tearoom was next to the house where Keats had died, which enhanced the romantic flavor of his fruitless afternoons. My mother was a young university graduate student on her first holiday abroad—she came from a modest family in southern Ireland and knew very little of the world. She was staying in a cheap pensione by the train station, counting every lira she spent and falling in love with all that was Italian. But on that rainy afternoon she was longing for a proper cup of tea and a scone. It took my father two minutes to invite himself to her table. He wanted to fall in love with someone different; she was dreading the idea of going back home, to the drab, smelly rented room she had in Dublin. They didn't speak the same language and talked in broken French. This thrilled them even more.

In their honeymoon pictures my mother smiles on a bridge in Venice in a short-sleeved yellow sweater and a checkered skirt, a headband holding her curly red hair in place. My father looks thin, more interesting than handsome, impeccably dressed despite the little money he was making at the time as a public school teacher, surrounded by the flurry of pigeons that every shot in Piazza S. Marco includes. Every year afterwards, on their wedding anniversary, the two of them would travel from Milan to Rome and would go back to Babington's for high tea; even when the trip and the tearoom's pricey meal had become too expensive, they still made a point of going. They said they feared it would jinx their marriage otherwise; I think it cheered them up to keep this one extravagance. They maintained the ritual till Leo and I were out of school and had left home. By then the traveling had become too tiring and the joke had lost its audience—us—and run out of steam.

The end of the ritual didn't affect their marriage. But maybe they were right about the jinx. Because it was right after they stopped that my mother got sick.

My mother had the romantic look of a Pre-Raphaelite painting, but she didn't know it, and never carried herself as such. If anything, she was self-conscious of her freckles and flaming hair. Her taste in clothes was funny, very un-Italian. She was not quite frumpy, but she wore all the wrong colors. I remember watching her on the nights of parent-teacher conferences; I'd be praying that my teacher wouldn't think her ridiculous, and that the other kids wouldn't laugh at her. They never did, yet I worried: she looked so helpless to me, cloaked in her funny caftans, or in those large, bold prints she liked to wear, the blouses with ruffles and puffy sleeves she saved for special occasions. I loved her and feared for her—could sense her anxiety, the insecurity that seemed to follow her wherever she went, whether on the bus, in a grocery shop or at the beach. She blushed when people didn't understand her pronunciation, or when she got the tenses wrong. No matter how many years she'd lived in Italy, she seemed never to belong.

I worried too much about her; over the years, that worry spilled into my personality and became my own.

· · ·

Pierre was, he said, *aux anges,* "to the angels." A flamboyant expression for ecstatic, which conjured putti trumpeting on clouds.

He sent me links to some of the stories Imo Glass had written in the past for the *Guardian* and the *Observer* and articles on the situation of women's rights in the southern provinces. He also sent me via courier a guide to Afghanistan that had just been published in England. I spent the next few days online reading the *Kabul Daily,* looking at ads for new restaurants and at the classifieds, scrolling Wikipedia like mad on different Afghan entries, checking from geography to literature to food. I waited anxiously for the guide to come, as if the book had the power to dispel all my fears and answer all my questions. In the meantime my mother's yellowing edition of *The Road to Oxiana* provided wondrous descriptions of what Kabul, Herat and Kandahar had been like in the forties: "Hawk-eyed and eagle beaked, the swarthy loose knit men swing through the dark bazaar with a devil may care self confidence. They carry rifles to go shopping as Londoners carry umbrellas."

The guide finally came through. Its content proved more up-to-date than Byron's journal but far less alluring. It wasn't aimed at travelers—there had been none for decades and none seemed to be coming anytime soon—it had been conceived for use by aid workers, reporters, donors, local NGOs. The security tips went something like "Don't walk off the road into the bushes for a leak! Mines are everywhere; minimize your time in bazaars and crowded areas, vary your routes to and from office/residence as much as possible. Do not go outside while there is shooting. What goes up must come down."

A short paragraph on women and photography stated that photographing Afghan women had often proved difficult, particularly in the most conservative Pashtun areas. Taking their portrait without their consent could lead to an ugly situation. A

CNN crew who had been filming women in a hospital without their permission had been detained at gunpoint.

Pierre rang to say that the insurance for me and Imo Glass was going to cost the paper a fortune. His voice was crisp, ebullient almost.

"You're going away covered by a policy that's the Ferrari of insurance," he said. I guess he thought this sounded reassuring.

"Great. Does that mean they cover the ransom in case we're kidnapped?"

Pierre laughed as if I had said something really funny.

"Probably. In any case you're most welcome to go over the policy here at the office when you come to London. It's thirty pages long." And then the laugh again.

"And how about the assignment for *Gambero Rosso*?" I asked. "I was scheduled to shoot for them the first week of December. What are we going to do about the—"

"I'll take care of it. They're my next phone call, in fact. They will find someone else, no problem, so don't you worry about that."

He was brimming with enthusiasm, as if canceling that shoot was a personal victory. I heard paper rustling from his end. It pissed me off that he should be so efficient. He told me that the insurance required us to take a course.

"Hostile environment training," he said. "It's the least they can expect, with what they're covering."

"Which means?"

"They teach you how to behave in situations of potential danger. It's like going to school and taking classes about safety, first aid and stuff like that. There are only two companies in the world who provide this kind of training and they're both based in England. People who have to go off to hot zones come here from all over the world. So we'll fly you over, you'll start the course on Monday, meanwhile we'll take care of your visa and so forth and then you and Imo will leave together from Heath-row the following week. It works out very neatly like that."

I said nothing. He was beginning to get on my nerves with all that optimism and positive feeling about everything. My brief fantasy about the two of us in the south of France seemed to belong to another era of our relationship, eons away.

"There'll be about fifteen of you in the course. They're holding it in the country, here, just outside London."

"What do you mean *in the country?*"

Pierre cleared his throat.

"Yes, they're deporting you to a sort of mansion in Hamp-shire, in the middle of the English countryside. All the partici-pants have to live there for the duration of the course. You'll go to classes from eight till six. It's going to be hard work."

There was a pause. I didn't fill it.

He chuckled. "Basically you're going to boot camp."

My silence grew deeper. An absence of breath, more than a suspension of sound.

"It'll be fun, you'll see. There'll be a whole bunch of interest-ing people who work in interesting places. It's an experience, Maria. In fact, you don't realize how lucky you are. I'd be in it like a shot."

Sure he would. I heard the papers rattle again in the back-ground.

A couple of days later I met my father for lunch in a trattoria in his neighborhood, where they've known him for years and call him "Professore." We sat at his usual table in the back, facing the faded Miró print and the old wooden cupboard. The table was covered with a sheet of paper and a quart of cheap white wine *della casa* had been placed between us. Naturally, my father had now printed more pages from the Internet about my survival course.

"I did a search and in the end I found this group. They're

called 'Defenders.' " He grinned. "It must be them, they're the only ones who do this kind of thing. It's like something out of James Bond!"

The photos he downloaded looked pretty muddy in the smudgy black and white of his old printer. I could scarcely make out a group of people sheathed in bulletproof vests and helmets. Another picture showed a table covered with firearms of every kind: rifles, machine guns, grenades. A close-up showed a man in full camouflage gear, his face blackened like in the poster of *Platoon*.

"I don't know about James Bond," I said. "They look more like mercenaries to me."

"They're *not* mercenaries. These are ex–British marines. It's a totally different ball game, *mia cara.*"

Domenico, the owner of the trattoria, came over in his apron and tried to tell us some very fresh scampi had just come in. But my father wasn't ready to pay attention to food yet.

"Look at this, Domenico," he said, handing him the pages. "Maria is going to Afghanistan on assignment for the *Observer*. But first she has to do a survival course with these guys. *Guarda qui,* they simulate all kinds of scenarios: a shooting, a car bomb, whatnot. What they do is they teach you how to react, how to avoid getting in trouble, *capito*? It's proper special forces training, look at this."

Domenico put down his order pad and leaned over the table to thumb through the pages that my father promptly started to translate.

"See," my father said. "Look what big bruisers they are. These people have all been to Iraq, Kosovo, Afghanistan. When she gets back she can teach us a few tricks!" He laughed and reached across the table to squeeze my arm with fatherly pride. Domenico looked at me and laughed too, shaking his head in disbelief.

I looked at them both, their reading glasses lowered onto their noses: my father, bony and creaky; Domenico, short of breath, a paunch, layers of fat and cholesterol level off the charts.

They surveyed the photos with the greedy eyes of a couple of kids handling someone else's toys.

"Brava, Maria!" said Domenico. "Send us a postcard and I'll put it by the cashier. But make sure you come back in one piece."

Then he raised himself up and resumed his professional manner.

"So, today I have linguine with scampi, the fresh ones I mentioned before, or else I recommend paccheri di gragnano with zucchini flowers . . ."

I left for London with two very different pieces of luggage. I pulled out my beat-up old canvas Domke bag from my photojournalism days to stow my two 35 mm camera bodies, a digital Leica, a multitude of lenses, flash cards, batteries, notepads, pens. I packed it exactly in the same sequence as I used to, with the efficiency and speed of a surgeon laying out his instruments. It felt good to take along such a light bag instead of the heavy metal case packed with my studio cameras and another with my lighting equipment.

The second bag, a much heavier suitcase, was the result of an endless search through my closet that had taken up a whole afternoon and a good part of the night. The outcome was a bundle of stockings, sweaters, scarves, odd gloves, twisted in a formless clump of soft, loose material that made me nauseous just to look at it. I carried and dragged these two different weights with an equal measure of pride and contempt for the reassuring firmness of the first and the suspect lumpiness of the second, which looked like a vital organ about to burst.

. . .

The *Observer* had booked me into a small but fashionable bou-
tique hotel in Kensington, furnished with minimal furniture.
The room had orchids in vials on the night table and lounge
music CDs in the bookshelf. I was under a gigantic showerhead
in the black bathroom when the phone rang. I ran to answer,
dripping water all over the crisp sheets. It was Imo Glass. She
told me in a flurry of hyperbolic adjectives that she was very
happy to work with me and that she found my photos "absolutely extraordinary."

I, on the other hand, asked her if she was by any chance
Japanese. A foolish question—I knew it as soon as I blurted it
out—but the minute I had heard her name from Pierre I had
established, for some reason that now escapes me, that she must
have a Japanese mother and a Jewish father. I had subsequently
proceeded to form my own mental picture of Imo Glass: tiny,
with glasses and sleek jet-black hair cut short, with the studious, genial air that certain Japanese girls have.

She laughed. "I wish. Unfortunately Imo stands for Imogen."

Her voice was rich, throaty, her vowels precise. Another
image instantly superimposed itself onto the studious Japanese
girl: a tall blonde with fair skin, an English rose, delicate and
yet unyielding, able to survive anything in spite of her fragile
appearance.

"Let's meet for coffee at my club. You know the Front Line,
don't you?" she asked. "It was founded in memory of journalist
and photographer friends who were killed in war zones."

"Excellent," I said, but frankly it didn't sound like such a
great omen to start with. When I arrived—late, I took the wrong
line on the tube and had to change trains—she was waiting for
me in the bar, ensconced on a purple velvet couch under an
enormous photograph of a fair-haired man swathed in a keffiyeh and pointing his telephoto lens at a tank in the middle of a
desert. I wondered if he was still alive.

. . .

Imo, as it turned out, was languid, round, like a reclining beauty by Rubens, with thick, wavy dark hair, tanned skin, dark red full lips and the aquiline nose of a Nefertiti. The partially unbuttoned white shirt offered a glimpse of her cleavage beaded with a light film of sweat and of her generous breasts. She wore an oversized cashmere cardigan with rolled-up sleeves that could've been left behind by a lover (she didn't look like the marrying kind). Thick Indian silver bracelets clinked at her wrists and as she hugged me I caught a whiff of patchouli. Imogen Glass emanated body heat, female humors and fluids. She appeared to be someone who loves to walk barefoot and doesn't burn in the sun. I confessed to her straightaway that she didn't look anything like I had imagined. She laughed.

"I bet. Genetically speaking, I have nothing in common with Imogen Glass. My real name is Lupita Jaramillo."

"Oh, that's why," I said, not really getting what she meant.

"My adoptive mother decided to name me after her own mother. Unfortunately she was called Imogen. But I was born in Medellín."

She paused and then specified, "You know, the hometown of the cartel?"

She laughed again and I did too, not knowing what was so funny about that.

"I didn't expect you'd speak such fluent English," she said. "That's another bonus."

"Well, my mother was Irish. At home my brother and I spoke English with her."

Imo noted the "was" and gave me a sympathetic smile.

"Anyway. I can't wait to tell you what the plan is. Pierre has told you more or less what this is about, right?"

"Yes, he's sent me a couple of stories on forced marriages. I looked online and—"

"Yes, yes, of course," she interrupted me dismissively. "I

know the story has been done a million times already. But we're going to do something slightly different."

She leaned across the table, closer to me, and lowered her voice in a conspiratorial manner. "In case you're interested in desserts, they have these chocolate éclairs here which are amazing. I've already ordered you one."

She took out a notebook and some newspaper clips and put on a pair of reading glasses with rectangular red frames. They made her kind of look silly and I appreciated her insouciance in wearing them.

"I call them the Vaginas of Journalism, you know," Imo said, arching an eyebrow.

"Who?"

"Oh, those women reporters who have built their career on women's abuse and sufferings around the planet. You know, genital mutilation, rape, incest, you name it. They couldn't believe their luck when the Taliban came on. A big story that only a woman in a burqa could do? Too good to be true."

"Right," I said a bit warily.

"A few of them still give speeches about their experiences at the time of the Taliban rule, of how they risked their life traveling through Afghanistan incognito pretending to be some Pashtun man's wife. Right in this club, for instance. Oh, you should have heard them."

She gestured vaguely around the room.

"The lectures, the talks. They just couldn't stop telling the story."

I gave a snicker, eager to show her how boring that sounded to me too. But how our assignment was going to be different from what the Vaginas had done was still unclear to me.

"A few of them still keep the burqa they traveled with in their closet, like a trophy. I've seen them wear it to parties. Talk about bad taste."

A waiflike waitress brought the éclairs. They were enormous.

"What we're going to do instead has a totally different angle. First of all, not much has changed for women in the rural areas since the end of the Taliban regime, and that's a fact. But one thing has changed: information. What is happening is that now, with television, radio, the presence of NGOs and all the infor mation that is beginning to seep through from the West, the women arc beginning to realize what their rights are. Before, and under the Taliban, every girl knew she belonged exclusively to her father and then to her husband, and that was the end of the story. But now the more they know, the more desperate they feel about the condition they're in. As a result, the suicide rate among women who are forced to marry has increased. Numbers are sketchy, but they're on the rise."

Imo gulped down half her éclair in a couple of bites—I could tell it was filled with custard and not real cream. She let out a little moan of pleasure and wiped her lips with her middle finger.

"You could draw a stunning graph of what this is about. Basically, the more information, the more suicides. The women are ready to take their own lives now more than ever because they know the world is watching them. Isn't that just the perfect paradox?"

"That's really interesting. I had no idea," I said, unable to find something more clever to say.

She looked at me, squinting slightly as if to get me in focus. I feared she might think me an idiot. But she smiled, lifted a smudge of chocolate left on her plate with her finger and licked it.

"I know. It's a great story."

She shuffled through her papers.

"First of all we go and speak to this one here, what's-her-name, let's see . . . Roshana Something from the Afghan Human Rights Commission, she's the woman on top of the statistics and from her we'll get the numbers right. Then we go to the villages where these girls have immolated themselves. We try and talk to the girls who are about to be forced into a marriage and see what they have to say about that. And then—you'll snap!"

I told her what I had read in the guide about photographing women.

"I must admit it made me quite anxious," I said.

She smiled and grasped my hand across the table. She pressed it between hers, leaving me stunned.

"I know, I know, it's always the same story, isn't it? It all seems impossible from here, then once you get there . . . Oh well, one always finds a way, as you must know from experience. You'll see—I'm sure we'll manage to come home with incredible material. Besides, I don't know whether you feel the same, but the harder it is to get a story, the more excited I get. I become even more obsessed."

I cleared my throat and nodded, perhaps too weakly. I got the impression that she was disappointed by my lack of enthusiasm. I had a pretty long list of questions I was anxious to ask, mostly about vaccinations, the medicines I would need to bring with me, the actual danger of land mines, of being kidnapped and so forth. But in the face of her fervor, I didn't want to sound small.

Imo glanced at my plate and realized my éclair was almost intact. Her eyes widened.

"Are you not going to finish it?"

I shook my head. She took the éclair between her thumb and forefinger and swallowed it whole, in one go. And this, in the secret language of women, especially one with hips as broad as hers, is a clear manifestation of self-esteem and strength of character.

By the end of our first meeting in London, Imo Glass's personality had had a sort of miraculous effect on me. I felt like a teenager who had developed a crush on the new girl in class. She had won me over completely. She told me bits and pieces about herself, none of which was of much consequence. Her bio sounded as if it belonged to four different people. She grew up in London but had lived in St. Petersburg as a student; she spoke fluent Russian (on top of French and Spanish, which she had learned while living for a year in Mexico City with a boy-friend). She had covered wars in Sudan, Sierra Leone, Kosovo; she practiced Tibetan meditation and adored soccer.

"I'm in love with Francesco Totti," she declared. "He's my number one favorite, along with Ronaldinho."

I wasn't prepared for so much personality, charm, or for that overflowing effusiveness that she kept expressing with such ease (she grabbed my hand again twice during our conversation and then on the street she casually put her arm around my shoulders). I was flattered by so much attention, and the prospect of spending a week in Hampshire with those marines together with her made it all more acceptable. I had actually envisioned myself in a flak jacket running through the English countryside with Imo, together escaping a terrorist attack. Suddenly the idea of doing the course with her seemed an opportunity for a great adventure that would consolidate our friendship. Essentially, I realized in a flash that anything done in Imo's company would take on a whole new light.

I was gratified by the respect she seemed to grant me for no reason I could discern, and I decided it wasn't necessary to remind her I hadn't been out there on the streets in years and never once in a war zone. The Barbie doll picture seemed to have had enough power to make her trust me completely. Whatever the reason, I didn't want to deter her faith in me.

"We could take the train together tomorrow," I suggested, as we were saying good-bye in front of the cab she was about to climb into. "Unless you were planning to drive."

"Where?"

"To the country. Wherever this place is. For the course, I mean."

"Oh, right. The Defenders," she said, letting the name dangle for a second in the air. "Oh, no, darling, I'm not going to come. I did that course already *years* ago, when I went to Sudan. The insurance only needs you to do it once. But don't worry, I'll see you next Monday at the Emirates check-in at Heathrow."

She hugged me tight and kissed me on both cheeks. The disappointment must have redrawn my face, as I felt my cheeks sag, my nose lengthen. What an idiot. Someone who hops from one war zone to another, what was I thinking? She didn't need the Defenders to defend her.

"They'll do all sorts of things to you, just wait and see," she said, wrapping her black cashmere coat around her. "You might just love it!"

And with a devilish grin she disappeared into the darkness of the large cab, leaving behind a sweetish, spicy scent.

I walked back to the hotel in order to digest the meeting, constantly checking my "London from A to Z" map for fear of getting lost again. I felt Imo Glass was a person whose definition eluded me. Perhaps because a little girl born as Lupita Jaramillo in the slums of a South American city ruled by drug traffickers, and who subsequently mutated into a woman by the name of Imogen who grew up in Notting Hill with an art historian (father) and a psychotherapist (mother) as adoptive parents, was a unique creature whose DNA had flourished in total anarchy. That's probably why she seemed able to effortlessly shift from one language to another, from one country to another, as if she were always swimming in the same water and consequently managed to feel at home just about everywhere. But what struck me the most about her was her total lack of fear in the way she approached complete strangers—the waitress at the club, the taxi driver, me—enveloping everyone with festive familiarity, a secret weapon that tamed them on the spot, neutralizing any aggressive potential.

The following morning at seven, I had an appointment at Paddington station at the platform with my course companions. Pierre had told me over the phone that it was going to be a short trip and that one of the instructors was supposed to meet us at the other end, at Hampshire station.

I was the last to arrive. I spotted them right away as, tottering and sweaty, I lugged my big suitcase along. They had all gathered under the platform roof and were watching me as I wobbled toward them. I knew right away I was the only Italian of the group. I guess they had only just met, but already they looked to me like a well-bonded team that was about to set off on vacation. A consolidated group that viewed with suspicion the only stranger, the one no one wanted to share a room with. They shared a similar look: casual and contemporary, equipped in Nikes and North Face; their snazzy cell phones, literary magazines poking out of bags, iPods and woolen caps. They greeted me and my about-to-burst suitcase with incredulous grins, since they were all carrying hand luggage. We quickly introduced ourselves to each other and I didn't even try to memorize a single name; for the whole journey I pretended to be reading the *Guardian,* half listening to their wry comments on what was awaiting us.

The redbrick station was in the middle of the countryside—it looked like an idyllic English countryside, all right, with Jersey cows and lots of green. I picked the awaiting Defender at once because he was watching us from a distance and didn't move forward. He stood next to a brick pylon, a cigarette dangling from his lips, waiting for us to go over to him like a gaggle of anxious geese waddling up to their feed.

"Welcome. My name's Keith," he said with an accent that

sounded coarse to me as he crushed the cigarette butt under his shoe—although my ear was untrained to the endless nuance of English class pronunciation. "Defender" was written on his jacket in light blue against a yellow background. He looked around fifty, albeit a pretty trashed fifty; burly with the gravelly voice of a smoker and the watery gaze of someone who drinks a lot of beer.

"Come on, let's get a move on. The first lesson starts at nine." Then he looked at my bags.

"No, it's just that"—the urge to justify myself rose like a wave—"as soon as I'm done with the course I'm flying straight to Kabul. There are cameras in it and . . ."

"You're free to bring whatever you want."

Keith's eyelids lowered slowly and he shrugged.

"Your whole wardrobe if you like," he said, turning his back on me.

In the small conference room of the country inn—fluorescent lights, folding chairs, gray carpet and a screen for slides—the Defenders turned up in full force, with the spirit of a soccer team at a photo shoot. They showed no interest in being liked, had no time for formalities or pleasantries. There were about ten of them, all wearing identical blue Defender T-shirts. They had a weathered look, scoured by the elements and by late nights at the pub. In fact, as I walked past them, my nostrils caught a blend of beer notes mixed with toothpaste and pine shower gel, the same sharp scent that wafts through every subway in the world around eight a.m.

They were standing in front of the slide screen with their arms crossed over their mighty stomachs, biceps on display, legs apart, in a menacing bouncer stance. I noticed how one of them—a sort of Celtic mountain who looked like Obelix, the gigantic Gallic cartoon character with braids and horns on his helmet, ready to uproot a tree—wore his thin blond hair in a ponytail, despite being well over fifty, which struck me as sad. A couple of them were younger, not as bulky but scary nevertheless. These had the sinewy, diabolical look of martial arts champions, ice-colored eyes and tattoos on their forearms. They introduced themselves one by one, mumbling their names under their breath: "I'm Roger, I'll be giving you the first-aid course." "I'm Alan, together we'll take a look at weapons, munitions and land mines." "Hi, I'm Toby, with me you'll be doing outdoor war games, we'll be simulating emergency situations together."

They surveyed us with an air of polite superiority. It was obvious we didn't arouse the least curiosity in them. There we were, a bunch of middle-class civilians shrouded in expensive layers of polypropylene with BlackBerrys stuffed in our pockets, who had only ever seen war on television. I could detect it in their eyes, the tedium of having to put up with us for a whole week.

At that point, the one who appeared to be the oldest, Tim— a mild-faced man with sky-blue eyes and a King Kong physique—invited us to introduce ourselves and name the organization we worked for.

"Please state your destination as well," he added.

Nobody moved, eyes met all round.

One after another, my course mates stood up and declaimed their personal details as if they were introducing themselves at an AA meeting.

"Hi, I'm Bob Sheldon, I work for Reuters in Sydney and next month I'm going to Indonesia to cover the elections."

"Um . . . My name is Monika Schluss, I come from Bonn and I will travel to Belize to work with Christian Aid."

"Hi, I'm Liz Reading, I'm from London and in six months I'm going to the Congo to . . . well . . ." The sexy brunette hesitated, then giggled. "I'm with an NGO that helps local people make cheese," and there were nervous titters all round to break the tension. The Defenders did not laugh.

"Hi, my name's Jonathan Kirk. I work for AP. I'm American, but I live and work in Bogotá. I'm not going anywhere. I just need to survive my own neighborhood."

"Hi, my name's Nkosi Mkele, I work in Johannesburg. Like Jonathan, I'm not going to any hot spots because I already live in one that's at boiling point."

More titters of approval, zero reaction from the Defenders.

When I stood up, I stammered my name and said I was a freelance photographer.

"On Monday I'm going to Kabul," I added before sitting down again. All my course buddies whipped their heads around to look at me, and I noticed, or perhaps I just thought I noticed, more respect in their eyes than I had seen before. Tim wound up, addressing me.

"Well, Maria, keep your ears open in the coming days, because everything you'll learn could turn out to be very useful to you. And with that, thank you, everybody. We've finished here and we can begin."

By ten I had already fainted.

I came to in a sort of slow fade-in. The utter darkness discolored into different textures of gray, then blotches of color began to emerge and separate themselves from the rest and more distinct sounds surfaced from the background hum. I realized those colored blurs were faces leaning over me; then the muffled sounds turned into voices and familiar sentences. "Water, get her some water. There, now she's coming round. Hey, everything's okay. There, drink, good girl, that's the way."

Water doesn't do a thing. I know because I'm prone to fainting and there's always someone who thinks that making me drink will get me back on my feet.

Roger—one of the ones with the ice-colored eyes and raven hair who looked scary—had asked before starting the slide show if anyone in the room was likely to be affected by the sight of blood. No arm was raised and I didn't move.

"Always better to ask," Roger had said. "People have passed out before."

My companions had giggled. I had kept quiet, hoping that I wouldn't, this one time.

We had been sitting on the folding chairs, each with our own notepad with Defenders letterhead, complete with pen with the same logo, while Roger went through the slides, illustrating the basics of extreme first aid.

He had just started on the subject of hemorrhages and, in particular, arterial bleeding when I began to feel strange. The description of blood pressure, but mostly the use of the word "gush" caused a sort of softening in my stomach. I tried to stay focused as Roger called Tim over to act as a guinea pig and went on to show where to tie the tourniquet on the thigh, higher than the wound, and how to exert pressure on the artery by pushing a fist into the groin with as much force as possible. When he started to demonstrate how to push to stem the blood flow, emphasizing the speed with which the victim can bleed to death, I started to get that languid feeling I know so well. Monika Schluss, the German from Christian Aid—a Louise Brooks haircut dyed red, oval glasses—was diligently taking notes next to me, unperturbed, whereas I could not stop the image of spurting blood, of lips turning whiter every second and most of all of the pool of thick red liquid spreading on the floor.

How can everyone listen to these sounds, I asked myself— *firearm, severed vein, gushes, squirts, puddle, blood*—and not feel the same atrocious chill that is slowly taking hold of me?

Everybody looked perfectly calm, interested, some actually even amused. My body instead started to simulate the same process Roger was describing. I could actually feel life flowing away from me like river water, the blood streaming away from my wrists, down my legs, away from my heart and lungs, emptying my body, leaving me dry. I pointed my toes to ward off that familiar somnolence, that desire to be elsewhere. It's the first warning that my body has decided to give up on me. There's nothing I can do. My body seems to possess a personality of its own, like a difficult friend who will walk out of a scary movie without a word of warning.

A split second before I passed out, a last thought flashed through my mind. It is truly unbearable to accept the idea of how vulnerable our bodies are in the face of elements, accidents, attacks. How can we possibly walk around our whole lives carrying this tangle of veins, organs, tubes, valves, glands, air chambers, filters, juices, membranes, protected by only two millimeters of epidermis? Madness, I thought, that such a delicate load—doesn't our life depend entirely on its correct functioning after all?—should be wrapped in tissue paper . . . Then I was out.

At dinner I had decided to join Nkosi, the South African journalist and the only black person in the group, precisely because I noticed he was sitting by himself. The others had already formed small cliques all around, and I got the impression that he might be feeling out of place as well, in this wet and wintry English countryside.

"Of course you can sit here." He smiled. "Maria, right? You're the one who's going to Kabul, isn't it?"

He was wearing a pair of dazzling yellow glasses and a black-and-orange-striped sweater, which made him look like a bee. You could tell he came from a country where there was plenty of sunshine. He wasn't scared of bright colors. With old-fashioned charming manners he had moved a chair for me to sit on.

Just then Liz Reading crept up behind me. She had been heading toward a table of journalists rigged out in black and gray Patagonia gear when, as if on an afterthought, she approached my table with the false concern whose sole purpose I knew was to humiliate me. She leaned in towards me.

"Roger told me tomorrow's class will be on amputated limbs. I just thought I'd let you know, in case you . . . you know . . . might faint again. There may be lots of blood on the slides, so . . ."

"So what?" I asked abruptly.

"Nothing. But he suggested I tell you, in case you prefer to leave the room," she advised in a mellifluous tone.

"I'm *not* scared of blood. It's just that it freaks me out how easy it is to die," I said, coldly glaring at her and stressing every syllable like a mad person. She hastily withdrew, holding her overflowing plate of roast beef and potatoes close to her chest, as if she'd run into a Jehovah's Witness on her doorstep, ready and eager to discuss the Last Judgment.

When she was gone, Nkosi was gracious enough to pick up the conversation where we had left it and ignored my fainting spell as if it had never happened. He asked what I was going to do in Kabul. I muttered something about arranged marriages and diverted the conversation to him and the situation in South Africa. I wasn't really listening, just nodding occasionally whenever I heard the familiar names, like Soweto, Mbeki, Mandela, Truth and Reconciliation Commission. As Nkosi mentioned how one of his best friends had been shot by the police back in the eighties and how he himself had been to jail, I lost myself gazing at the roast with mashed potatoes and baked carrots sitting on my plate. I began to nudge it imperceptibly with my fork, imitating the way Nori assembles the food for a shot, creating neat symmetrical mounds of vegetables next to the entrée.

The Defenders were all sitting together at a long table at the back of the room, hunched over their plates, their heavy shoulders caved in, elbows resting on the table. They were gnawing meat from bones like characters in a medieval painting. They were taciturn and gloomy, doubtless not looking forward to another interminable week of lessons repeated all over again to a bunch of fools who passed out at the mention of blood.

I had the impression I could actually hear their teeth grinding the bones.


"I've had dinner with this very nice South African journalist," I said on the phone to my father, who called me that evening.

I could just picture him, sitting on the checkered sofa in front of the mute TV screen tuned to the satellite news channel, cigarette in hand, eager to hear my report.

"Which paper does he write for?" he asked, as if he read the Johannesburg dailies regularly and knew the names.

"Um . . . I didn't ask. He's very smart. I think he was an activist during the apartheid years." I sighed, realizing that I hadn't listened to Nkosi with enough concentration to appease my father's insatiable curiosity.

"How's the weather?" I asked.

"November weather. The same as you left. What do you care about the weather, anyway?" He sounded impatient now. "Tell me more about this South African journalist."

"What do you want to know? He seems bright, he's nice, he's . . . I don't know. It's not as if he told me his life story."

"*Va bene.* What is it like over there? What about the marines? What kind of place is it? *Allora?* Do you think you could give me some kind of description?"

By now he would've had his plate of pasta and the one glass of red the doctor allowed him for dinner. He had probably saved this phone call till the end of the day, in order to savor it with his last cigarette. I could feel his excitement buzz through the phone line.

"All right. What would you like me to tell you? It's like, let's see—there are all these aid workers and journalists, the food's terrible, the hotel is like a badly refurbished manor house they rent out for weddings, with fluorescent lights and blue carpeting on all the floors; it looks like a rest home. Actually it's almost funny. The Defenders are . . . I don't know, kind of impenetrable. They look like a herd of bison. Quiet and dangerous. How does that sound?"

"A pretty caustic description."

I heard him chuckle. I had succeeded in amusing him. Now—I knew it—he would put down the phone and repeat all I had said verbatim to Leo.

The next day I woke up at five. Outside it was pitch-dark and rainy.

My room was tiny, not much bigger than a closet, and I was feeling claustrophobic and unhappy. Another source of anxiety was the lesson on firearms that was scheduled to open the day. I certainly didn't want to pass out again.

I started surfing the satellite channels and suddenly came across the images of one of the English hostages in Iraq—a middle-aged, kind-looking man in an Day-Glo orange jacket— pleading with his government to help and listen to the kidnappers' requests. I immediately switched to the next station, where a family was pouring breakfast cereals in slow motion and smiling at one another. In the background I could hear a cheerful jingle.

"Right, this morning we're going to learn something about weapons," Alan announced with a grin. His hair was still damp from the shower and combed back like a schoolboy's. Despite the freshness of his cologne, the withered look of someone fighting a fierce hangover was still plastered all over his face. Laid out in front of him on two long, narrow tables was an array of guns, automatic weapons, machine guns and bazookas, like a window display of a spooky toy store.

"Now, on this table we have various types of weapons, those we call low and high velocity. Some of these can pass through the body without significant soft tissue damage, some can shoot up to four hundred rounds in three seconds, others will cause extensive crushing in the wound. On the other table we have more of the nasty stuff. M-16s, rocket launchers, grenades. Naturally, it's important you know how to distinguish one weapon from another, because in case you find yourself under fire, there are vital choices you'll need to make rapidly. For example, some of these weapons can penetrate even concrete, so hiding behind a wall wouldn't do you much good. But let's look at them one by one and learn to recognize them by their shape first."

I had been the last to come in, and Alan had greeted me with a little cough and motioned to me to take a seat in the back. Liz Reading was sitting in the front row and was already taking notes. Nkosi was busy talking to the Australian Reuters journalist. He waved at me, but I didn't want to seem clingy, so I sat at the very back, next to a guy named Mike—a balding, short fortysomething who didn't wear gear and looked just plain and old-fashioned, more like a priest than an adventurous reporter.

Alan showed the class one gun after another, running his fingertips over the barrels, triggers, levers and mechanisms with the same expertise and admiration that mechanics have for engines. He described caliber to us, power, wound volume, kinetic energy theory, entrance and exit holes. Then he proceeded to hand the bullet corresponding to each weapon in question to Liz Reading, who was sitting in the first row right next to him, so she could pass it on to the rest of the class. Liz examined the cartridge for a while, ruminating on its shape and weight as if it could disclose precious information, then reluctantly passed it to the person next to her, so that after a lap of the room the bullet finally reached me.

Two hours later we had covered only the weapons of table number one and we had handled about twenty bullets of various sizes. My companions were growing excited, they kept asking questions and took notes. The women especially, I noticed.

Mike, the silent guy in gray sitting next to me, had begun to give almost imperceptible signs of impatience. I seemed to remember he belonged to a Catholic organization that worked in the Amazon. As I passed the shells to him I noticed he didn't even bother to turn them over in his fingers, feigning interest like the others (some actually knitted their brows as if the object presented unexpected characteristics); Mike instead passed each bullet straight on to the person next to him without even bothering to look at it, as if he found the whole thing silly and didn't want to be part of it. I tried to intercept his attention. I wanted him to know I too was beginning to feel that the whole thing was ridiculous. We started handing our bullets incrementally faster, as if they were getting hotter by the second, averting our eyes from them with identical disparaging expressions.

"Now," Alan announced three hours later (by which time we were supposed to have memorized the names and functions of about forty weapons), "we'll go outside and get cracking on what we call the 'awareness path.' You'll find the suits on that table; put them on and I'll see you outside in two minutes."

Alan went out for a smoke with some of his pals while we clambered into navy blue overalls conceived for extra-large-sized men. Through the glass doors I could see the Defenders smoking, heedless of the rain, kidding around amongst themselves. Then I saw Obelix, Roger and Toby set off for the woods, guns slung over their shoulders, an image that looked sinister and foreboding. I had rolled up my navy blue overalls at the wrists and the ankles the best I could, but I felt strangely humiliated having to wear them. Now that we had on identical uniforms we looked like a group of convicts. We stared at one another with sudden wariness, a bunch of unwitting victims of something that was yet to happen.

The earth was soaked, blackened with peat and chestnut leaves.

Toby explained to us that now we had to set out along a path and things would happen. We would have to react accordingly, bearing in mind what we had just learned.

"Don't be afraid, whatever you hear, don't panic. Everything we use in the scenarios is harmless, no one can get hurt. Go on, off you go now," said Keith, pointing to a path leading through the trees. "And good luck." He grinned.

We set out, hampered by the extra-large suits, timid and hesitant, like Little Red Riding Hoods who know they're about to stumble upon the wolf. Although we knew perfectly well that this was only a scenario, we pushed on unsteadily, clinging together.

At the first volley of gunfire we all flung ourselves to the ground. We landed one on top of the other—a human pyramid of legs and arms tangled together—flattening ourselves, heads down, the whiff of wet leaves in our noses.

"No, no, no!" yelled Toby. "What are you all doing on the ground? You're a perfect target like this. What would it take to do this, for example?" He raised his rifle and mimed a mass execution.

"No, when you hear this kind of shot, from a low-velocity weapon, you've got to find shelter behind a tree, a bush. Your only hope is to hide. Throwing yourself to the ground is the worst thing you could do. Come on, get up, let's get a move on."

We laughed. It didn't even take a second to see that Toby was right.

"What idiots," someone said.

"Automatic reaction," someone else added.

Smeared with mud, we got up and continued to advance, our ears pricked, ready to detect the slightest signal. As we kept walking, the wait became nerve-wracking. Then suddenly, four sharp shots, close together. I ran for all of one and a half seconds, then dived again, flattening myself onto the frozen ground. The others all did exactly the same. Toby emerged from the bushes shaking his head.

"No! I told you, that's not an option. You have to learn to think when you hear gunfire, not panic. You have to try and work out, first off, where the shot's coming from, and then, by the sound, you will have identified the type of weapon being fired. For example, what kind of gun you reckon that was?"

Nkosi, Jonathan and Liz Reading seemed the most prepared. They stammered some of the names and numbers we were supposed to have memorized. Toby merely shook his head disapprovingly.

"Nope. Sorry. It was a Beretta. A handgun. Anyway, come on, keep moving and keep your ears open."

We were hit again and again. First, going past Toby, we were caught in a cross fire, then by a sniper with a high-precision rifle, then by an M-16 and lastly by a grenade. Unfailingly, we ducked down each time, without trace of a strategy of any kind. Each time we leapt as if a heavy shutter slammed down as soon the shot fired and all our bodies wanted to do was disappear. There was no way of ramming any other reaction into our brains. It didn't help to remind ourselves the guns were fake.

The sequence was identical for the entire awareness path: we would get up from the ground, learn what we did wrong, and then go for more. Another bang, another leap, more mud, more leaves in the nostrils.

At one point I even held my breath, thinking I could get away with just playing dead.

· · ·

Dinner found us all lined up, plates in hand, in front of the usual buffet of roast meat and pale, frozen veggies.

Nkosi beckoned me to sit at his table, next to Jonathan Kirk, the American journalist who lived in Bogotá, a forty-year-old who definitely worked out at the gym a lot; square jaw, sandy hair and that bespectacled-superhero look that some women find attractive. To break the ice and get it out of the way, we joked about our failure on the awareness path. Nkosi, however, went on to recount a hairy five minutes he'd spent in Sierra Leone at a checkpoint held by trigger-happy rebels. Jonathan Kirk seized the ball and in turn described a demonstration in Jakarta where bullets had been flying everywhere. This ping-pong braggadocio between the two went on for a while. It wasn't the least bit interesting.

"Maria leaves for Kabul on Monday," Nkosi said to Jonathan, as if giving me the cue that it was finally my turn to recount a dangerous adventure.

I nodded, offering no further explanation. Jonathan smiled. Nkosi cleared his throat.

"She's doing a story on arranged marriages," he continued.

"A good friend of mine lives in Kabul," proffered Jonathan. "He used to be a correspondent for the *Financial Times,* but now he works for an NGO. You may know who he is—Steve Gilmore? He knows everyone there. I'm sure he can give you a hand."

"Ah, yeah, Steve Gilmore," said Nkosi. "I think I know the guy. Wasn't he based in Nairobi about five years ago?"

Jonathan and Nkosi discussed Steve Gilmore for a while. I learned he had just divorced his wife, a brilliant CNN correspondent who had moved to Shanghai and whom they both described in glowing terms. They then turned back to me to bring me into the conversation, in the hope I would say something, anything, as long as I contributed to this map of names, places and adventures that seems to bind all correspondents who live in war zones.

"I heard Steve lives in a rambling old palace in the center of Kabul," added Jonathan. "I ought to have his number some-where, I can give it to you if you like. And then what's-his-name will probably be there too, the BBC correspondent, the one who was in Tehran—you know who I mean."

"Actually, I've never been anywhere like that. I mean, I've never gone to a war zone in my life," I said, dismantling the vegetable compositions on my plate. I looked up at him evenly.

"I did some photojournalism in the past but I'm more of a food photographer now. I do cookbooks, gourmet magazines. Sometimes I illustrate food articles for the papers."

Nkosi and Jonathan looked at me, their eyes blank.

"It's by sheer chance that I'm going to Kabul," I added quickly. "This is something completely out of the ordinary for me. Actually, I'm really nervous."

Nkosi and Jonathan smiled feebly, trying to figure out whether I was putting them on.

"No, really. It's true," I said, smiling back at them, as if to reassure them that it was okay, that my confession had not embarrassed me, that being an ordinary person who doesn't live surrounded by gunfights and kamikaze attacks is not some-thing to be ashamed of.

"So, all this, I mean, the classes, their scenarios . . ." Jonathan darted a look at Nkosi. "I mean all that we're doing here must seem completely nuts to you."

"Nuts? No, why? If anything it makes me even more aware I haven't got a clue as to what awaits me."

Nkosi shook his head and laughed. He poured some wine in my glass and then raised his, as if to invite me to a toast. I think in a way he was impressed I had outed myself. I guess it took guts, among war correspondents.

I glanced at Mike over at the back, who had chosen to eat alone at a table by himself. He had brought a book to read and was avidly turning the pages. I envied him. I could've done with a bit of peace and quiet myself.

Each morning we started at eight sharp with a first-aid theory lesson. Roger illustrated increasingly complex situations, more like an escalation of horrors. We went from multiple fractures to tracheotomies to the retrieval of severed limbs.

Roger had a businesslike attitude about injuries and wounds. He treated the human body as if it were something that could easily be patched up, at least temporarily. He said there was always something you could do to keep the victim from dying. For a few hours anyhow, until you got to a hospital.

"What would you do if, let's say, your casualty's intestines were hanging out?"

No one had a clue, nor was anyone inclined to put a hand up with a suggestion. How could we? For all we knew, in every war movie the soldier holding his entrails in his hands is a goner. That's usually the scene where he dies in his buddy's arms. End of performance.

But no, Roger reassured us, the intestine is just like a sausage.

"You can stick it back in, no problem. All you have to do is push it back in and tape it."

Moans and murmurs of horror and disbelief.

"Yep. Regular tape. The paper one's actually best, but duct tape'll do. But if it's bleeding," he warned us, "it gets a bit trickier because a bleeding intestine will last no more than six hours. In this case you just tie it with string."

"Tie it *how*?" someone asked meekly.

"I told you," said Roger, "just think of sausages, the way they're tied up. That's all."

He mimed winding string, knotting it and pulling it tight.

"Severed hand? Rinse, wrap in damp gauze and put it in a plastic bag. If there's any available, use ice. Never put a severed limb in direct contact with ice or you risk burning it. You have no idea how many hands and fingers could have been reattached if this simple procedure had been followed."

I was struck by this new way of conceiving the human body. If only a couple of days before I had still been thinking of it as a complex and fragile apparatus, so tenuous that it made me swoon, now, thanks to Roger, my vision had begun to change. The body, I was beginning to see, was something you could put your hands into without fear. More like a thick slab of meat in the kitchen that you could cut open, stuff, tightly truss and shove in the oven.

Roger insisted, "The human body is more resilient than you can imagine. It takes a lot of damage to shut it down. When you give first aid in an emergency situation always remember you have more time than you think. It's rare that a casualty will die on you. Do your assessment, think, don't rush and then do all that you need to do without panicking. Ninety percent of the time, you'll succeed in getting your casualty at least to a hospital."

It felt reassuring. I took a mental note that this was the most important information I'd learned so far.

Roger added, "A few years ago a team of scientists tested the resistance of the human body in the lab on that of a pig. Of all the animals, the pig's system is the most similar to ours. Well, they did everything they could to it for a whole day. They shot it four times in the chest, they cut off its ears, they severed its legs, performed a tracheotomy, cut out a huge piece of intestine, took out part of the stomach, took out a lung. Guess what—by the end of the day the pig was still there. Yup, Porky gave no sign he was ready to bite the dust."

. . .

In the following days we began the more intense part of the training, what the brochure called "traumatic scenarios under controlled conditions." Horrific events were carefully staged every afternoon—explosions, shoot-outs, accidents of all sorts. We had to get into our extra-large overalls, by now stiff with mud, and go outside to put into practice what we had just learned in the morning in Roger's first-aid class.

Two or three Defenders took turns playing the casualties. Each one wore different gear—military jackets, Afghan caps, camouflage cargo pants, turbans—and mixed them together in imaginative ways that unapologetically suggested potentially aggressive ethnic groups. They also had a variety of latex prostheses (the sort that might be used by a special-effects crew in a horror film), which were strapped to their legs, chests, arms in order to simulate multiple fractures, stumps, gaping wounds. To add verisimilitude they also squirted jets of blood with a little pump to produce arterial hemorrhages in large quantities.

There were different themes, all carefully staged by invisible set designers. The first one we came across was a very realistic road accident—two cars had crumpled into each other, one driver slumped over the wheel, the horn blaring, the other trapped under the seat.

On a different occasion we stumbled upon a refugee camp where a gas-cylinder explosion had caused third-degree burns to a group of crazed and drunken militiamen (for this one the set was dressed with tents, a campfire and guns stacked against a tree). On another occasion we encountered a shoot-out at a checkpoint, and here the victims were lying facedown in the mud by the barrier, in puddles of blood.

We were usually split up into small groups. We always ventured out with the same hesitant gait, expecting the worst. Invariably, after only a couple of minutes along the country lanes, all sorts of explosions, loud bangs and catastrophes would be sprung on us, followed by piercing screams. This was the signal that some disaster had taken place and our help was needed.

We would run to the site of the incident, shouting (rule number one: approach only if it's safe to do so, always announce your presence, Roger had recommended), and rush to help the victims. There was no time to determine who was the most seriously injured, or to pick the victim who presented fewer complications. It was pure chance that threw rescuer and casualty together.

With his seasoned Viking air, Obelix was, out of all the Defenders, the one I had begun to nurse something akin to a feeling for. During our daily scenarios I'd happened to pick him as my casualty more than once and this—unknown to him— had made him strangely familiar to me.

The day of the car accident, I rushed to the crumpled car and found my casualty slumped over the wheel, his face and hair spattered with blood, his foot planted on the accelerator. The horn was blaring and the engine was roaring, racing, lending a distressing urgency to the scene.

It wasn't until I approached, yelling at the top of my lungs, "I'm here, everything's going to be all right now. I'll get you out of there," that I recognized him. His hair was caked with blood—clearly a head wound.

On this particular occasion Obelix was drowsy but awake (during the exercises the Defenders had the option to decide whether to remain conscious, pass out, or die in the arms of their rescuer, depending on the gravity of their wounds and the efficiency of the rescuer's assistance).

"Don't panic, this is only an exercise, try to think," I kept repeating to myself as I felt the adrenaline pumping and panic seizing me by the throat.

First off, I cut the engine (rule number two: check for any danger to yourself, the injured person or others around you). I grabbed him by the shoulders and lifted him off the horn. He fell back against the seat, his head slumping against the head-rest, and silence descended at last. I checked to see if his airway was clear and he was breathing. I also made sure that the head wound was only superficial and quickly stanched it with a bandage before the sight of all that fake blood could make me faint. Then I inspected the body for other wounds, while he kept moaning in a slurred chant that everything hurt and he was surely going to die.

Roger had taught us that you had to feel the torso, running your hands under the jacket to make sure there was no blood. I had to get my hands under his shirt to do so. I felt his warm, clammy skin. As I brushed his body I became aware of the intimacy of the gesture. It unsettled me.

"Nothing here either," I said out loud. I then ran my hands along his thighs and legs, trying to touch his body lightly, impersonally, in the same way airport personnel search passengers at metal detectors. I noticed a protuberance on his shin. I touched it and realized something was out of place. I took out the scissors from the first-aid kit we carried in a pouch and cut through the fabric of his trouser leg to see what was underneath. I did it with a show of self-assurance to counteract the embarrassment I actually felt at what I was doing.

"Don't worry, it'll be all right, you're fine," I whispered to him the way I'd seen camp doctors do in movies.

"Aha. It looks like there's a fracture here," I declaimed, staying in character for the scene we were both playing. A latex prosthesis strapped to his leg revealed lacerated flesh and a bone poking out of his shin.

At this point, Obelix was still sitting back against the driver's seat while I was trafficking with his trousers. He kept flopping his head repeatedly onto his chest as if to hint he would be better off lying down. And, of course, the bandage I had tied around his temples had come undone and the gauze was dangling over his face.

"Now, in just a minute we'll get you out of here, all right?" I offered tentatively. Obelix did not reply.

"I can't fix up your leg unless you're lying on the ground," I explained.

He ignored me. Nevertheless, I managed to get him over my shoulder and haul him out of the car, adopting the method we had been shown in the lesson on casualty evacuation. There was actually a way, by using leverage on arms and shoulders, by which even someone of my size could move a man of Obelix's bulk.

"You're hurting me like that, you stupid bitch," he snarled as I was helping him to drag himself along.

It shocked me that he would insult me. I had assumed personal affront wasn't part of the game.

"Yes, but what else can I do? I can't fix your leg up if you don't—"

"Fuck off, you're hurting me, can't you see? Who the fuck sent you?"

In class, Roger had warned us that the injured may not be polite. I tried to remember what he had said exactly and the specific way to respond: "A person who is suffering tends not to follow etiquette, but you have to be firm and keep doing what you know is right, even if it's painful."

I laid him on a blanket (rule number three: always try to cover the victim, or put a layer between him and the ground; shock and loss of blood lower the body temperature and create hypothermia), then I started to work on the fracture, bandaging it tightly in a splint.

"Don't touch me, you bloody idiot! Call a doctor. You don't know what the fuck you're doing!!"

"Stop being such a pain in the ass. Now," I hissed with a forcefulness I didn't know I had. "And let me work in peace."

I was amazed at the speed with which I'd shut him up.

I wrapped him in the cover and while I was at it retied the

loose bandage on his head. I thought I'd fixed him up pretty nicely. It was a treat to look at him all snug under the blanket, his bandages tight, looking so much cleaner and tidier than when I had found him.

Now I knew for sure he was going to survive.

More or less at this point, once we had all assisted our wounded, or evacuated them from the accident sites, the casualties leapt up like blood-spattered zombies, their heads and arms bandaged somehow or other, gauze hanging, their clothes slashed, and, in front of the group that had gathered around, gave their evaluation of the assistance that had been provided. It was a sort of quick, very technical overview, where oversights and errors were pointed out.

Obelix jumped up like a bloodied jack-in-the box and, in front of everyone, graded my intervention.

"Let's see what we have here. Maria, you acted quickly, you turned off the engine straightaway—well done, it was the first thing to do. You immediately checked the airway and response and that was good too."

He had resumed a detached, impersonal tone, gone back to being an instructor. For some reason I didn't fully understand yet, I felt a certain disappointment. Only two minutes earlier, I had been comforting him as he moaned, reassuring him that he was not going to die, that everything was going to be all right, and now this sudden change in our relationship had caught me off guard.

"You realized right away that the head wound was only superficial, and you handled it quickly—which is right, although your bandaging technique needs some improving."

He coughed a thick smoker's cough that seemed to originate from deep inside his lungs. He wiped his mouth with the back of his hand.

"So far, so good. But there's one thing you didn't pay attention to."

He pointed to his ear and asked the group, "Can anyone tell me what this is?"

A few of them gingerly stepped in to look, but shook their heads.

I felt a pang of jealousy. Obelix and his injuries were my responsibility, they belonged to me and I didn't want anyone to come between us. I stepped in and studied the rivulet of dried yellow liquid that ran from his ear down his neck. I hadn't the faintest idea what that was supposed to be. I looked at Obelix, hoping he'd give me a clue. I shook my head.

"Cerebrospinal fluid leakage," he announced darkly. "It tells you there's a serious head injury, possibly a skull fracture. You wouldn't have thrown me backwards and forwards like that if you'd been aware of it."

"Yes, actually, I didn't—"

"You forgot to check to see if my neck, or spine, was broken," he went on, ignoring me, "and that was a serious mistake. What else. You dragged me out of the vehicle rapidly and you remembered to lay me on a blanket to prevent hypothermia. Well done. The splint wasn't bandaged securely enough. But all in all, I'd say you didn't do too badly."

"I think I'm beginning to get the hang of this." I was bragging to my father, who called me again that night. He was thrilled by my daily schedule and didn't want to miss a detail.

"Tomorrow we've got a class on land mines and after that we go into a checkpoint situation."

"What's that supposed to mean?"

"Okay, what they do is they stage a checkpoint, like in one of those countries where there's a revolution going on, a civil war, something like that. Then they split us up into groups and each group in turn pretends they are a news crew that needs to go through. One of us plays the producer, another one is the cameraman and the other one is the journalist."

"Hmmm . . ."

"We get to the checkpoint in our vehicle and the guys, the militia or whatever, start asking for money, passports, documents, bribes. In other words they start giving us a hard time, saying we can't go through, our papers are not in order, blah blah blah. Basically they threaten they'll have to keep us there. Stuff like that."

"But what are they actually teaching you, *tesoro*? I still don't understand."

Despite the endearment my father suddenly sounded irritated.

"Well, the point is we have to figure out how to extricate ourselves from the situation, how to react without getting us into more trouble. There are all these unwritten rules one needs to know, like always take off your sunglasses, keep your hands on the dashboard."

"On the dashboard?"

"Yes. Then you have to know how much cash you need to have at hand in case they decide to keep your passport, how to handle the really aggressive guys, who to pay and how. Apparently checkpoints in danger zones are where the most incidents occur. People get shot at checkpoints all the time, you know."

I had started talking like Nkosi and Jonathan. It felt good to use the jargon.

"Basically, what you're saying is they teach you how to *bribe* guards at checkpoints, yes?"

"Well, basically, yes. If necessary," I said, defensively. "Should the situation get hairy."

It annoyed me that my father, of all people, wouldn't see the point of this. Wasn't he supposed to be Mr. I Know It All on coup d'états, guerrillas and tribal clashes?

"But, Maria, it sounds more like an acting class than a training course to me. More like you're playing danger," he said.

"I'm just wondering how this is going to help you once you actually find yourself in the situa—"

"Afghanistan is one *huge* checkpoint."

"Right," said my father skeptically.

"What?"

"Nothing, it just sounds a bit sinister, at least from where I'm standing. Besides, I know how impressionable you are. I wouldn't want you to—"

"No, I'm fine, I promise you. The first couple of days, maybe. But now I'm getting into it."

Perhaps he was beginning to feel guilty for having pushed me into this, now that he could see how the adventure was taking shape in all its gruesome details. However, at this point I didn't need him to remind me how ill-suited I was to all this. Not now that I was beginning to cope. Not when I'd just managed to shut Obelix up.

Even the first-aid classes had taken a different light. All that talk about blood and amputations didn't freak me out as much as it had two days earlier. Something had shifted in the last forty-eight hours. I had acquired an unexpected faith in the resistance of the human body now that I had begun to see it in a new way, as a solid chunk of flesh and bones, or better yet, as sausages. It seemed that, after all, everything could be fixed up with a snip here, a few neat stitches there and a good, tight bandage.

At dinner, Liz Reading had commandeered a position at Nkosi's table and was now sitting between him and Jonathan Kirk, laughing and tossing her thick dark hair as Jonathan poured her a generous glass of wine. Bob Sheldon, the Australian journalist—a corpulent, hairy man with a gentle, bovine air—had joined them. I waved at Nkosi as I waited in line holding my plate in front of the shepherd's pie and the cauliflower au gratin, but quickly turned away again, fearing he would ask me to join them. I could already hear Jonathan's booming laughter as, heedless of the volume, he was telling a funny story about meeting once with Chavez. I headed over to Mike, the quiet, balding rebel, who was sitting at a table at the back all by himself.

"How's it going?" I asked him.

He put his book down.

"I guess the novelty wore off."

"Who did you have as a victim today?"

"Alan, the one with the blue eyes. He was wounded in his thigh. An arterial hemorrhage."

"Ah!" I said. "Was it difficult to handle?"

"Oh, I gave up straightaway. He kept squirting blood in my face with that pump thing, and he just wouldn't stop. They do it on purpose. It's their private joke. They pick one victim and then laugh amongst themselves afterwards. I wasn't in the mood to play along."

He snorted and went back to his roast.

"You mean you just left him lying there on the ground bleeding to death?"

"Yes. Anyway, I didn't have a clue what to do with all that blood spurting on my glasses."

He'd gone on strike. Incredible.

"You see, I'm only an accountant for an NGO. We do work for refugees," he explained. "I sit all day in an office with air-conditioning and a doorman. I don't think I'll get too many opportunities to save someone with a severed artery. If anything like that does ever happen, I think I'll call an ambulance with my cell phone and let them deal with it."

I took a better look at Mike. Glasses with silver frames, sagging eyelids, lusterless hair; the texture of his clothes was soft, fuzzy, lifeless. I wasn't sure he was being sarcastic. Candid, more like it. We ate in silence for a few minutes.

"Excuse me, but can I ask you something?" I said.

"Sure."

"You're not by any chance a priest, are you?"

"No."

He shook his head slowly. He looked amused.

Only then did I notice the book he was reading all this time—*The Artist Within: A Journey to Discover Your Hidden Creativity*.

The following day, the checkpoint scenario didn't exactly go as planned.

It was almost dusk and we were all packed in the van; Keith was driving us to the location of the action. The landscape had taken on a spectral appearance; it was drizzling again and the cold got into your bones. It wasn't the kind of afternoon one longed to spend outdoors. I would've preferred to read a book by the fireside. The others were laughing and telling stories, a raucous animation like on a school bus.

Just then we heard the shots. The van slammed to a halt, and we were swept up in shouting, volleys of gunfire, blows to the side of the van; someone yanked the sliding door open. I caught a glimpse of camouflage suits and black balaclavas. Everyone was screaming like crazy. It felt like the end of the world.

"Get the fuck out! Out, I said, get out, bastards, move!"

Hands grabbed me and flung me out together with the others. Before I could get an idea of what was going on, someone shoved my head forward and stuffed it into a thick, dark, rough sack. There was screaming and banging all around. I couldn't think straight.

"Down! I said get down, you motherfucker!"

I felt a blow in the back of my knees as two heavy hands bore down on my shoulders. The next thing I knew, I was facedown in the freezing, slushy mud. My heart was beating wildly, the cloth of the bag was stuck to my nostrils like a suction cup and I was gasping for air.

Then the voices subsided all at once; a preternatural silence fell. All I could hear now were the men's footfalls in the wet grass (how many were there? and *who* were they?). They moved slowly, intentionally. All I could make out was muffled, rustling sounds, as if heavy bundles were being moved around. I heard footsteps approaching; someone kicked my ankle, forcing me to spread my legs open. The hands grabbed my arms and wrenched them away from my body.

There I was, crucified, facedown in clods of frozen earth with a bag over my head.

A cold rage started mounting. It was unbelievable, what they were doing to us. The bastards. This was too much, completely over the top. To pay money to be pushed down, face in the mud. One could easily catch pneumonia lying in the rain like this.

"I'm not bearing with this another second. I'm getting up."

But I didn't. One side of my brain instructed me it was better to remain there on the ground, perfectly still, if I didn't want to get into more trouble.

I listened to the footsteps shuffling around me, stealthily. I could tell our kidnappers were busy doing something but had no clue what it was.

I tried to fully inhale the bit of air that passed through the cloth—I badly needed to breathe—but the sack clung to my nostrils even more. I started hyperventilating.

Great. I'm going to die of asphyxiation.

I furtively began to move my hand towards my face, I wanted to at least pull the cloth away from my nostrils in order to create enough space so that some air could filter through. But something hard hit me on the head (was it a boot, a rifle butt? I could no longer tell what anything was). A pretty heavy blow, mind you. I felt a hand grab my wrist and tug my arm out, thrusting it violently to the ground.

I tried to recall this breathing exercise I'd learned years before that helped release tension and anxiety. One had to breathe in very slowly, hold the breath for six full seconds, then slowly breathe out.

I couldn't work out where my companions were, how far from me, whether they had been dragged away. I could no longer hear their voices, or feel their presence. Could it be that we had all sunk in this horrid silence, lost to each other, without the courage to even send a signal?

Was that all it took? We had been a group only moments before and now we were isolated, blind, each of us caving in to this frozen solitude.

I don't know how much time had passed. I could hear the light rain pattering on the leaves of the trees, the footsteps, more sounds I couldn't identify, like metallic clinking against something here and there. I had gradually begun to breathe more normally; at any rate, it didn't feel like I had cotton wool up my nose anymore.

Footsteps approached me. The violent, brutal grip again. I felt the hands rifle through the pockets of my jacket, my pants, flipping me left and right like a deadweight, as they kept pushing something sharp into my back. The hands removed my wallet, my cell phone, my glasses and my room key. They touched me with an impatient, dangerous feel. They wrenched off my watch and my bracelet, clamped my wrist trying to snatch my silver ring, which was too tight and wouldn't come off.

Somehow, although I knew the man was only playing a part (it could have been Tim, Alan, Obelix—someone I knew), I just couldn't make myself speak to him and explain that I hadn't been able to get the ring off for years, that he probably needed soap if he really intended to take it. He was determined to take everything off me, and wouldn't let go of my finger till he succeeded by twisting it this way and that. Then the hands lifted my hair and fumbled around my neck, looking for earrings. The fingers were coarse, smelly. Their touch disgusted me. They yanked off my mother's gold chain.

I had worn that chain since the day she died without ever taking it off. It had been ten years I'd had it around my neck. I wanted to cry.

"I hate you," I mouthed. "I fucking hate you. You didn't have to fucking do this to us."

A leaden silence had descended. More than silence, it was an absence of life, as if someone had turned off the background hum of the insects, birds and plants and silenced nature's breath.

In that eerie emptiness a shot suddenly rang out. A distant, isolated shot, like a lonely instrument. Then rustling sounds, scuffling all around me. I heard feet dragging on the ground as if they were being pulled against their will; I sensed fear in those footsteps.

They're taking them away now. One by one. Maybe they're dead, I thought.

There was another shot. No shout, no struggle. Why didn't any of us react, or at least try to find out what was happening to the others? Why didn't anyone call out anyone else's name?

Jonathan, Mike, Nkosi, Liz? I didn't want them to die, I didn't want anything to happen to them. They were my buddies.

Yet we were passively complying. Each one closed up in his own black hood, all spatial references, all sense of orientation gone; now merely victims awaiting execution. Another sharp report in the distance. Was there someone pointing a gun at my head as well, ready to shoot me if I moved or if I even called out someone's name?

I heard footsteps coming quickly in my direction. Somehow I knew it right away. My turn had come.

They pulled me up like a heap of rags and shoved me forward. I stumbled into bushes, on the uneven ground, the hands prodding my back. I could hear the heavy breathing of the man shoving me. Then the hands pressed on my shoulders, forcing me down again. I fell to my knees on the wet grass. The hands grabbed my arms and made me cross them behind my head.

So this is it.

On my knees, hands crossed behind my head, waiting for a bullet that I can't even see coming. Like an animal in a slaughterhouse.

This is how one dies, in the cold and the dark of a night like any other. Without a voice calling you by name, without even the sight of another human being. Your head stuffed inside a bag, alone. And you don't even know why this is happening to you.

Memories and images muddled. The English hostage, the kind middle-aged man in the Day-Glo orange jacket. One moment in his car. The next on the ground with a gun at his head. Panic shutting my throat. Now the metallic taste of death.

It's just this simple, and the same for every one of us. I thought I knew. But now I really knew.

I felt the hands loosen the tie on the bag.

Beheading, I couldn't help but think.

They pulled the hood off my face. I saw Tim, the senior Defender.

He put a hand on my shoulder and leaned over me with a gentle smile.

"Everything okay? You all right?" he whispered while Alan was filming my face with a small video camera.

He smiled and spoke softly so he couldn't be heard.

"You can go back inside with the others and have some tea. I'll see you in class when we're finished with this."

I nodded. He handed me a plastic bag containing my ring, wallet, chain and the rest of my things. "Thank you," I said.

Before I left, I saw Keith shoving a hooded Jonathan Kirk
towards us. I watched him get down on his knees in front of
Tim and the camera.

I saw the way Keith forced him to cross his arms behind his
head.

I turned back towards the hotel. I didn't want to stand there.
I didn't want to see his face when they took the sack off and
uncovered his eyes.

"First of all, take a good look at yourselves," said Tim, as the
video started on the screen behind him. "Then we'll go through
what happened and analyze it."

The sequence was identical for each of us. There we were,
trotting along, dark bags over our heads. Stumbling, laden with
fear, a bunch of grotesque hooded figures no longer recognizable, no longer human. The image of our bluish, grainy silhouettes lurching from the woods towards the camera was straight
out of some sinister news footage.

We now slump to our knees, crossing arms behind heads. A
hand pulls the sack off. The terrified, contracted expressions,
disheveled hair, wide, staring eyes. A dress rehearsal for horror.

No one laughed when we saw our faces slip out of the bags.
In fact, the room was mute, cold. It was like looking at yourself
from the hereafter, staring into your pupils the moment before
the trigger was pulled. There was our last glance, immortalized.

There is no dignity in terror; if that was to be our last image,
then none of us looked the way we wished we had.

"Secondly, please forgive us for playing this—let's call it
trick—on you without any warning," Tim continued, throwing
his arms out, a faint note of embarrassment, "but the whole
point of this exercise is that it has to be totally unexpected. In a
hostage-taking scenario, the surprise factor is crucial."

Just then the door opened and Liz Reading came in. She
must have gone to wash her face and touch up her makeup; her

eyes were still puffy and red from crying. She sat next to me, swathed in a hooded sweatshirt. We half nodded at one another as if we wanted to acknowledge a shift in our relationship. I felt like patting her on the shoulder but I restrained myself.

"Let's go through the various phases together, now. The first is called 'initial takeover.' It's the phase when kidnappers use lots of shouting and gunfire to induce shock and subdue the hostages. This is the most dangerous phase of the abduction; adrenaline is sky-high and a wrong move could cost you your life."

That was exactly what was shameful. To be sitting there, cup of tea in hand, watching ourselves on the screen and analyzing what had happened as if it were an incident that could be split into phases, that had variables, unknown quantities of danger; an event that presented a problem but possibly had a *solution*.

The shame lay in the astronomical sum—didn't Pierre say just that?—we had paid to experience our own execution, to then be able to play it back in the warmth of the classroom and go over the behaviors that would save our hide. "The search," Tim continued, "is the next phase, where the hostage is stripped of his identity. Its purpose is mainly to create a sense of disorientation. Who among you tried to react?"

Hands slowly raised, the others were starting to come back from the daze and take part again. Gradually the atmosphere thawed, everyone relieved to have to answer questions. After all, it was just an exercise, a reenactment, wasn't it? That way what had just happened would slip away faster.

Tim went on, explaining that—once the initial violence had subsided—that would have been the moment to establish the beginning of communication with your captors through small, tentative gestures. He instructed how this new phase—number four, I believe—was crucial because it enabled the hostages to negotiate for water, food or blankets. My companions took notes. By now they had turned back into the diligent students they had been all week. Only Liz Reading, the enterprising top of the class ready to flirt with danger, seemed incapable of getting hold of herself. She kept blowing her nose and dabbing her eyes with tissues, to stop the tears that slid down slowly, like a dripping tap.

Tim droned on.

"It can be very long. Months, sometimes even years. If the negotiations aren't successful straightaway, you have to resort to some tricks to stop yourself from going insane. An American soldier was taken hostage by the Vietcong for five years. They kept him locked in a bamboo cage and every day they lowered him waist-deep into a rat-infested river and left him there to rot until nightfall. Well, I'll tell you how he succeeded in not losing his mind. He found a method, a kind of mental discipline. For five years he worked every day at building a five-star hotel in his mind. He began with the foundation, then he put in the pillars, the reinforced-concrete structure, the plumbing, wiring, fixtures, and so on. Every day he added a piece until he had done all the floors, the windows, right down to the beds, the table lamps and the towel racks. In a situation like that, you've got to find a way out, and if there isn't a way out, then you have to find an escape into your own head."

Liz Reading choked back a sob. I gave her a gentle smile. She tried to respond with a grimace. Her face was all red and blotchy. I laid a hand on her shoulder. She clutched it and didn't let go.

The dress rehearsal for horror had changed everything. We bonded.

Now, as we came together once again for dinner, lined up in front of another roast leg of lamb and mint sauce, we looked at each other with a sort of gratitude, a newfound complicity. Not only were we now a group of survivors, but another bonding factor was the shared knowledge that we had all behaved the same way. The film had given us unblinking proof of this:

we had watched the grim parade of our close-ups. Trembling, frightened and, worst of all, passive, reduced to silence immediately, without exception. There hadn't been any heroes in the group, we had all been incapable of even attempting to save ourselves, let alone the others; nobody had reacted, not even when we had been robbed of our most precious and sacred belongings. All of us had felt an identical terror, as the succession of stares striking Alan's camera lens had testified.

This was no time to brag about bullets, car bombs, minefields or thugs at borders. No previous real-life experience had outdone the event, simulated though it was, that we had just experienced together. Because through that cold rain, alone in our burlap sacks, each one of us had just had a close encounter with that cowardly self we didn't know we harbored—that rather contemptible being we would have felt sorry for, been irritated or embarrassed by, had it manifested itself in someone else. But now, to have discovered it in ourselves, to have been forced to recognize it and accept it, had made us more open, humbler, lighter.

We piled into a car after dinner, riding the crest of this new camaraderie. Someone had suggested it; after all, we needed to celebrate.

The pub reeked of beer and smoke, damp shoes and rancid breath. There were six or seven Defenders sitting at the bar in front of a row of empty bottles. They were kidding around with each other, flirting with the barmaid, who looked like she'd known them for ages. She wasn't young—hair dyed shoe-polish black, puffy eyelids, smoker's wrinkles around her lips—and was leaning on her elbows on the bar in a pose that showed her generous cleavage. She had that slightly wayward, coarse look that sensible women who live in small places often have, who wear stay-up stockings under their aprons and know how to comfort a tired man.

The Defenders had given us a weak sign of recognition—a half smile, a nod, the slightest raising of a bottle—to confirm that the unwritten rule was that you weren't supposed to fraternize. This was their pub where they let off steam at the end of the day. The last thing they wanted was to listen to us rambling about our trauma as pseudo-hostages. The implicit message was to leave them in peace. So, disheartened by this cool reception but still flush with the event of the day, we headed for a shabby couch at the back and ordered our drinks.

The simultaneous presence of pseudo-hostages and pseudo-kidnappers in the same place put something of a damper on our mission, which was to throw ourselves into a postmortem of the day's events with alcohol-fueled ardor. This was the payoff we had been craving: to be by ourselves at last, free to repeat, compare, elaborate details and dramatize.

Obelix turned slightly, without a flicker, let alone a smile, of recognition. I passed by him, hoping he would send a signal at least to me, if for no other reason than because of the extremely personal contact there had been between us. After all, my hands, soaked in fake blood, had felt his skin under his shirt. But he only darted a glance and turned back to the barmaid, who was laughing, slowly stroking her bare forearms.

Maybe those two had something going on. Having to bear this desolate countryside for months on end, the Defenders had to find some distractions. Maybe they each had a lady friend in town they could spend the night with, some hot divorcée they'd met at the café, or the supermarket.

The sight of Obelix's mighty back turned to me, the breasts spilling from the barmaid's low-cut top, the proximity of their bodies and the perfect intimacy between them vexed me.

By the end of the week, I had gotten used to the military routine of our days, to the exhaustion that fell upon me around five, to the cold during exercises in the fields, to living in a group, to eating together and to collapsing into bed at ten.

We had learned how to get out of minefields in one piece by prodding the ground section by section with the same metal skewer one uses for kebabs. We put together makeshift stretchers with blankets folded a certain way, we practiced mouth-to-mouth resuscitation and CPR, we were told how to dig a shelter in the snow if caught in a blizzard, we gained some notion of navigating by the stars, we learned to give our position by the compass, to recognize a package full of explosives and to check that the ignition wasn't connected to an explosive device. I had filled pad after pad with notes, watched an infinite series of videos and slides; my head was full of rules, warnings, procedures.

I'd gotten used to waking before dawn every morning and going straight to the hotel gym, a small, sour-smelling room. I would usually find Monika Schluss already there, working out on the machines with methodical slowness, listening to her iPod. We'd give each other a quick smile, then I'd get on the treadmill and run for twenty minutes. I'd stare straight in front of me and think about my life and how unadventurous it had been in the last few years, until the sun would start to come in through the window and the silhouettes of the fir trees formed outside; that was the signal that it was time to take a shower and start another day of war.

The last day of the course I woke up earlier than usual. I didn't feel like going to run on the treadmill and so I started zapping between TV channels while it was still pitch-dark outside.

The hostages in Iraq were still wearing their Day-Glo orange jackets and their faces looked grainy in the livid light. I watched the mute images as the newscaster gave an account of the latest, slim developments. Nothing had happened, it was just a matter of waiting, he said. Almost two months had gone by since they had been abducted. Who knows how they had been spending the time, who knows if they'd found a technique, a mental escape route, to avoid insanity while they kept on waiting.

Although the footage was always the same—the video the kidnappers had sent to Al Jazeera had been played over and over again in the last few weeks—it looked different to me now. It was as if their ghostly pallor, the tufts of dirty hair plastered to their foreheads, their empty gazes now appeared to me like the foreshadowing of their certain death. It was as if their destiny lay hidden in those details, and with each rerun it was beginning to come to the surface.

I had to switch channels. A documentary about the aftermath of the tsunami showed archival footage shot immediately following the catastrophe. An arm sticking out of the rubble, a mother beating her fists in the sand beside the body of her child, tourists' bodies washing ashore like dead fish, a redheaded woman in a floral swimsuit bobbing facedown in the water like a puppet. I switched channels again. A bombing in Tel Aviv. Police sirens, blood-spattered kids fleeing a discotheque, stretchers, dogs, rubble, dust, people screaming, bodies under plastic sheets. I heard the muffled sound of an alarm going off in the next room. It was time to get up. I turned the TV off with a snap of the grimy remote.

The final scenario the Defenders had conceived was like a Fourth of July fireworks display where the bangs go on forever. It was the summa of all catastrophes, Armageddon, the Atomic Mushroom.

We heard screams somewhere in the distance and headed in that direction. When we reached the clearing by the artificial lake, we stumbled upon a massacre.

It wasn't clear what exactly had happened, but maybe that wasn't even the point; it looked as if every accident, attack, explosion, fire, shooting that one could conceive of had taken place at the very same moment.

Our casualties lay in pools of blood, hair matted, clothes soaked with blood. They had shards of glass rammed into their flesh, gunshot wounds, hands lopped off, bellies hacked open Some were screaming, some gasping for breath, some looked dead or unconscious.

I grabbed a body by the shoulders, the first that came to hand. I struggled to turn him over, I could hear him wheezing. It was him again—my casualty of choice, the man I had lent more assistance to than any other in the history of my life.

I pulled my hands away; they felt sticky and wet and, in fact, were already covered with blood. Under his shirt, which I had promptly cut open with my scissors, I felt something soft and warm. His intestines, the famous latex intestines, spilling out of the gash in his belly. I dragged Obelix by the shoulders towards a tree and I leaned him against it, bending his legs to prevent the intestines from slipping all the way out. There was blood everywhere; he was missing a hand too.

All at once, something came undone in me. The tension, the anxiety that until that moment had kept me going, responding and acting promptly, drooped like a parachute touching the ground.

By now Obelix was barely breathing. The wheeze he emitted and the bloodstain that was rapidly spreading around his lungs told me I had to act fast, that I had only a few minutes before the lungs would collapse and he would bleed out from his wounds.

But I didn't even attempt to pull out bandages or tape from my backpack. I kneeled down next to him and took his hand. He let me hold it without resisting. I stroked it. I just sat there, still, looking at him as the rain pummeled my face and my boots slowly sank into the mud. I waited until Obelix's wheeze turned into a hollow rattle. I didn't move until he stopped breathing

altogether. Only then did I let go of his hand and close his eyelids with my thumbs. I gently laid him on the ground and covered his face with a blanket.

I left him there and slowly started walking away down the
path.

Behind me I could hear the shouts and moans of the injured
grow fainter, as did the orders my companions were calling to
one another—what a perfectly synchronized rescue team they
had become—as they stanched, bandaged, sewed, revived and
evacuated the casualties of this mise-en-scène.

Only then did I start to sob uncontrollably.

Because I knew there was nothing to be done. At least nothing I could have done, whether in a scenario or in real life.
Because I knew perfectly well I would've never been able to fix
something so tragic as Obelix's mangled body; there was nothing anyone could do to prevent life from slipping away from
him. Because watching a man die is an unbearable sight no
matter what, much more than I could bear.

And because that gesture—walking away from Obelix and
leaving him in the mud—had triggered something deeper than
just fear.


It was like a crack beginning to run along steep walls. They
were my walls, and they were crumbling.

I saw it now: death facedown on the side of the street, death
in a war, was a different death than the one I had experienced in
the whiteness of the hospital ward when my mother died.

Yes, I saw it now. One could actually walk away from a body,
leaving him or her in the mud, like an animal rotting in the rain.
Swollen, bloody, half naked because his clothes had been ripped.
One could—or had to—walk away from it in order to move on,
because the dead bodies were too many, or simply because there
was nothing one could do. Death in the dust, on the ground,
was about the dead body; it asked us to close its eyes, wash its

dirt, wipe its blood, using our hands, hoisting its weight on our shoulders.

And this is what death looks like every day in so many parts of the world.

As sanitized as my mother's death had been in her hospital bed, I hadn't been able to bring myself to touch her either. There had been other people in charge of washing, dressing her body, maneuvering it from the bed to the morgue to the coffin. People whose job was to perform this procedure every day on the dead bodies of strangers. Instead I had done everything I could to avoid looking at her afterwards, when she had become just this frightening thing and not my mother anymore. I had desperately wanted to run away from it.

I was crying out of rage, for the sinister game I had been forced to play all week had left me weaker than before. What was I thinking, that some tailor's or butcher's trick would suffice to patch up a body riddled with holes? That it would be enough to stop me from fainting at the sight of blood? My father was right—we had only been playing danger, playing death. But on Monday I was going to a place where nothing sounded like a game.

My final surrender hadn't surprised the Defenders. It's true that I had let Obelix die on me without even attempting to save his life, but I doubt I was the first one ever to have hoisted the white flag. Nor the first to have had a breakdown that required chamomile tea and a tranquilizer.

My buddies had all succeeded, without exception, in completing the last exercise seamlessly. Even Liz Reading, in spite of the initial crisis after the abduction, had fully recovered and had finished with flying colors. During the final evaluation, Keith, her victim of the day, had complimented her. Liz had blushed, still breathless from the effort, her face spattered with blood, her helmet crooked on her head, her hair caked with mud, incredulous and radiant, like a teenager taking a bow at the high school play. Even Mike, the rebellious accountant, had thrown himself headfirst into treating the wounded from the *War of the Worlds* and had amazed everyone with his presence of mind and his quick responses, issuing orders left and right, revealing unexpected leadership qualities.

On the last night, the euphoria in the dining room was palpable. Everyone was busy swapping cell numbers and e-mail addresses, promises to keep in touch and send photos.

My companions all felt compensated for their efforts. Thanks to the Defenders they had discovered a second nature that lay asleep in the depth of their souls, whose existence had been unknown to them till now. It had taken only a little training to awaken it as if it were an atrophied muscle. During the week they had seen the anxiety and the panic abate and the ability to make rapid, efficient decisions grow. What had terrorized them on Monday didn't bother them anymore by Saturday.

I saw them wholly transformed by this new discovery. They had gained strength, character; they were walking away from this rejuvenated. This renewed confidence in themselves didn't irritate me, but my personal defeat—my cowardice—if anything, felt infintely more real to me.

Tim handed out the certificates to everyone, the usual piece of paper with your name in calligraphy. He handed me mine without comment (the Defenders had been courteous enough to ignore my failure and never mention it in front of the others) and they wished me—without irony, I believe—good luck in Afghanistan.

That piece of paper was worthless. It was just a certificate of attendance that some of my companions would have framed and casually hung on a wall of their offices, with the idea of making humorous remarks whenever asked about it. But as far as I was concerned it did certify one thing for sure: that I didn't possess a second nature.

There was no dormant one within me, awaiting a Defender to awaken it.

I was going to take the first train for London at seven in the morning the following day. Before going to bed I went to say good-bye to my instructors. I felt uneasy dragging myself over to their table on my own, but there would have been no other time to say good-bye.

They were still sitting around, their table strewn with the remains of dinner and empty bottles. Obelix was cleaning his teeth with a toothpick.

"Hi, I just wanted to thank you all. I'm leaving tomorrow and in the evening I'm catching my flight for Kabul," I said.

The Defenders grunted. Keith, who was the closest, shook my hand.

"Good, well, have a good trip, then. If you can put to practice even just a tenth of what you have learned, then the course will have had a purpose."

It was probably just a stock phrase, he had said it mechanically, as if it was the hundredth time he'd uttered it.

I glanced at Obelix; he was really the one I had meant to say something to. I wanted to find a way to let him know he had meant a lot to me, that I had felt sorry I'd abandoned him.

"I'm sorry I blew it. I just couldn't do it," I said, hoping to meet his eyes.

Obelix shrugged, still busy dislodging what was stuck in his teeth. His hair looked stringy and bleached, tied in that sad ponytail. His tan was too dark to be natural.

"It happens," he mumbled, looking at the ceiling while he maneuvered the toothpick; he coughed and turned away, covering his mouth with his hand.

"All right, then. Good-bye," I said.

I stretched out my hand. I meant to say something like I hope to see you again. It was my last chance to let him know his body had been more than an anatomy specimen to me. He wasn't just a guinea pig I had experimented with.

But Obelix didn't turn around to meet my hand. He kept coughing as if his lungs were about to burst.

Two

"SO? DID THEY STICK YOUR HEAD IN A BAG?"

On Monday night Imo was waiting for me at the Emirates check-in wrapped in a full-length black coat cinched at the waist with a wide men's leather belt. With a pair of worn old boots and an astrakhan cap, she looked all set for the Afghan adventure, at least costume-wise. I assumed that her inspiration lay somewhere between Clint Eastwood and Tolstoy, yet somehow it looked as if she'd always dressed like that.

"Well . . . yes," I stumbled. "They kidnapped you as well?"

"Of course. It's their pièce de résistance. Everybody knows that at one point you get hauled out of the van with lots of screaming and they stuff your head inside a burlap sack. Big surprise."

She started rummaging in the large bag she had over her shoulder.

"These guys, the ones who run it, have all retired. I mean, come on. They have to do something to bring home the bacon, right? Oh, *please,* where did I put it . . . ? I swear it drives me crazy, I can never find anything in here."

She was kneeling down emptying the contents of her bag onto the floor. The wallet had come out, a voluminous makeup pouch, a perfumed candle, a pair of perfectly folded cashmere socks, a very soft shawl—probably one of those outlawed shahtooshes— a biography of Catherine the Great, the latest Nano, a jar of La Mer cream.

"Ah, here it is." She snatched up her tiny phone and started putting everything back in again. "Remind me later I have to

call the paper and get the number of this guy in Kabul where
we have to pick up our stuff."

"Which stuff?"

"You know, the flak jackets, the helmets and the satellite
phone." She flashed her eyes and sighed as she zipped up her bag.

"Oh, good," I said, reassured. I had been waiting for her to
mention the fact that we were going to take that sort of equipment along.

We'd had an entire lesson on various types of bulletproof
vests, we'd looked at different kinds of material—it was called
Kevlar, but I had learned there were various kinds of Kevlar with differing capacities to absorb the impact of bullets.
By now I felt something of an expert and I couldn't wait to
show off.

"Did he tell you what kind of vest we're getting?"

"Oh, I wouldn't have a clue, but it doesn't really matter, darling," said Imo, standing up and taking me by the arm. "We're
not going to wear them anyway. We'll have them in the back of
the car just in case, to keep the insurance and my editor happy.
He was adamant that we should keep them handy. But there's
no way we're going around looking like soldiers."

"We're not going to wear them, then?"

"Of course not. That's all we need, to show up in helmets and
flak jackets. It'd be like having 'Western target, please kidnap'
written on our foreheads. Come on, let's go, they'll be calling
our flight soon. God, look at the size of that suitcase. How much
stuff did you bring?"

"No, it's just that . . . I thought . . . But listen, Imo, about the
flak jackets: you know, at the course, the Defenders were saying
that one should be—"

"Forget the course now, Maria. It's useful but they also tell
you a bunch of crap. Believe me, it's better to go around looking
like locals, you know, like normal people. The point is to blend
in as much as possible."

Imo was evidently privy to information I did not have and that appeared to be at odds with the basic rules of personal safety I had just learned.

"I see. Then we should wear what? Burqas like the Vaginas of Journalism?" I tried to sound sarcastic, wanting to conceal my disorientation.

"No, I mean we shouldn't stick out like a sore thumb, that's all. Regular clothes. Without showing any tits or legs, of course."

She eyed my coat.

"You haven't got anything less bright than this, have you?"

"No, this is the warmest thing I've—"

"Hmm." She gave a slight shake of the head. I could tell she wasn't crazy about my thick green quilted jacket. The color was hideous and it didn't suit me. I'd bought it on sale at the last minute, terrified by the polar temperatures in Kabul I'd seen online.

"Why, what's wrong with it?"

"No, it's just that in this color they'll see you coming a mile off. Besides, only a Western woman would wear a Day-Glo green down jacket. The idea is to camouflage ourselves with the colors they wear up there, you know what I mean?"

"Right. Unfortunately I'm not sure I brought any—"

She grabbed me by the sleeve.

"It's okay, don't worry, I'll lend you something. Come on, let's go buy some silly magazines. It's an endless flight."

Just then her cell rang. She read the name on the display and did a graceful twirl on her toes, curving in on herself.

"Hello?" Then she roared with laughter and started speaking very fast in Russian.

She grabbed my arm and moved away in long strides, her expression becoming suddenly serious and attentive, asking one question after another of her interlocutor. She kept a strong hold on my elbow throughout the conversation and directed me towards the newsstand. Still talking and sounding a bit more concerned now, she pointed with her chin towards *Vogue, Harpers & Queen* and then moved to the next shelf and indicated *The New Yorker,* which I dutifully picked up along with the other two. She then proceeded to guide me to the cashier, where she made a gesture with her hand, holding her cell between ear and shoulder while fumbling in her bag, meaning that she wanted to pay, now listening to her caller's monologue and interjecting a series of sparse *"Da . . . Da . . . Da"* as she pulled out her wallet. She paid and mouthed a silent thank-you to the cashier, still on her Russian conversation, then guided me to the gate. When they finally called the flight to Dubai, she was still pacing up and down a distance away, immersed in her phone call. I had to wave my arms wildly to attract her attention, gesturing to her that all the other passengers had boarded and we were the only ones left. She walked over, shut the phone and sighed.

"Work, work, work. You know what it's like."

On the plane, Imo slept almost the whole time, curled up in her shahtoosh with her Nano buds in her ears, wearing that very soft pair of cashmere socks she carried in her bag.

I couldn't close my eyes for one second. I spent most of the flight staring at the monitor that showed our progress. As we advanced, the names of the cities I read on the blue screen acquired an increasingly fabulous sound: first Baden, Budapest, then Tehran, Baku, Tashkent, Samarkand, Dushanbe. Enclosed as we were in the cocoon of the plane, cradled by the hum of the air-conditioning and the muted sounds in the cabin, it was mind-blowing to think that these two realities—the plane with the randomly assorted crowd it contained and the lands below—had actually merged into one. I looked at the sleek Arab businessmen working on their laptops, the noisy Pakistani children running up and down the aisle, the Eastern European stewardesses in their veiled Emirates uniform handing out juice from the trolley, the young Australian couple checking their Lonely

Planet. If we'd had to make an emergency landing, would we have found ourselves surrounded by nomad tents? Or would it be the steppes? The desert? Or rather, wasn't Mongolia the one with the desert and the nomad tents?

By the light of dawn, the Hindu Kush suddenly opened out beneath the belly of the plane. Glinting in the first rays of the sun that tinged it with pink, this gigantic range of mountains was a herculean apparition that evoked blaring trumpets, a Wagnerian sound track. I wanted to wake Imo and yell to her that we were flying over the Himalayas. I was possessed by an unexpected, mad euphoria (but then, what was that, actually? the Himalayas or the Hindu Kush? weren't they the same thing? how annoying that I shouldn't even know that), but she was sleeping so soundly it didn't even seem like she was breathing; she looked like a bundle of expensive wool forgotten on the seat.

Beyond the peaks I saw the stony desert begin to spread from the foot of the mountains announcing Afghanistan. The Wagnerian sound track went up a notch. I knew that desert. I had seen it drawn on the maps I had looked at in the previous weeks. As the plane started its descent I realized that the desert's vastness, the ruggedness of its terrain, were no longer just abstractions, mere colors on a map. In just a few minutes, once the cabin door opened, I was going to fall right into this place called Afghanistan. Just looking at it from above, that immense, corrugated territory ringed by mountains, was enough to tell me that here the game was of immense proportions. Suddenly the whole week spent with the Defenders—the slides, the dummy shots, the pumps squirting blood, the latex intestines and the explosions among pruned hedges and wet oak trees—seemed like a pathetic attempt to put some order into an expanse ruled by titanic forces.

Once I had reached as far as this no-man's-land, I felt I was back to square one.

· · ·

Hanif had been highly recommended to Imo by a colleague at the BBC and was supposed to be the man who would solve our every problem from the moment we set foot in the country. He'd been described to her as an excellent fixer, someone who knew lots of people in the various ministries, who could easily get permits, get us through checkpoints without a problem, who spoke English well and who was used to working with Westerners. In the early days of the Taliban regime, Hanif had fled to Pakistan and had lived in Peshawar as a refugee; he'd been back in Kabul for only a couple of years and currently worked for the recently revived Afghan TV. In short, Hanif was reputed to be number one as far as efficiency and charisma went, and Imo had bent over backwards to secure his services.

"He's the guy who actually *reads* the six o'clock news. Apparently for the last couple of months he's also the presenter of a quiz show that goes on air once a week. Everyone will ask for his autograph on the streets. It'll be like traveling with Madonna," Imo said as we were beginning our descent.

Kabul looked like a dusty patch with no color.

"Why does he need an extra job if he's a TV star?" I asked.

"Because we pay him one hundred and eighty dollars a day, which is probably more than half of his monthly salary, that's why. I don't think you get it: there's still no electricity, no roads, in this country." She looked me in the eye. "Everyone is poor, everyone is struggling. Nobody is a star in Afghanistan, Maria."

She pulled out from her diary a printout of an e-mail he had sent her.

"Good day, Miss Glass, I trust your health is fine and so too is that of your family. I wish your profession may proceed as you desire and I wish you much prosperity. I shall be honored to work at your complete disposal, but I am obliged to warn you, the road to the village you wish to visit is greatly in disorder because of debris from an explosion and presently it is not possible to surpass the crater, but inshallah, perhaps the detritus may be removed before your arrival and we may proceed."

The first thing to greet us on Afghan ground in the early-morning light was three big posters plastered on the outside of the airport building. One was a huge portrait of President Hamid Karzai in his astrakhan cap, quoting a phrase in English on peace and democracy. The second one was an even bigger image, of the great Afghan hero Commander General Massoud, the Lion of Panjshir, leader of the resistance against the Taliban—a handsome man with slanted eyes and a *pakol*, the Pashtun woolen hat. Below his face was a sentence explaining how peace and democracy had been his mission but unfortunately he hadn't lived to see it fulfilled. The third, truly gigantic poster, was an ad for Roshan, the new mobile telephone company, welcoming incoming passengers to the new Afghanistan.

"Excellent," said Imo, eyeing the Roshan ad. "They have no electricity yet, but they already want to sell them mobile phones."

We looked around, expecting to find a rugged guy with Ray-Bans in a multipocketed jacket, leaning on an SUV. Instead, Hanif—rotund, with a prominent nose, double chin, tired black eyes—looked more like an Eastern version of Inspector Clouseau, with bushy eyebrows and a well-trimmed moustache. Despite the subzero temperature, he wore a navy pin-striped suit—the same one he wore to read the six o'clock news, it later turned out—with a red tie, a light trench coat and black patent-leather shoes. I had spotted him right away at the arrivals, holding a sign that said "Imo Glass." My heart sank: he looked more like a limousine driver than a fearless hack working in a war zone. He helped us collect our bags and quickly led us outside to the parking lot. There were lots of people moving quickly, in and out of cars, waving and calling to one another. Everyone had guns. While our flight companions were all screeching out of the airport car park into high-tech diesel 4WDs driven by sturdy men, Hanif swung open the doors of a dusty old Ford— the car was included in his daily rate—whose exhaust pipe seemed to be dragging on the ground. No Defender worthy of the name would have approved the security standards of this vehicle.

"Are you sure this will get us to the village?" Imo asked.

"No problem. In this we have been everywhere. It is perfect. Very safe."

"And the crater?"

"There is still rubble, but I think we can get through. Not a problem."

"Mmmm."

Imo eyed the exhaust pipe dubiously. Then she turned to me and shrugged.

"What can I say? He's probably right. And we sure won't stand out in this thing."

I cast a glance at the drivers of the 4WDs in camouflage jackets and mirrored shades, wishing I could clamber into one of their cars instead. But Imo held a different view.

"Suicide bombers aren't going to waste time blowing up two women in a clapped-out Ford. Those guys look way more promising as far as hostage material."

Right outside the airport the first thing we came across was an Italian army military vehicle crossing the road. Neapolitan and Sicilian faces, strangely familiar, looking tense and drained in their heavy camouflage. I felt like waving to them, as if they were a good omen. I knew that since 2001 there had been thousands of troops deployed to Afghanistan, from thirty-seven countries, but mainly American and British. ISAF, the International Security Assistance Force, had about 32,000 men spread between Kabul and the provinces. American soldiers seemed to be everywhere, manning the roundabouts, waving guns outside buildings protected by high blast walls.

On top of the troops, Hanif told us, there were thousands of foreign civilians living in Kabul: UN personnel, consultants of all sorts, NGO workers, contractors and dodgy businessmen. Thousands who needed proper housing, working telephones, good restaurants, good cars, satellite dishes, pasta, Crest toothpaste, ketchup, white bread and cornflakes, soft toilet paper, Coca-Cola, alcohol. There was a black market that catered to these extravagant needs. It used to be called the Brezhnev Bazaar at the time of the Soviet invasion and it sold Russian items. Now it had been renamed after Bush.

"You can find Oreo cookies and Aunt Jemima pancake syrup at the Bush Bazaar. It's crazy what they sell there. Even coconut tanning oil." Hanif chuckled. Because of the foreigners, prices for nearly everything had skyrocketed to such an extent that life had become unaffordable for the Kabulis, more now than before the American intervention. Although the city was a mound of rubble, "the cost of housing is higher than Manhattan," Hanif told us. And prices were still rising.

"I should've bought the house where I live when my wife and I came back from Peshawar. Now it costs twenty times more," he said and, without bitterness, he shook his head.

Hanif took us straight to the hotel that he'd booked for us. It was a brand-new guesthouse that belonged to a cousin of his wife's.

"Maximum comfort," he assured us.

"Are you sure it has an Internet connection?" Imo asked suspiciously.

"Yes, yes, connection. There's a phone, television, everything. My cousin came back from London six months ago and he built this guesthouse European style." Hanif chuckled with satisfaction. I saw his face smiling at me in the rearview mirror, from which dangled a tasseled plastic gizmo in the shape of an Arabic letter.

Outside the window was Kabul.

I peered out, squinting my tired eyes. Only one word came to mind to describe it. Brown.

The city lay like a cloak spread over two hills. It had been climbing obstinately over them like strangleweed, leaving no space, and had managed to cover both and spread at their feet. Everything was brown: the color of the houses, the bare trees, the dirt resting on every surface. Brown were the faces of the men who walked in groups, brown were their cloaks, brown the burlap bags of coal stacked along the roadside. The sky was brown. A camel-colored city covered with a layer of dust: a panorama that by the first light of morning was already looking worn.

Hanif's cousin's guesthouse was a work in progress. Someone was mixing cement in the courtyard. Two workmen were building a wall in what was supposed to be the lobby. An enormous refrigerator was parked in the hallway, still wrapped in its plastic packaging. Other men were doing the wiring. Hanif led the way, smiling as he elbowed through the workmen, dodging paint tins, wooden boards, ladders.

"This way, please, follow me." There was a smell of plaster and paint and the sound of a drill. Hanif called out to someone, his voice booming in the empty room.

"Everything is going to be okay, just a little more work, but your rooms are ready."

His cousin appeared; he was the slim one with the drill. His name was Rashid. He'd been a minicab driver in London for ten years, he said, and braced by his metropolitan experience, had decided to return to Kabul and go into tourism. Imo and I were herded to just-painted rooms. One was empty, the furniture was all piled up in a pyramid in the center of the other one.

"The water will be on tomorrow," Rashid said. Hanif nodded, convinced. There were no tiles, no toilet bowl, no sink in the bathroom.

"But the room is ready . . . there's a big bed, the desk, a television . . ."

I felt my heart sink. The temperature in the room couldn't have been above five degrees, given that a white puff issued from my mouth with every breath. Imo moved away.

"Great. Now, listen, Rashid, there are just a couple of things."

Imo hadn't stopped smiling. She sat on a chair she had pulled from beneath the pyramid and crossed her legs. She was looking around, sizing up her surroundings as if she were the editor of *The World of Interiors* and was scouting a shoot.

"First of all, I'd like to compliment you; this is going to be a sensational guesthouse. Well done, really. I think you've had a brilliant idea. It's true that Kabul needs more hotels; there'll be more and more Westerners who need a comfortable place to stay." She gestured towards the furniture. "Look at this lovely bed, the desk, all these antiques. The main thing is to put a lot of beautiful rugs in the rooms, you know? Rugs really help. But—"

And here she stood up and took me by the arm, drawing me to her as if I were her suitcase.

"We really need to go now, because we can't wait another five minutes before we have a bath. We've been traveling for eighteen hours, you see. Maria hasn't slept, I'm absolutely dying for a plate of scrambled eggs with bacon and some fruit, and it looks to me like you're not ready yet to organize the kind of breakfast I have in mind. Thank you for everything, my compliments again, my friend, keep up with the good work. Come, Hanif, let's go."

Imo held her hand out to Rashid, who gaped at her, perhaps unprepared for such a swift reaction.

"All the best to you and your family, to your business, I wish you great prosperity and success. It has been a great pleasure meeting you, really. My compliments again."

Hanif's smile drooped. He exchanged a disconcerted, disappointed look with his cousin, but decided against further persuasion.

In the car, Imo avoided any reference to Hanif's clumsiness. She was flipping through a guidebook.

"Let's see. Right, here it is: Babur's Lodge, or the Kabul Garden, for example. Hanif, what do you think? Do you know where they are? Do you have a phone number for either of these places?"

It was a call to order, it was clear she wasn't into wasting any more time, but she had made it sound as if she were asking his advice and cared about his opinion. Hanif stammered that yes, he knew both places, it was not a problem, and he started fumbling with his old-fashioned Nokia.

The roads were slowly filling up with people. Streams of men were walking in columns, or pushing carts on the side of the road. A pallid sun broke through the sand-colored clouds and now illuminated the festive splotches of color on the street stalls: mountains of pomegranates, red apples, dark green leaves.

Now and then a woman crossed the road, a sky-blue blur, a ghost, an azure flutter that swelled with air and disappeared behind a car. It was like coming across a giraffe for the first time in Africa. After all, isn't a giraffe just an oddity in a photograph? Somehow I always found it hard to believe that such a prehistoric animal, with such a long neck, does really exist somewhere. Crazy to think one could actually come across it, placidly grazing on a spiny acacia. And now, surrounded by absolute indifference, women in burqas too appeared—just like the ones I'd seen in so many pictures, of course—but these women were busy doing their shopping, counting money in their purses or waiting for the bus on the side of the road, seemingly taken by their daily chores, as if it were completely normal to be living under a tent.

The Kabul Garden had closed down, but after some haggling, Hanif succeeded in convincing the manager of Babur's Lodge to give us two rooms, with the promise that we would vacate them in a week, as they had already been booked for some time by someone else.

My room was spacious, with heavy, dark furniture, rugs on the floor, mirrors. Under the window was a collapsed green velvet sofa, an old lacquered desk and a wooden swivel chair. A gas heater in a corner diffused a pleasant warmth. I inspected the cushions on the couch, I ran a finger along the windowsill, peeked under the rugs; there was dust everywhere. The rugs were threadbare, the upholstery on the couch ripped. The electric sockets looked like they dated back to World War I. The hissing of the stove made me anxious. I wondered about the gas fumes, they smelled so toxic.

The bathroom was on the landing and had no heating. Going in there was like entering an igloo. On the windowsill stood a number of clues indicating male presence. A jar of shaving cream and a skimpy slice of yellowed soap, a cheap shampoo bought in an American supermarket. I made out two thick black hairs embedded in the soap.

An hour later, I knocked on Imo's door. I found her curled up on the couch, her hair wrapped in a towel and a triumphant smile on her face. She smelled of shampoo. She had lit a stick of incense and connected her Nano to a pair of portable speakers. She was listening to some strange electronic music mixed with what sounded like Tibetan monks chanting. Colored shawls and clothes dangled in the wardrobe, books were stacked neatly on the desk. It looked as though she'd been living there for ages.

"Look at this. Isn't it perfect? I'm starving, how about you?"

On the low table was a tray with scrambled eggs and bacon for two, orange juice, a pot of black tea and two slices of cake. She patted the couch next to her, the way you'd call a little dog.

"Come here, Maria. We deserve a proper breakfast. Look out there."

She pointed to the window, which offered a view of one of the two hills, its slopes carpeted with mud-brick houses. The sky had cleared—from brown it had suddenly become an intense blue. A light wind was blowing, sweeping away the dust and ashen clouds.

The plan was to spend a few days in Kabul doing interviews, getting permits in order to be able to travel outside the city, then to head off for the villages. There we would try to speak to the families of the women who had immolated themselves, and possibly to other girls of marriageable age. On paper it looked doable. But by lunchtime both Imo and I had already realized that in Afghanistan the concept of movement needed reinterpretation.

After our sumptuous, cozy breakfast we met Hanif in the big dining room of the hotel. At the back, the guests of the lodge were having breakfast seated together around a long table like a family. They seemed to be all Westerners and males. I only dared to cast a glance and caught a glimpse of powerful backs, army jackets, desert boots. I overheard a nasal drawl from the south of the States. Something about their attitude had instantly discouraged me. Maybe it was their lack of response to our appearance. Not a single head had turned, not a greeting was uttered, not a smile was produced. If anything, judging from the chill that came from their table, it seemed that our arrival had disturbed them.

Imo sat at a smaller table, turning her back, openly ignoring them. She spread a map of the country on the table and showed Hanif where she wanted to go. He seemed dubious about the possibility of covering great distances. Many stretches of road were interrupted, but above all, traveling wasn't safe anywhere.

Every time Imo asked him about a village, I saw him tilt his head in a movement that expressed some apprehension, but he never openly said no. It was almost as if he feared that his prudence could be interpreted as rude. He invariably assumed a vague, falsely willing air, which in fact conveyed a sense of terrible uncertainty to me.

"Everything can be done, it's not a problem. We just have to go slowly."

"But are these safe areas? Could we be attacked?" I asked, alarmed, as Imo refolded the map, pleased with her plan.

"No, but maybe a good idea to travel with your heads covered outside the city. Better to look like Afghan women. That way nobody will bother us," said Hanif, satisfied that he had put forward a solution.

Did "bother" in his lexicon mean "kidnap"? I wondered.

In the next couple of days we realized that getting around the city was no easy feat either. Kabul had no electricity and when night came the city was plunged into darkness. Even though the curfew had been lifted, Hanif had told us it was better not to go out in the dark. And never, ever walk.

There were armed checkpoints at every main crossroads, barbed wire coiled along the walls, gigantic blocks of cement stacked around the embassies and the headquarters of military organizations, to shield them from possible attacks. The roads would be closed to traffic for hours if military vehicles had to go through and the traffic would go berserk; big American army guys in helmets stopped the cars, waving machine guns and shouting at drivers to give way to U.S. military vehicles. These roared out of their headquarters with screeching tires, accompanied by intimidating shouts, by a wave of tension that presaged danger, anxiety, imminent unforeseen events.

The war was over and this was a time of reconstruction, the politicians kept saying. Pierre had stressed this too in his first phone call; the military presence was only a force to ensure that the process of peace and democracy followed its course. Yet this felt nothing like peace. Not just because of what I saw out on the streets—a half-destroyed city besieged by soldiers and guns—but because of what I felt in the air. It was plain to see we had entered a world out of bounds, a world of a far greater insanity than anything I could've envisioned back home. What was worse, I could tell nobody was in control of the situation. I just sensed it like a dog sniffs fear in people around him: everyone had to be constantly ready for any eventuality. No, nothing looked like peace to me on the streets of Kabul.

The first thing we had to do was collect the equipment that Pierre had recommended we carry with us at all times. He had instructed us to pick it up from the office of Jeremy Barnes, a freelance reporter with Sky News. Imo had turned up her nose.

"I know who he is. He used to work for the *Guardian* ages ago. I've never met him, but he had an affair with someone I know."

I had no doubts that Imo knew him and had him classified. Before getting in the car, she dug her elbow into me.

"Don't say anything about this guy in front of Hanif. He has worked for Jeremy and totally adores him. He says he's the number one journalist in Kabul."

She arched an eyebrow.

On the way to Jeremy's office Hanif repeated to me how he and Jeremy were old buddies, and he stressed enthusiastically how Jeremy was the best reporter he had ever worked for.

He lowered the car window and waved to the armed guard in the sentry box at the entrance. The guard lit up when he recognized Hanif and leaned into the car, wanting to shake his hand.

We walked into an unassuming building. The ground floor was empty, there was no furniture, and an icy wind came in through the broken windows. A man in a woolen vest had a chair next to a stove, with a teapot on an electric cooking ring. He hugged and greeted Hanif.

Barnes's office was on the first floor. It was a large room with military maps and photos stuck on the walls, a couple of computers, an antiquated TV, linoleum curling at the corners on the floor. Jeremy was sprawled on a swivel chair with his feet on the desk, his head tipped back, speaking animatedly on the phone with a pen in his hand. He vaguely waved to us and indicated with the tip of the pen that we should sit on a low couch covered with the brown woolen shawl I had seen all the men wear. He made a gesture that meant "I'll be with you in just a couple of minutes." Hanif didn't sit but wandered towards the wall to study the photos with an air of satisfaction. He took one down and brought it over to us. It showed him and Jeremy on a rocky, snow-covered pass, a tank in the background, their arms swung around a couple of bearded characters with machine guns and bandoliers strapped across their shoulders. All four were wearing Afghan hats whitened with snow.

I passed the photo to Imo. I feigned more admiration than necessary to compensate for Imo's evident lack of interest.

Just then, Jeremy put the phone down and got up to hug Hanif with great enthusiasm, uttering what was apparently a series of Dari niceties.

"Welcome to Kabul," he said in what sounded like a decidedly upper-class British accent, shaking hands with us. "So what can I do for you?"

"Nothing," Imo blurted out. "We don't want to disturb you, we've just come to pick up the phone and jackets."

"Ah, yes, of course, the jackets. I hope you're not planning on wearing them, because—"

"No, of course not," Imo said. "We wouldn't dream of it. It's just a formality, to keep my editor off my back. You know, the insurance."

"Right, of course," Jeremy agreed. "These insurance companies, it's all so crazy."

He was quite attractive. Very, actually. High cheekbones, hair a bit longer at the back, around thirty-five. Intelligent eyes, good teeth.

"Don't tell me you had to take that mad course too, the hostile—"

"No, I didn't have to," Imo quickly pointed out. "I had done it pre-Sudan, luckily. But Maria had to, poor thing. By the way, this is Maria Galante, the photographer."

"Nice to meet you," he said, turning to me. "I did it too, ages ago. I remember it was a nightmare."

"Well, yes. Even though—"

"I mean, I guess there are a few things that could come in handy, provided one remembers them, of course. But all that bollocks about firearms, explosions, land mines . . . the whole thing, Jesus, is *such* a circus, isn't it?"

"Well, I don't know," I said as the man in the vest came in with a tray laden with glasses of steaming tea. "I had no clue about any of those things, so for me it was compl—"

"Sure," he interrupted me, "I guess if you've never been in a conflict zone."

At this point, Jeremy turned to Imo, sensing that out of the two of us, she was the pro.

"These are things you only learn from experience. You can't learn them in a classroom watching slides, right? Anyway, at this point, I figure people like us have probably spent more time in war zones than any of those guys, don't you think?"

But Imo wasn't into being responsive. She shrugged with an offhand expression that meant she didn't have an opinion or didn't care to share one. Jeremy's smile vanished. He then turned to the man who had brought the tea and said something to him quickly in Dari. The man immediately left the room.

"I told him to put the vests, the phone and the first-aid kit in your car. It's been a while since I checked the kit, perhaps you should make sure it has all the stuff you need. People here borrow it all the time and never restock it. And the phone needs recharging. I never use it, so the battery's flat."

Imo nodded vaguely again, like she didn't care to register.

Jeremy lit a cigarette and blew the smoke to the ceiling as he settled back in the chair, stretching his arms and legs as if he had just woken up.

"And what kind of story are you—"

"Forced marriages and suicides," Imo preempted him.

"Ah, yes. Of course," said Jeremy smoothly, yet somehow condescendingly, as though for a veteran like him this was too much of a hashed and rehashed topic to stir any particular excitement.

By now it was obvious that Imo and Jeremy were engaged in some sort of unspoken competition and Imo was losing it.

Jeremy scratched his head.

"The road to those villages has been closed for quite a while and I doubt you'll be able to—"

"Yes, I know there's still a crater, but Hanif says that—"

"Right, Hanif's the man. He knows everything. You'll be safe with him. He's the best fixer in the whole country. He saved my bacon once."

Jeremy turned to Hanif. "Remember, my friend?"

Hanif nodded and laughed. Jeremy took another voluptuous drag, then pointed to the photo Hanif had shown us.

"We were traveling to Bamyan, it was snowing quite hard and we were crawling along, do you remember? At one point Hanif noticed a dodgy car was following us."

"Yes, a car I did not like, it would not leave us. I decided we must lose them," Hanif said.

"So Hanif accelerated. We were in his beaten-up Ford, right? And I thought, oh, my God, one of the tires is going to burst any moment. We managed to outstrip them a bit and after a while we came across a truck loaded with people and goats and God knows what else; Hanif made me get out in a flash, barked orders to the chap at the wheel and shoved me up in the back. He drove off in the Ford, tootling along slowly, so the others could catch up and stop him."

"Yes, yes, I was going too slowly on purpose so they would catch me." Hanif was excited. It must have been a great adventure, told and retold many times.

"Then the guys who had been following us in the dodgy car stopped him, they made him get out and searched everywhere, even in the boot, but I was long gone and they had to go away empty-handed."

Jeremy and Hanif laughed as if the whole thing had been a hoot.

"We'll be off, then. I don't want to take any more of your time," Imo said, standing abruptly, avoiding to make a comment on the story.

Jeremy threw his arms wide.

"Well, please, if you need any help, information, I mean if there's anything I can do for you . . ." He escorted us to the door. "Please drop in at our place anytime for a drink, a plate of pasta, whatever. We're always home in the evening."

I wondered what the plural implied. A wife? For some reason it seemed unlikely.

"Shall I give you my number?" he offered Imo.

"Yes, of course, but my cell's turned off now. Could you save it on yours, Maria?"

I keyed in Jeremy's number on my cell as Imo haughtily turned away.

"What a puffed-up jerk," she hissed under her breath as soon as we were in the car.

" 'People like us . . . I've probably spent more time under fire than any of those guys'? *Please.* Who talks like that? No, I mean, I'm asking you, is he ridiculous or what?"

She closed her eyes and shook her head vigorously.

"And I'm not even beginning to tell you the way he behaved with my girlfriend two years ago!"

We moved through the city past collapsed walls riddled with holes, through gaping chasms, a sort of unending backdrop of skeletons and hollows. My heart sank. Although I had seen images of Kabul so many times on the news, I was shocked by the actual extent of the destruction. And yet everywhere, despite the devastation, I saw Afghans moving quickly, busily, skirting heaps of rubble and sagging buildings, like ants following an ordered and constant flow, heedless of the obstacles. Everywhere there were street stalls, kiosks selling detergent, condensed milk, mountains of almonds and raisins, donkey-drawn carts preposterously overloaded with goods.

Money changers fished rolls of soiled banknotes out of their cloaks, counting out blackened wads; children were begging and laughing—children with no trace of melancholy or piteous attitudes, but cheeky and dazzling, displaying that same comic talent of certain Neapolitan street urchins—and giving the impression they were asking for money more for a lark than out of necessity. The brown and dust-coated city revealed unexpected gashes of intense color, enhancing the contrast between the archaic and the industrial: made-in-China plastic thongs with the Nike swoosh next to handwoven rugs and blue Herat glass, piles of bootleg DVD copies of *Titanic* side by side with fighting cocks and caged falcons.

I pulled out my camera. Everywhere I looked, I saw a photo. I suddenly realized I hadn't shot a single frame since we'd arrived and I needed to familiarize myself with the light.

"Hanif, can we stop, please? I want to take a couple of pictures."

Hanif hesitated.

"Can you pull over? Just for a sec."

"It's better not in this area. Too many people."

He looked at me through the rearview mirror with a contrite expression.

"I'm sorry. It's not safe here," he said. As if it was his fault.

"It's embarrassing, how attractive these men are," Imo blurted out as she stared out the car window, her nose practically pressed to the glass. "They're the ones who should be veiled."

She was right. Everywhere we looked I saw incredibly handsome men. Children, elders, younger men, the flat-nosed Hazaras with their almond-shaped eyes, round faces that had Tibet's and China's imprints in their features; the Pashtuns and Tajiks with stunning green or blue eyes that shone in the piercing light like lapis. The old turbaned men with thick white beards stained by orange streaks of henna, who walked behind their donkeys like biblical kings.

I asked if we could stop so that I could take some pictures. But, again, Hanif hesitated.

The men held hands as they talked, held them as they walked, held them as they greeted one another. Big, fiery warriorlike men, guns strapped around their shoulders, holding hands like young girls.

A light blue burqa knocked on our window in the traffic jam. It had no face. Just a dried hand, beating on the stomach, mimicking hunger. She knocked relentlessly, aggressively. Hanif gave her a coin before Imo and I could reach for our wallets, and told her—kindly—to let us pass.

Hanif stopped the car in front of a barely standing two-story building. He got out and we followed.

"This was once a famous cinema. We came to see movies here, when I was a boy," he said, with the sweep of the arm that a Roman would use to show the ruins of the Forum or the Colosseum to a tourist.

"We can go up. The staircase is still holding but be careful. Please take the camera, here you can take photographs, no problem."

I took the camera out of the canvas bag and followed Imo up the half-collapsed staircase. It looked as if it was resting only on a couple of steel rods sticking out from underneath it and it couldn't possibly hold our weight. I went along holding my breath, but Imo looked bored.

"I've seen this place already in a documentary. This must be one of those sights where they take every Western journalist," she hissed to me sotto voce.

On the second floor the facade of the building had giant holes from which twisted metal bars—what was left of the window frames after the blast—dangled in the air. They seemed like tendrils swaying in the breeze and about to fall off, but had probably been like that for years.

The city lay at our feet like a termite mound flattened to the ground. Imo looked down at the destruction below, pointing in different directions.

"Soviet bombs or civil war?"

Each ruin had had its different killer. The destruction had come from outside first with the Russians and then from the opposing factions of mujahideen later. And then, when that was over, there had been American collateral damage and Taliban revenge.

While Imo and Hanif continued their conversation, I wiped the camera lens with chamois and walked out on what was left of the roof.

Short gusts of wind made my scarf flap, tufts of hair got into my eyes. This was the moment—I wanted to savor it.

On top of that crumbling building I felt like a photographer again.

I shot the rubble, the gaps, a group of men below who were loading carts with wood and huge burlap sacks. Across the street I shot a sign displayed on a newly built housefront. It said "Aryana Billiard Club" in bright pink and green lettering. It seemed like the beginning of something new in this Hiroshima-like neighborhood.

Imo and I were quiet in the car on our way back to the hotel. An unexpected sadness had seeped into our pores with the dust. It was almost dark, people were still moving around, although there was a sense that everyone was heading back somewhere. To their shacks, half-destroyed houses, who knows where they were going. Everyone carried something, a bundle, a basket, wood, a sack filled with coal. There would be a fire and some food in every house tonight, and tomorrow they would start again.

On the landing on our floor at the guesthouse, there was a door to a third room. I strongly suspected it was occupied by the owner of the hairs caked in that bathroom soap.

We met him at the communal table where all the guests of Babur's Lodge had breakfast every morning, like a family. Or not him—actually it was them—for there were two occupants to that room. They were both American, and after the third day at the lodge they had become a familiar sight. One was tall, blond, with Scandinavian skin, long hair and white albino eyelashes. He must have been twenty-five at the most and looked like a basketball player or a student; he seemed to lack the savagery of the others. He always wore the same faded T-shirt, a pair of cargo pants and a *pakol* on his head. At breakfast he never said a word, but kept his eyes glued to the paper, hiding behind the *Kabul Daily* as if it were a fence. His buddy was smaller, with a leaner, nervy physique, black hair and a goatee.

He had a good-looking face, a bit too pointy for my taste, like the snout of a weasel. There was something darker, more menacing about this one.

Every morning the smaller one had ordered scrambled eggs and refried beans with onions and ketchup. A disproportionately large plate would arrive and he would attack it slowly, with method. I thought that this eggs-and-beans affair must have been some kind of ritual that held a special meaning for him, as if those eggs were an umbilical cord to some diner back home, in some forsaken town where he'd had breakfast every day. He must have spent a considerable amount of time instructing the kitchen on exactly how to prepare his plate. The young Afghan waiter who brought it to him did so with great pride, as if every morning a miracle had taken place in the kitchen. The waiter would place the eggs in front of him, each time seeking his approval, which the American accorded with a slight nod.

These two guests hadn't introduced themselves, they had never even acknowledged our presence or spoken to us, but I thought of them as *il Biondo e il Bruno*. Whenever we passed each other on the landing on the way to and from the bathroom, I felt I'd intruded on their space, that our presence across from their room annoyed them. They were intimidating and always made me feel on edge.

Imo was oblivious to their existence. She had already invaded the bathroom, pushed their stuff into a corner of the windowsill, filled the edge of the tub with her bottles of sandalwood and tangerine shampoo, aromatherapy conditioner, jars of day cream, night cream, the whole female arsenal of cleansers, makeup pads, non-alcohol deodorant, brushes, as if it were the most natural thing in the world.

Although I had carefully avoided leaving any clue of my existence and kept all my stuff in the room, I felt responsible for this territorial invasion. After all, there wasn't a tag with Imo's name above this cosmetics store that was now on display in their bathroom and I knew they must resent me as well for it.

When they finished eating, il Biondo and il Bruno went off together without saying good-bye to anyone, pushing their chairs back and dropping their soiled napkins on the table. They went out the door, and a few seconds later a roaring engine carried them away.

"Security," Imo whispered in my ear.

"Meaning?"

"They're bodyguards."

"Whose?"

"I don't know. But they look like killers to me."

"How do you know?"

"I just can tell, and then I asked the waiter, the older one. I sneaked a peek in their room when the cleaning woman was in there. They've got automatic weapons right on the bedside table next to their mineral water bottles."

The other guests were equally graceless and made me feel uneasy. Another American—salt-and-pepper hair, chunky and compact like an action doll with pumped-up muscles—always sat at the head of the table in a crisp shirt and multipocketed vest. His breakfast seemed as if it were part of some weight-loss plan: a small glass of orange juice, oatmeal and fruit. He spoke in a steady rhythm without inflection. It wasn't clear who exactly he was talking to; he seemed happy to keep talking indefinitely until the charge ran down. The others chewed on, nodding now and then, all except il Biondo, who kept his eyes steadfastly planted on the front page of the paper. The only one who actively paid any attention, commenting at intervals, was a mousy-looking little guy with a tiny moustache and a strong South African accent.

The second day, as we were all sitting at breakfast, the chunky American had been banging on at length about a specific type of tank that had been used in Korea. Imo looked up from her bowl of yogurt and interrupted him.

"I don't understand this thing about frozen terrain."

There was a moment of general ruffling of wings around the table.

The American looked at Imo as if he were noticing her for the first time. The others all moved their eyes from him to Imo, then back from Imo to him, as if they were following a tennis ball. The man considered the question and didn't miss a beat. He kept talking in the same monochromatic tone, like those military spokespeople who brief journalists in the pressroom at the White House.

"These are tanks that we used in Korea, but the heat they produced during the day melted the frozen surface of the terrain, so they used to sink into the rice paddies at night. We'd have to keep moving them back and forth to prevent them from bogging down. But I think they could work over here, because Afghan terrain is pretty solid and stony. They wouldn't sink here like they did over there."

Imo held his gaze and popped a piece of buttered bread in her mouth, squinting slightly.

"What is it you *do* exactly?"

The question landed on the table with a clunk.

I cringed. I thought it was a given that one shouldn't ask such direct questions to people like that. It was more than rude, it was against the rules.

"I'm General Dynamics," he replied, as if he were stating, "I'm Mormon," or "I'm Spanish," or "I'm a vegetarian."

"That is to say?" Imo countered.

"We supply war matériel, armaments, communications systems, to the Afghan government based on our acquisitions experience."

"And what does that mean *exactly*?"

The man curled his lip in a patronizing smirk and translated.

"It means I go around the world shopping on behalf of the Afghan government, using my connections and my expertise to buy arms, munitions and vehicles suited to this terrain and climate."

"Funny, isn't it, that they should ask Americans to do this kind of shopping on their behalf," Imo commented with her mouth full.

The man didn't move a muscle.

"They don't have a choice. They're still fighting with guns from the eighteen hundreds; they have no idea how weapons have evolved, or where to buy them. If it were up to them they'd still be going to war with swords."

The others gave a snicker to bolster him. Then General Dynamics wiped his napkin across his mouth, pushed his chair back and left.

He too, without bothering to utter a good-bye or a see-you-later.

In order to travel outside Kabul we needed a written permit from the Ministry of Information. Hanif explained it was necessary to have it with us at all times, in case we were stopped at any of the checkpoints outside the city. The ministry was an old building inside a beautiful shady garden, the only patch of green I had seen so far.

We walked up a creaky wooden staircase and sat in a spacious room furnished with office furniture from the thirties that my brother, Leo, would surely have appreciated. Two sleepy clerks gave us forms to fill out. I noticed there was a Bakelite telephone sitting on one of the desks; I saw no computers. I looked out the window at the view of the garden below and recalled how in *The Road to Oxiana* I had read about the lush gardens of Kabul, the sweet smell of oleaster, the shady arbors planted with Canterbury bells and columbines. And how once, after a reception for the king's birthday at the British Legation, all the Afghan ministers—mad rose lovers—had sent their gardeners to request cuttings of the rosebushes they'd seen in full bloom. "British diplomacy now hangs on the Minister's roses," Byron laconically wrote.

While we waited for our permits to be issued, Hanif took us to see the Darulaman Palace. It was built for King Amanullah in the twenties, designed with an eye to European aristocracy, all cupolas, swirls and turrets. Sitting on a hilltop just outside the city, it was a solitary structure, imposing, neoclassical, overlooking a flat, dusty valley. You could see it standing out against the mountains on the horizon, commanding the landscape, but already at a distance you sensed that something wasn't quite right. The palace had kept its shape, but it had been riddled by mortar fire everywhere and was slumping to the side, chipped and gaping. Not one single arch, capital, or column was intact. It might have been professional deformation, but it reminded me of a wedding cake that had been knocked around too much and the wisps and curlicues of the icing had gotten smashed. I took its picture from a distance; I liked its lopsided bearing against the deep blue of the windswept sky, the way it looked as if it would topple at any moment. A grandiose dessert, planned for a great event that didn't turn out as it should have.

The soldiers behind the barrier warning "Military Zone No Pictures Allowed" looked bored. They gestured towards me and yelled something that sounded menacing. Hanif went over and introduced himself, I guess explaining who we were and what we were doing. There was an unusually long and cheerful exchange of greetings, shaking of hands and excited laughter. Hanif walked back to where Imo and I were standing.

"They want you to take their photo. They said they want me to be in the picture with them."

"Oh, okay. Sure."

"They see me on TV. Some of them also know me from the quiz show on Tuesday night," he added shyly.

I moved behind Hanif towards the soldiers. They all seemed very young, barely in their twenties. I moved my hands quickly, pointing at the position they should take in order to get the right lighting. They giggled among themselves, exchanging jokes as they shuffled. Maybe they were excited by the presence of a Western woman, maybe they found it exhilarating that a woman would tell them what to do. I changed the lens, put in a 35 mm film and pointed the camera at the men. Their expressions changed immediately, the laughter and the smiles giving way to grave, serious faces. They stiffened and puffed up their chests, holding on to their guns. Hanif stood in the midst of them like a general among his troops.

"Okay, Hanif, what's the best restaurant in Kabul?" Imo asked when we got back in the car. "I want to splurge on real Afghan food."

Hanif laughed and nodded.

"The best? Sure. The best. Okay, I will take you there."

Imo's extravagance amused him but also daunted him. Her self-assurance, the way she moved as if she owned the place, had made him uneasy from the start. I watched him roll down the window and speak with an obsequious expression to a guard who had pulled us over for an inspection. The man asked him questions while unabashedly checking me and Imo out, the tip of his gun brushing Hanif's moustache. In spite of his current status as a star, there was a mix of courtesy and fear in Hanif's eyes whenever he had to deal with authority, like a dog that's been beaten in the past and fears it could happen again, at the snap of a finger, without any warning.

• • •

The restaurant had no atmosphere whatsoever. It was vast, with very high ceilings, and badly lit. Long tables and plastic chairs were scattered about as in a factory cafeteria, and every sound reverberated with an echo. The few customers looked like Afghan politicians or businessmen shrouded in woolen shawls. There was also a long table of what seemed to be a group of aid workers lunching with their Afghan colleagues. At the head of the table sat a blond man in a beret, constantly talking on his cell phone.

Imo took out her glasses and studied the menu with great concentration while Hanif explained every dish in detail. Finally we settled on a very elaborate platter of grilled meat and chicken, Kabuli rice with pistachio nuts, cashews and saffron, and curd.

"But will that be enough for the three of us?" Imo asked. "I'm starved, aren't you?"

Hanif confessed he was on a diet and he was going to eat very little.

"Oh, come on!" Imo nearly shrieked with laughter. "Why on earth do you want to lose weight? You look very good like this, you shouldn't be any thinner."

Hanif blushed at the compliment and patted his belly.

"My wife, she says I should lose a bit . . ."

"Really? Well, then, if your wife says so. She's the one you should please."

Hanif laughed and nodded.

"Tell us a bit about your wife." Imo lowered her glasses on the ridge of her nose and smiled at Hanif.

"She is very young," he admitted with a touch of embarrassment, his cheeks pinkening, as if he, a big-nosed forty-year-old with a few extra pounds to shed, had received an unhoped-for gift from heaven he felt unworthy of.

"She is pregnant, almost seven months," he said radiantly. "My first child."

"Oh, that's wonderful. Is your wife beautiful?" Imo asked.

"Very beautiful." Again, Hanif seemed to blush.

"Show us a photo. You've got a photo of your wife, haven't you?" Imo pressed him.

"No, no photos, sorry."

A waiter arrived, smiled and greeted Hanif, whom he either knew or recognized—I couldn't be sure—and Hanif proceeded to order.

"See? They don't do that here," I said under my breath while Hanif was talking to the waiter.

"Do what?"

"Carry photos of their wives in their wallets. It's not done, to show your wife's face to strangers, you see? If Hanif, who works as a television presenter, doesn't like to show her picture, just imagine what it's going to be like for us in the villages."

"He just doesn't carry a photo with him, that's all. Don't get neurotic about this, Maria, I beg of you. You're making me nervous."

The food came. It was a feast, but Hanif placed only a bowl of spiced yogurt in front of him.

"This is very good for the digestion. It's the secret for longevity." He laughed. "Had it not been for the war, Afghans would reach a very old age thanks to this."

Imo poked me with her elbow.

"Look at that group photo session. So much for that not being done here."

Then I saw the French aid worker with the beret and all his coworkers posing in front of a woman taking a snapshot. None of the Afghan girls were wearing headscarves. They were all laughing and had their arms around one another. I felt ridiculous and wished I had kept my mouth shut.

Before he dropped us off at the hotel that evening, Hanif had revealed with a certain amount of pride that his quiz show was going on the air at seven p.m., as it did every Tuesday night.

"Everyone wants to win the prize!" he said. "A Japanese racing bike, brand-new."

Imo and I told him we would watch it for sure. After dinner we asked one of the waiters to show us where the TV was. He knew right away what we were after.

"Mr. Hanif?"

"Yes!" Imo immediately replied. "Would you like to watch it with us?"

I wasn't sure he understood any English, but he nodded vehemently and we followed him into a small room on the first floor where there was a couch and a few chairs. There were full ashtrays and empty beer bottles everywere, a pile of DVDs on top of the TV. The waiter fumbled with the antenna and the remote control till Hanif came into focus.

Imo slumped on the couch, pulled out a pack of cigarettes and lit one.

"I love it. Here's our Hanif. Look at that. Amazing."

"I never knew you were a smoker," I said.

"I didn't either. But, you know, just one to unwind at the end of the day."

Hanif was reading from a sheet of paper, standing up. The studio was very basic, just a dark blue background without any props, only the racing bike right behind him, which glittered under a spotlight like a totem. Two young men with slicked-back hair and Western clothes were sitting at a small table, their hands ready to press the buttons. The setup was weird: it didn't look like a quiz show, but more like an examination or a job interview. There was no music, no audience, and Hanif didn't look anything like a presenter of a variety show. He looked more like a bureaucrat. Yet, despite the awkwardness, one felt that this timid beginning of consumerism—variety shows, prizes and glitter after years of Taliban restrictions—was the most exciting thing that had penetrated any Afghan household that could afford a TV set. The waiter seemed entranced.

"What is he saying?" Imo asked, pointing at Hanif.

"Yes, yes." The waiter nodded, excited. He grabbed a chair and sat only a few inches away from the screen.

"Is it good?"

"Yes. Very good."

Just then the door opened and General Dynamics came in with the Blond and the Dark One, followed by another two men I'd never seen before. The Dark One stood in front of the screen, obscuring the image, fumbled with the DVD jackets till he found what he was looking for and slid it in the player.

"We're going to watch a video," he announced, more to the wall than to us, as he grabbed the remote.

Imo stood up and pointed to the screen.

"We were actually trying to watch this TV show, if you don't mind."

The men sat down and lit their cigarettes, ignoring her comment. *Jarhead*'s title credits appeared on the screen.

Imo opened her arms and rolled her eyes to the ceiling.

"I don't fucking believe this," she said loudly.

Nobody reacted. The Dark One turned up the volume and swiftly plopped down in Imo's place on the couch with a sigh of satisfaction. Someone switched off the main light and the room sank into the dark.

The next morning we were sitting in the sun on a lumpy old sofa in the open courtyard of the office of an NGO that supported women's rights. A kitten was rubbing up against my ankles and purring. A French girl with a headscarf and *shalwar kameez* had received us—not too effusively, actually—and told us, in a heavily accented English, to wait. There was an important meeting going on, she said, and Roshana Habib, the person in charge, would be with us as soon as she could. She'd pointed to the old sofa, plunked in the middle of the courtyard, and disappeared without asking if we'd care for some tea. Imo was scribbling notes in her Moleskine notebook and looked grumpy. Perhaps she hadn't been pleased with the French girl's reception, or maybe she construed the wait as a mark of disrespect.

"If there's one thing I simply cannot stand it's European women in Afghan clothes and headscarf," she grumbled without lifting her eyes from her notebook.

"Maybe they feel more comfortable walking around like that because they blend in more?" I offered. "In fact, didn't you say we needed to blend—"

"As if people on the street didn't know they're Westerners. No, it spells 'Don't fuck with me, I'm a local,' not to the Afghans, of course, just to other foreigners. It's so smug."

I was beginning to see what were the things that infuriated Imo the most. The presence of other Westerners, seen as potential competitors, was one.

"How's your tummy?" she asked me.

"What? It's all right, I think. Why?"

"Mmm. I've got the squitters. If you ask me, that meat we had yesterday at the restaurant was off. Had to run to the bathroom all night long."

"I don't know, for the moment I don't feel any—"

"I was running to the bathroom in the dark and I bumped into that blond guy, the tall one who never talks? He was completely naked."

"Oh no."

"Yep. And he had a hard-on."

"You're kidding."

"I swear. He slammed into me as I came out of the bathroom, and he didn't even bother to say 'sorry,' like, you know, he owned the place. Just like yesterday in the TV room, as if we didn't exist. Those two are such pigs, they totally disgust me. They never bother to clean the toilet bowl, have you noticed?"

The idea of the Blond, crossing the landing stark naked terri
fied me as much as the idea of a nighttime attack of diarrhea
that would force me to encounter him.

We saw a woman cross the courtyard and come in our direction. It was Roshana Habib, a minute, handsome Afghan
woman in her forties with stern eyes. She smiled at us as she
shook our hands and apologized for making us wait, but kept a
formal, almost suspicious, distance.

She asked without smiling, "I'm sorry, could you just remind
me which newspaper you are from? We get so many journalists
in here . . . I'm afraid I forgot."

Imo told her it was the *Observer* from London and made a
reference to the e-mail exchange they had had in the previous
week about the women's self-immolations.

"Yes, yes, of course. Now I remember." Roshana sat down
on the sofa. "I'm sorry but unfortunately I only have half
an hour. Today there's an ongoing meeting which I need to
return to."

She wore a bulky man's watch around her wrist, a touch of
lipstick, a heavy sweater over a long skirt and a scarf over her
head. Her English accent was almost flawless, her vocabulary
extremely refined. She answered Imo's questions without hesitation, reeling off numbers and statistics like a lesson she'd learned
by heart, while Imo took notes. Her cell phone rang a couple of
times and she apologized again for having to answer—it was a
crazy day, she repeated. She gave quick, to-the-point instruc-
tions in Dari to the person at the other end and shut the phone
with relief.

Imo was looking for evidence of the theory she had put out to
me back in London.

"Would you say these suicides have increased in the last couple of years? Is it true that women who have more access to outside information have become more aware of their situation
and—"

Roshana shook her head. "I don't know that there's a connection. I've read something about it, but I think it's just one of those stories journalists come up with. In the rural villages of Afghanistan nothing has ever really changed. Not before, not during and not after the Taliban. Women are sold as slaves by their families and have been since the beginning of time."

Most of the self-immolation cases occurred in the Helmand Province, and it was true that numbers were growing every day, she conceded.

"It may be just because there's more communication than before, that's why we come to know about the deaths whereas before we wouldn't even hear of them," Roshana acknowledged.

She strongly advised us it wasn't wise to travel there. The security situation was critical. Only a few days before, there had been heavy fighting between the U.S.-led coalition forces and Taliban militants; suicide bombings and small-arms attacks had increased exponentially since the reprisal of the insurgence.

"You also have to consider there is a strong social stigma attached to suicide in Afghanistan, and many families are reluctant to seek help for victims of self-immolation or talk about the reasons behind the attempt. You'll see. It's going to be hard to get people to talk about that."

"We'll find a way," Imo said. But I could tell she was disappointed by how unimpressed Roshana seemed by our project.

"May I ask you what is it exactly you intend to do?" Roshana asked.

Imo sighed.

"I'd like to go a hospital and talk to the women who have attempted to burn themselves. I was wondering whether you had any contact with doctors or families who'd be prepared to talk to us. And then I'd like to get some pictures of wedding preparations, the part of the ceremony that takes place in the women's quarters."

Roshana nodded, but something in her expression seemed, if

not hostile, skeptical. The kitten had come back and jumped on my lap. I scratched him behind the ears as he kept purring.

"So sweet," I said, to lighten up the atmosphere. "What's his name?"

Roshana looked at me and shrugged as if I had asked the dumbest question.

"I've no idea." She then turned to Imo. "And how long are you planning to be here?"

"A week, ten days. It depends."

"Ah. Then I don't think it will be possible."

"What?"

"To go to hospitals, photograph women, shoot wedding ceremonies. This is a country where until a few years ago photographs of human beings were outlawed."

"I know, I know. But this article is precisely intended to—"

"Of course," Roshana agreed. "But I'll tell you right now that in the rural areas no woman with a father or husband will let you take her photo without the veil. As you probably know, they live in a very traditional way. And who would the photographer be?"

"Maria."

Roshana shifted her gaze to me. She looked down at the camera I was holding. I gave her a friendly smile, to counteract the fact that I had been practically mute till then. Roshana turned back to Imo, unimpressed.

"That French girl who let you in, Florence, she's a photographer too."

"Oh. Is she?" Imo started tapping her pen on the Moleskine.

"Yes. To give you an idea, she's been working on your same story for . . . let's see . . . four years now. She lived in Herat Province, where our organization has a branch, and she's spent months and months just earning the trust of these women and of the village chiefs, explaining what the photographs would be used for, et cetera, et cetera. All in keeping with the work our organization has been doing over this territory for a very long time. She still hasn't finished, and she's been working on it for four years."

"Unfortunately we don't have four years, so we'll have to manage," Imo said, somewhat icily.

The sun had disappeared behind the building and it was getting cold outside in the courtyard. I wished Roshana would ask us to continue the conversation inside. But obviously there was a far more important meeting going on in the office.

"And as far as the weddings are concerned," Roshana went on, "the part of the ceremony that takes place in the women's quarters is secret. No man has ever been allowed to see it and so that is also something that can't be shown in photographs. Ours are very ancient traditions, Miss Glass."

"Imo, please."

"Sure. Imo. Not even Florence was able to do that."

"I see." Imo looked at her watch. We didn't have to go anywhere in particular, but I could tell she was getting restless.

"Maybe you should speak to Florence. She might be able to give you some advice," Roshana said.

"Yes, of course, that's a good idea," said Imo, faking a smile. "But I'm afraid we really have to go now. Perhaps I'll call you tomorrow and see if we can drop by again and have a chat with Florence."

It didn't take much to figure out that the last thing Imo wanted was to have a French girl in a headscarf explain to her why it would take years to get what she needed to get in ten days. I, on the other hand, could have done with a bit of advice. All I had so far was ruins and teetering buildings. I picked up the camera from my lap.

"I'm going to get a picture of Roshana. A portrait, just to have it. I don't know, you might be able to use it."

Imo eyed Roshana—who was taking another call on her cell and pacing up and down the garden—sizing her up.

"Sure, why not. I don't think I'll need it, but what the hell."

Roshana, when asked, looked at me with an unfriendly expression and said it was not doable.

"I'll explain why. Obviously it's not for the same reason as the other women that I don't want my picture published. It's just that we've created a shelter here, a secret place in Kabul, for women who've run away from home to escape the violence of their husbands. It's for their safety that my picture must never appear in the papers. I have to protect them, so my identity must remain hidden."

I put the camera back inside the bag. Roshana had started to escort us to the gate.

"And how about the shelter?" Imo asked. "Could we take some photos in there? That would be just perfect for our story."

"Oh, no. That isn't possible. We're protecting women who are in danger of their lives. If they were recognized and found, they would risk having their throats cut."

Imo began to forcefully twist her hair in a bun, in the attempt to conceal her exasperation.

"But listen, Roshana . . ." Imo mimicked her politeness and diction. "This story will appear in the *Observer* magazine in London. It'll get serialized and receive a lot of thoughtful attention. And I'd be happy to print the details of the shelter, where readers could send their contributions."

Roshana gestured to the guard at the sentry box to open the gate to let us out.

"It's a matter of principle for me—call it professional ethics if you like. If their faces, or my face for that matter, started appearing in the papers, *any paper,* even in Papua New Guinea, these women wouldn't trust me anymore."

"Frankly, I doubt that in the villages where these women's husbands live there will be newsstands that sell the *Observer.*"

"*Frankly,* their safety is more important to me than the

careers of Western journalists," Roshana replied, holding out her hand. Obviously our time with her was up.

"But without Western journalists, there wouldn't be an international public opinion, and without a public opinion, there wouldn't be NGOs or the funds you need to do what you're doing," Imo insisted, withholding her hand.

"I realize this. Of course I do. And I also realize it may seem a vicious circle. But everyone has their priorities. If I were you, I'd speak to Florence. She's an exceptional woman and her experience on this issue, even as a foreigner, is worth ten times more than anything I could tell you. Thank you for your visit," she said, and smiled.

"That went really well," snapped Imo as she slammed the car door. "Go figure, women sabotaging stories about women. We're not going to get any help from Lady Roshana, I'll tell you that much."

"We knew it wouldn't be easy outside Kabul. It said just that in the guide."

"But if what she said was true, then we would've never seen a single photo of an Afghan woman since the Taliban fell. No, she clearly has a problem with Western journalists, except for her friend Florence with the oh-so-chic headscarf, whom she has a lot of respect for. And she's going to make it as difficult as she possibly can for us, believe me."

The surge of excitement I had felt the day before while playing with the camera around the city, acquainting myself with that piercing mountain light, with shooting outdoors for the first time in years, was already beginning to fade and give way to anxiety. I realized my real assignment was going to be incredibly tough and that I didn't have a strategy. I had no clue how to go about it. I needed to be more aggressive about making contacts, to talk my way in and gain access on my own behalf to get the photos we needed. I couldn't let Imo do it for me. I had to get into shape fast.

"Maybe I should try and talk to that French photogr—"

"Better not. You know what'll happen: she'll get all worked up the minute she finds out you want to take the same photos she's shooting. The only thing we need to do is get out of the city as soon as possible and head into the interior. Can't you see how *controlling* everyone is? It's just so annoying. Hanif, excuse me, we need to stop somewhere with a decent bathroom. A hotel, a restaurant, anywhere civilized."

She had lowered her voice and clasped my hand.

"It's come."

"What has?"

"Montezuma's revenge in the Hindu Kush. The nightmare begins."

Imo collapsed in the space of two minutes as if she'd been struck by lightning. One minute it was her, with her cool hand, spicy perfume and light makeup, the next she came undone, her features gone slack, her body shuddering.

The minute we got to Babur's Lodge she bolted up the stairs three at a time to the bathroom. I waited for her on the landing, still shocked by the force of the thing that had struck her down, and I couldn't help hearing her grunting, gasping and groaning. After an agonizing silence, the door swung open and another Imo emerged, a Medusa bathed in sweat, her curly hair plastered to her face like swirling snakes and dark rings under her feverish eyes. She waved a hand, as if to say "don't speak," and lurched to her room.

"I have to be very still. If I don't move I'll be okay."

I followed her all the way into her room, unrolling a petulant string of questions.

"Shall I call a doctor? Should we go to the hospital? Do you think you've got a temperature? Maybe a good idea to call

Hanif? Do you need antibiotics? Do you want some water? Some tea?" But I was really the one who needed help. Seeing her like that had sent me into a panic.

Imo raised her hand with her palm facing me, as if to keep me at a distance. She pulled her sweater and undershirt over her head in one go, got out of her pants, boots and socks, dropping piece after piece on the floor as she went towards the bed like a sleepwalker. She stood for a moment in her black lace bra and matching panties—way too elaborate underwear for the place we were in—her hair damp, her body trembling. Then she collapsed under the duvet.

She kept her eyes closed as she whispered, "I don't need anything, I just need to close my eyes and stay still. Can you just close the curtains, please? The light is killing me."

I drew the curtains and sat on the edge of the bed.

"Where's the first-aid kit? There should be some medicine in there. Do you want me to call Pierre and get the insurance to send a doctor?"

Imo shook her head. Her teeth were chattering under the duvet.

"With what they paid for the insurance, the least they can do is—"

"Please, Maria, *be quiet,*" she managed to say through her clenched teeth in a weak but firm tone. "Go to your room now and leave me alone."

Not even an hour later, the same avalanche cascaded over me like a dam bursting. I'd gone down to the dining room, ordered a cup of tea and was checking my e-mail on the hotel's old-fashioned computer.

There were messages from my assistant Nori saying that absolutely nothing new was happening in Milan, work was slow and she was dying to hear my exciting news. There was one from my father giving me an indignant summary of the latest misdeeds of the Italian government and sending me a link

for an article in the *Guardian* about an Afghan film director.
The food editor of a weekly magazine was offering me a gig
shooting an Easter lunch spread for the April issue of her magazine. She went on at length about the feeling the pictures had to
have, suggesting I scatter flower petals among the pizzas and
salamis.

Since I had arrived in Kabul I hadn't given a single thought
about what might await me once I got back to Milan. The
thought of how much energy, money, people there were behind
a table laden with food once again struck me as madness. But it
was the word "salami" that set off the alarm bells. My body
started to perceive a sort of distant thunder, which, although
still in the distance, did not bode well. It wasn't yet a symptom,
just a churning. But before I could click on "Reply" I felt a claw
clutch my intestines and twist them inside out like a glove. A
wave of cold sweat broke over my forehead and in that precise
instant I knew that a frontal attack had been unleashed on my
system. Something had sunk its fangs in and was punching and
clawing at me. Something unknown, but above all, something
Afghan, and therefore potentially mortal.

I was stretched on the couch in my room at Babur's Lodge,
my nose pressed against the dusty fabric. This, I thought, was
how I was going to die. Murdered by a kebab. Was this a food
photographer's karmic punishment?

I knew for sure that none of those horrible men who chewed
beans at breakfast would notice my disappearance or Imo's. In
three, four days, someone—Hanif, possibly, or the Tajik cleaning woman with ruddy cheeks I'd run into every morning on
the stairs—would find us in our respective rooms still and composed, like little birds struck by lightning.

The fever rose and fell like a roller coaster. One moment I
was racked with the shakes, the next I was burning up. I could
feel the angry monster make way, destroying everything in its
path like a bombardier spraying napalm. I didn't have much

time left, I knew that it would annihilate me if I let it, but I didn't even have the strength to crawl on my hands and knees to Imo's room to ask her for help, let alone do a whole flight of stairs to ask General Dynamics to please find me a doctor. Anyway, at four in the afternoon, Babur's Lodge was deserted. Its occupants were out doing the jobs they were being handsomely paid to do. Some buying arms, some selling information, some watching someone's back with a loaded machine gun.

That was when I saw the cell phone.

The effort would be minimal. I would just have to press a key—his name was still saved as number three on the speed dial, I hadn't been able to bring myself to delete it. Besides, I was dying and I didn't have much choice. He would understand this was an emergency.

And, he was an immunologist.

The idea of hearing his voice after so long made me anxious. I hadn't talked or written to him in two years. I feared his name just like a sick person fears the name of his illness, even if only fleetingly reading it in a newspaper. A text message, maybe, would be a sensible compromise. To compose it I would have to press more than one key and that would cost me a considerable effort, but I had to hurry: the monster was goose-stepping through my system and my temperature was soaring.

AM IN KABUL, HAVE HIGH FEVER, CAN U HELP?

There, done. For the first time I didn't care if my name lit up on the display of his phone as he was eating or sleeping or reading in bed next to her.

Stella, that was her name.

From the start, when I first discovered Carlo had been having an affair, I insisted on never saying her name out loud. I called her *quella,* "that one." I didn't want her to be a real person. I wanted her to remain a secondary character in a film, whose face wasn't necessary to remember in order to follow the plot. But I was wrong.

Beep. Beep. Beep.

DIARRHEA? WHY R U IN KABUL?

There had been tears, late-night talks, desperate sobs. His clothing had been thrown in a bag and out the door, then retrieved in a bout of forgiveness. There had been frantic phone calls, more tears. He admitted he had made love to her at a medical convention in Turin. I wanted to know all the details, the where and the when so that I could retrace exactly what I had been doing (watching TV in my pajamas? eating dinner standing up in the kitchen staring at the microwave?) while he had been undressing her, kissing her, licking her body all over.

I told him he had to leave, that the damage was irreparable, and told him to sleep on the couch. He came to bed in the middle of the night full of grief and we made love magnificently, aroused by the pain. The next morning I offered some hope: maybe there was a way we could work this out? But over his cereal bowl he admitted he'd seen her more than once, that it hadn't been just a one-night stand.

Pressed, he confessed he had fallen in love.

I threw his clothes out the window. I threw an ashtray. My brother had to come at three in the morning and calm me down with a Xanax in his pocket.

HAD IT. NOW ONLY RAGING FEVER & ACHING ALL OVER. WHAT DO I TAKE?

I had allowed him to come back after a month. He had written e-mails, left messages, cried over the phone. He said he'd been in agony, that he had made the biggest mistake of his life and wanted to come home. He came back, but my victory felt like a defeat. We sat around the house in the evening sprawled on the couch like two rag dolls that needed stuffing. There was nothing we felt like doing together—being back under the same roof again seemed more than enough. Our unhappiness spilled all over our food, our clothes, our agitated dreams. Every time his phone rang the air in the room would solidify, the atoms hardened and I felt them pricking my skin, his skin, like Chinese torture. We couldn't wait for the other one to leave the house.

When he left again, I didn't scream. I wasn't even granted the dark splendor of rage to help me look dignified. I watched him pack his bags once more, feeling weaker and weaker, as if I were bleeding to death and he wasn't even bothering to call the ambulance.

Beep. Beep.

IBUPROFEN RIGHT NOW 2 LOWER TEMP. THEN BROAD-SPECTRUM ANTIBIOTIC. CAN U CALL A DOC?

Carlo had ended up moving in with Stella. He had made it sound—when he talked to mutual friends—as if it were merely a fortuitous arrangement, as if her address had been the first that came to mind when he entered the taxi.

NO DOCTOR. TELL ME WHICH ANTIBIOTIC?

I was pleased with my urgent, imperative tone. I couldn't have cared less where he was, who he was with, what he was doing. All I wanted was the name of the drug, the dosage, a cure. I had succeeded in moving from the couch and now was groping around in my medicine bag. I found the Advil and gulped down two tablets without water.

I had heard from friends that he and Stella were having problems. After two years of living together he had gained weight and she was on antidepressants.

Beep. Beep.

TAKE CIPRO OR BACTRIM. DRINK A LOT OF WATER PLS.

I could feel the insides of my body crackling and crumbling. The little monster was chomping away, devouring, setting fires here and there. Which pill, I wondered, among the many I had thrown into the bag, had the power to stop this descent of the Huns? I could barely focus on the names of the medications. I just wanted to close my eyes. With a huge effort, I keyed in:

CIPRO. OK

I had to somehow administer the same dose to Imo. I absolutely had to get out of bed and cross the landing.

Beep. Beep.

THAT OK FOR NOW. 1 EVERY 12 HRS. CANT SOMEONE GO W U 2 A PHARMACY, HOSPITAL?

I swallowed the antibiotic and prayed it hadn't expired, that it still retained all its power. I only had the strength left to key in two letters.

NO

It was an economical reply, more from the front line than from a desperate ex-girlfriend. The proximity of my end—or at least the possibility that the end was near—made me stronger, perhaps because it put everything in the right perspective. And although I was nearly delirious, I felt that this was the best perspective I had had in a long time.

Then I collapsed.

Babur's Lodge had not been set up to effectively take care of guests. It was more like a receptacle for men who came in from their missions tired and dusty, who dumped their weapons and muddy boots in a corner, asked for food and alcohol and then crashed into bed. More like a barracks than a hotel. At Babur's there were no working phones in the rooms, the idea of room service was a mirage, none of the staff spoke a word of English, you had to communicate with hand signals, the generator cut off at ten.

I awoke from something that resembled a coma more than sleep. I had no idea how much time had passed, but my room was dark and the heater had gone out. It could have been any hour of the night; it could have even been the day after. Everyone could have been dead.

More cold sweats, more nausea. I needed to throw up again, but I realized I absolutely needed to check Imo too, give her the antibiotic. Maybe by now it was already too late. In total darkness (why didn't I bring a torch? the Defenders in their lesson on personal safety had insisted one should always have a flashlight handy, no matter what) I started to grope my way along, using the display of my cell to light what it could of the room, find my boots, the packet of antibiotics and the roll of toilet paper. I managed to check the time—three twenty—and saw there were two messages.

HOW R U? TEMPERATURE DOWN?

He'd put an "X" after the question mark. The symbol for a kiss.

Interesting.

Then:

ANSWER ME. I FOUND NUMBER OF AN ITALIAN COLLEAGUE WHO WORKS IN A HOSPITAL, HE SAYS IT'S NORMAL TO CATCH THE VIRUS. IT IS DUST BORNE. THEY CALL IT KABUL BUG. CALL HIM.

There was a number.

I didn't reply.

On the landing it was like venturing into the Alaskan night: pitch-dark and so much colder than my room. I made my way, brandishing my cell, pointing the display in the direction of the bathroom and projecting a dim light on the floor. Just then, the door was thrown open and someone came out. I heard bare feet padding on the floor, got a whiff of beer and tobacco.

He walked right into me; I pushed him away with my hands. I touched, inadvertently, his hip with my fingertips. The skin felt warm and smooth. It was true: he was naked.

I saw it. The erection.

It looked enormous, perfectly horizontal, tinged with the greenish glow of my display. Something rigid brushed my hand. It couldn't have been anything else.

"What the fuck . . ." I heard him growl.

And he gave me a shove, angrily pushing me out of the way.

Of course, Imo refused to take medication—antibiotics? no way, she was homeopathic—and claimed she preferred to fight the virus with "hand-to-hand combat like they taught me in Sudan." I begged her, but she wouldn't listen to me. She said all she needed to do was drink lots of water and that she was genetically equipped to deal with weird bugs.

"Don't forget, I have Colombian blood," she grumbled under the duvet. She begged me to leave and let her fight in peace.

The next morning my door flew open. Imo appeared, smiling, freshly showered, with a breakfast tray. She put a thermometer in my mouth and opened the window.

"Look how much weight I've lost," she said. "My pants are falling off me."

She slid the thermometer out of my mouth. I felt like crap, all sticky, sweaty and dirty.

"Wow, still thirty-eight point five. You better get some rest. I'll tell the guys downstairs to bring you tea and toast. I'm going into town with Hanif to pick up the permits from the ministry and then I'm going to interview the deputy minister who handles women's affairs and see what she has to say. You stay in bed and drink lots of fluids. We're leaving for the village tomorrow and it's going to be a long trip."

I cleared my throat.

"What about the crater?"

"All sorted, we can get through. The main thing is to get out of this latrine of a city. You'll see, once we're out of here everything will change. Hanif has found a woman interpreter who will help us with the women in the village, so we're all set. I can't wait. It'll be fantastic."

She grinned. "Blue skies, open spaces and kind, traditional people at last who don't read international newspapers."

I had no idea what Imo had in mind, what she was expecting to find once we got out of Kabul. All I could think of was land mines, dangerous checkpoints, kidnappers on the warlords' payroll, anarchy. But what actually worried me the most was the idea of a journey through such a vast territory without a single toilet.

Imo sat on the edge of my bed, flipping through her notes. She could hardly contain her enthusiasm.

"And the best news is that, hang on . . . where did I put it?"

She pulled out a piece of paper with something scribbled on it.

"Ah! Here it is. This German NGO has given me the name of a woman who might be willing to talk to us. She tried to kill herself about a week ago and is recovering in some kind of tiny clinic outside her village, about two hundred kilometers out of Kabul."

"Fantastic," I said faintly. Then I had to close my eyes again.

Beep. Beep.

WELL? TELL ME HOW U R. IF U LIKE I'LL CALL.

I was still weak, but I could tell the monster had been dealt a lethal blow during the night. It'd been knocked to the mat and was all punched out. The bout was over.

AM MUCH BETTER. THANK U 4 TREATMENT.

I considered the possibility of adding HUGS & XX but I didn't mean it. Besides, I feared any mention of physical contact could prove incendiary. With each beep-beep I could feel the tension rising. Although he had been only a consultant over a clash between viruses and antibodies, the object of his attention had been my body. A body he knew rather well, and whose shape and outlines he now was certainly remembering. By allowing him to examine it again, I had also allowed him to regain some control over it and, in a certain sense, he was now claiming his rights of ownership.

Beep. Beep.

MARIA. DON'T EVEN KNOW WHAT U R DOING IN AFGHANISTAN. WANT TO HEAR YOUR VOICE. MISS U.

I stared at this message at length, studying the syntax, interrogating the letters the way a graphologist would examine an anonymous letter to decipher the personality of the murderer.

The period after MARIA was an important clue, I felt, a sort of invocation. That period stood for a theatrical pause. Had he been standing in front of me, he would have paused after pronouncing my name, with studied slowness. He would have touched me too, I knew it. Probably he would have taken my hand, or perhaps stroked my hair. MISS U stood for the final capitulation. It all felt very dangerous.

I turned the phone off.

By the evening I woke up from another bout of sweaty unconsciousness. I felt drained, inert like still water on a lake, but the fever was gone and I was hungry. I walked downstairs to the bar in search of something to eat.

Imo was having a gin and tonic by herself in a corner, intent on texting on her mobile.

"Oh, you're back! I was beginning to miss you," she said cheerfully. "Look at you. You're yourself again, thank God. I didn't want to scare you, but you were looking terrible this morning. I thought I might have to send for a helicopter or something." She laughed.

As for Imo, she was looking ravishing, swathed in her soft shahtoosh, several Indian glass bangles clinking around her wrist, her eyes darkened by kohl.

"Good thing you came down, it's so depressing in here," she whispered. "Look at these men, don't they all look suicidal to you?"

The bar at Babur's Lodge was one of the few places in Kabul that served alcohol, and in the evening it slowly filled up with Westerners. The South African and a middle-aged German who wore a mud-colored corduroy suit and hiking boots sat on stools at the bar, oozing loneliness and gloom from every pore.

"See that one? A mercenary or a criminal." Imo jabbed me with her elbow and looked over at the South African. "I bet he's one of those who enjoyed putting blacks on the grill instead of sausages."

"Jesus, Imo. What makes you say that?" The way she always seemed to know, without a doubt, who was who in this—at least for me—indecipherable world of men was beginning to irritate me.

"I just know because that kind of South African is always ex–secret police. Probably an escapee from a life sentence. What else would he be doing here otherwise?"

The German was drunk. He was the one paying for the South African's beer. He was railing into his beer in English, in that graceless accent full of *zees,* that Germany had fallen into the hands of pigs, that they were all Communists, and he didn't want to live there anymore, he was ashamed to be a German. The South African nodded distractedly, lost in his own thoughts, gazing at the bottom of his glass. It was obvious that neither of them was in any way interested in the other, and there was no connection between them, just bitterness alongside bitterness. Two elbow-to-elbow bitternesses, propping up the bar in a hotel a long way from home. The alcohol somehow stripped them bare: it was like seeing them naked through a keyhole; the German obscene and disheveled, the South African stony and still like a wrinkled lizard.

At a table behind us, the Blond, wearing his usual *pakol* and a sloppy sweater, was deep in conversation with a man I'd never seen before. He was all worked up and appeared to be in the midst of an elaborate explanation; he had the apprehensive look of a student justifying himself to a teacher. We passed by just inches from him, but he didn't give the slightest sign of recognition.

The German burst out in cavernous, raucous laughter. He raised his beer glass and proposed a toast in German to nobody in particular. The South African looked like he was asleep.

"It just blows my mind," said Imo, casting a sideways glance first at the Blond, then at the German. "We've been here three days and none of these guys has so much as acknowledged us yet. I'm curious as to how long they can go on ignoring the fact we actually exist. Would you like to order something, darling?"

"I was thinking maybe just tea and maybe a cup of soup later on would be good. I don't want to eat anything too . . ." I let my words trail off.

"You know, to me this seems to be the place where all good manners have come to an end," Imo continued, looking around the room. "And it's not a very good sign if you ask me. If there were any hope—if any of them actually believed this country could still make it and get back on its feet again—these people would still be engaged in some kind of civilized behavior. But could they care less? They know this is the last stop. After this one there's only chaos."

Imo called the waiter, the young Afghan boy who produced the huevos rancheros for the Dark One every morning, and ordered tea for me and another drink for her.

The man the Blond was talking to had longish hair, a ginger beard and the crumpled look of someone who'd been on a long journey and had collected a lot of dust on the road. Muddy army boots, a heavy military coat, a face tanned by the mountain sun. He was listening to the Blond intently, but I noticed out of the corner of my eye that he was also scanning our table. Our eyes met for a split second and I intercepted a sort of signal, a nod, possibly half a smile. The Blond picked up on this breach in the man's attention—it had been barely a power glitch—and immediately moved closer, hiking his chair forward a few inches, placing himself like a screen between us.

"He's paying him," murmured Imo. I turned around just in time to see the man with the ginger beard hand a roll of bills to the Blond, who counted, then pocketed them. The man with the ginger beard gave him a pat on the shoulder. It was a gesture of encouragement, almost paternal. They shook hands, then the Blond stood up and without looking at us at all, left the bar with his head down. The man with the beard stayed where he was and motioned to the Afghan boy behind the bar to bring him another beer.

"This is Paul. From Canada," Imo specified, as if I should rejoice that at least he wasn't another American. "He's explaining some very interesting things to me about the opium fields. This is Maria, the fabulous photographer I was telling you about."

The man with the beard had moved fast. In the time it took me to go to the bathroom and come back, he'd moved away from his table, joined ours and refreshed his drink. He pointed his thumb at Imo's gin and tonic with ice, and threw me a querying glance, jerking his chin up slightly.

". . . No, thank you, I'm not feeling . . . Maybe something warm . . . some green tea."

Paul called the waiter behind the bar by name and ordered in Dari, without a trace of an accent, or so it sounded to me. Imo had already pulled out her Moleskine and was taking notes.

"We were talking about the spray," she said. "The U.S. is pressuring President Karzai to spray the poppy fields, you know, to show the world that they're ridding Afghanistan of heroin. Which is actually the dumbest thing this government could do."

She then turned to Paul.

"You know of course how the U.S. did exactly the same thing in Colombia with coke. I'm actually from Medellín, so . . ."

But Paul had planted his eyes on me.

"Right. So, what would you say the alternative is?"

He was asking me, not because he thought I had an opinion, or because he was interested in hearing it if I did. It was a rhetorical question, something a teacher would ask the class dunce during a test. He lit a cigarette and exhaled the smoke slowly right into my nostrils.

"I wouldn't know. Sorry, but why is it so dumb to spray?"

Paul chuckled. He stretched and shook his head in amusement.

I'd obviously asked the wrong question.

"Well. First of all, it's a short-term, one-time effort and it would only push the opium prices up. Second, do you have any idea what the illiteracy rate is in Afghanistan? I'll tell you, it's close to seventy percent. How do you think this population of illiterates survives? What work can they do?"

"I don't—"

"Agriculture," Imo cut in, looking up quickly from the notes she was jotting down.

"Yes," conceded Paul. "And where do you think the farmers get the money to feed their families during the winter months when nothing grows?"

I looked over at Imo.

"Opium," she answered.

Paul approved with a movement of his hand and turned to me again.

"If they grow opium, then they get an advance on the harvest from the drug lords. And that money gets them through the winter. Then, when they harvest it in spring, they get the rest. But if the field is sprayed, then that farmer finds himself not only without a crop, but now he also has a debt to pay."

"And so the poor bugger is completely fucked," added Imo.

"Exactly. So, given that these poor buggers make up seventy percent of the country, how kindly do you think Afghans view the Americans who want to spray their only means of subsistence?"

"Not very kindly."

"Right. So even though in Washington this might sound like a really bright idea, the truth is, in this country they want to see every American dead."

He mimed the gesture of cutting his throat with his index finger.

"It's the worst thing they could do; it's actually why everything is going down the drain. That, not religion or culture or what have you, is the reason why the Taliban are coming back with the support of the people."

Imo wrote and nodded.

"But why don't the Americans help them with alternative crops?" she asked. "Then they can destroy the poppies but in exchange they get them to grow something else. You know, in Colombia and also in Bolivia they did exactly that."

Paul smiled enigmatically and stroked his chin.

"Okay. And what crops?"

"I don't know. Wheat, barley, for example?"

A glimmer of amusement flickered in Paul's eyes, then he shook his head as if Imo's suggestion was laughable.

"So how much do you think an opium crop weighs?"

Imo and I looked at each other.

"I'll tell you. I'd say you could transport it on a donkey's back. And how much does a wheat field weigh?"

"Obviously a lot more," I said.

"I'd say you'd need at least a truck," said Imo.

Paul nodded and took a slow sip of beer.

"Correct. That's exactly right. You'd need a truck."

This way he had of making us guess every answer was beginning to annoy me. He wiped his hand over his mouth.

"Do you have any idea what the roads are like ten kilometers out of the city?"

I was wondering if he was ever going to stop asking these questions.

"The tarmac ends, right?" I said to cut him off. I'd already figured out what he was getting at.

Paul raised his palms and shrugged, as if there was nothing to add. Imo lit up as if the obvious solution to a mathematical problem had suddenly been revealed to her.

"Right. Opium is the only crop that can be *transported* on the back of a mule. Wow. That's interesting." She was writing it all down, glowing from this bit of information. "Funny, one never thinks of that," she said defensively, not wanting to sound naive.

Paul sniggered.

"Everyone talks and writes about Afghanistan, but you've got to talk to the farmers, the villagers in the remote regions—and you've got to talk to them in their language—to figure out the details of how things work or why they don't work."

The waiter came with my tea and their drinks. Paul kept looking at me with a mixture of interest and insolence. He snapped his fingers and took a sip of his fresh beer.

"If they don't build roads first they'll never solve the problem of resources. If you can't transport it, you can't sell it. It's obvious, isn't it?"

We nodded.

"It'll be years before they build a decent road network here," added Imo with the air of an expert. Then she smiled at Paul. She picked up his cigarette from the ashtray without asking permission and took a drag. I realized she was on to something. In order to weasel as much information as possible she was actually flirting with him.

I took my pills out of my pocket and swallowed one with a sip of tea. Everything still hurt: my bones, my muscles, my nerves. The battle with the monster had left me aching all over.

"What's the matter?" Paul asked.

"Nothing, I've got a bit of a headache."

"There, you see, for example . . ."

He picked up the bottle of Advil and turned it around in his hand.

"Do you have any idea how many painkillers are consumed every day around the planet?"

He was driving me insane. Maybe it was a syndrome, this thing of closing every sentence with a question mark.

I didn't answer.

"And what is the main substance in an analgesic?"

"Morphine derived from opium," Imo said, twirling the ice around in her drink.

"That's right," conceded Paul once more. He took another sip of beer and smiled. He didn't say anything for a few seconds. He looked at us, expecting one of us to cry miracle, as if his beer glass was the Holy Grail and we still hadn't realized that whatever we were seeking had been under our noses all along.

"Precisely. There you go," he said triumphantly.

"Precisely what?"

"Pharmaceuticals would be the only solution."

"No, I'm sorry," I said wearily. "I don't think I get it."

"Simple. In order to produce the quantity of painkillers the world consumes every day, you need about ten thousand tons of opium a year, and the legal market can't produce enough. If Afghanistan sold its opium to the pharmaceutical market rather than to the drug cartel, we'd all be set. The farmers would be happy because they'd get paid, the American government would be happy because it could show the world that it had eradicated the drug problem, and you, with your headache, would get the drug you need. Does that make sense?"

We nodded again, obediently.

"But here's the point: Do you know which countries have the license to legally produce opium?"

"No," we said in unison.

"France, Spain, India, the U.K. and Turkey, to name a few."

Imo was stunned. Her pen halted in midair, her eyes widened.

"But that's absurd! I mean, sorry, but why don't they give the license to Afghanistan? Wouldn't that make sense? That way they'd have found a solution to the whole—"

Paul chuckled, as happy as a magician in front of children who pester him to find out where the bunny went.

"Why don't they? That's entirely another issue. But actually, it's the real heart of the problem."

He lit another cigarette, ready to start another round of question and answer.

Imo was excited. She slipped her shoes off and tucked her feet under her on the chair.

"No, I'm sorry, Paul, but I'd really like you to explain this to me. Would you like another beer? Maria, more tea? I'm having another gin and tonic."

Paul put up his hand to stop her. He wasn't the kind of guy who lets a woman buy him a drink. He called the waiter and ordered another round.

"I mean, this story about opium and licenses is incredible. This is actually something I'd like to research. What do you say, Maria?" She turned to Paul. "Please, Paul, explain why they give the license to France, of all places. How insane is that?"

I chose this moment to stand up.

"I'm sorry but I'm a bit tired. I'm going to bed."

I felt too weak to undergo another round of interrogation, and besides, the looks Paul was giving me were making me uneasy.

"What, you're going already? Sit down and have a drink."

He was pissed off that I dared to withdraw, that I wouldn't have a drink, but mostly, I thought, because I didn't have any questions for him.

"No. I'm going to get some sleep," I replied firmly.

Imo blew me a kiss on her fingertips.

"You go and rest, sweetie. Tomorrow's going to be a big day."

Paul gave an imperceptible nod, the way killers do in movies when they're in a crowd and realize it's not the right moment to make the hit, but they let the victim know that although they have gotten away this time, they won't the next.

The morning after, at seven, General Dynamics—freshly shaved and corseted in another immaculate multipocket vest—was describing the performance of a particular kind of bullet when it hit armored concrete as he carefully scoured his bowl of yogurt and muesli. The South African and the German in his pseudo-

Tyrolean outfit were listening like salt statues. The Dark One was eating his mound of Kabul-style huevos rancheros. The seat next to him was empty.

"Good morning, everyone," Imo intoned as she came down wrapped in a dark red shawl, flowing brown woolen pants and dangling Indian earrings. But no one replied. Only General Dynamics suspended the monotone flow of information for a fraction of a second, registering her presence with the slightest movement of his chin.

Imo sat down next to me, smiling at the audience, sending out wafts of sandalwood, and leaned over to my side.

"He got fired last night," she whispered, indicating the empty seat.

"Who, the Blond?"

She nodded.

"Paul told me."

"Did you go to bed late?"

"Two, three, I have no idea," she said offhandedly. "We had another four drinks each after you left. It kind of got a bit out of hand by the end."

She began to butter her toast.

I looked at her questioningly. She laughed and shook her head.

"No way, are you kidding? I just had to push him hard and slam the door on his face. Thank God he was so drunk he probably won't even remember."

"Was it useful at least?"

"He told me everything about what's going on in this country at the moment: who's in charge, who's corrupt, who's got money, who's got arms, who's got opium, who's in bed with whom. All of it strictly in quiz form, of course. I thought my head was going to burst. God, is he exhausting. But he knows a lot of stuff, that guy."

"What did he tell you about the Blond?"

"He says when you're working in security at the level the Blond worked at, all it takes is a split second's distraction and they send you home. Bang. Gone. Paul said he's sorry they had to lose him. He liked him a lot."

"I wonder whose bodyguard he was. Did he tell you?"

"Of course not. He just said he was very capable. That he doesn't muck around."

I thought of the Blond's milky body, his stiff prick bumping into me in the middle of the night on the landing. The brutal way he'd pushed me aside, the automatic weapon on his bedside table next to the mineral water. And then I remembered the desolate look on his face the night before as he pocketed the money from Paul, his head hanging low, his shoulders slack. He had morphed into some kid who'd been fired from his first job and had to start all over again.

"But why was Paul paying him? Is he his boss?"

"I think so. I don't know. I don't understand much about it. Around the third gin and tonic, I asked him, '*Who are you? How come you know all this stuff?*' But he just laughed at me and asked another question."

Imo turned to the Dark One and said out loud, "Could you pass me the milk, please?"

The Dark One ignored her.

"Hallo? I'm talking to you," Imo insisted, still smiling. The Dark One lifted his face from his eggs, stunned.

"The *milk,*" Imo repeated. Even General Dynamics cut short. There was a silence.

Imo held out her index finger, pointing decisively at the glass jug.

"Could you please pass it to me?"

The Dark One hesitated—all eyes were now on him—he picked up the jug, reluctantly, and held it suspended in midair for a second. Then he slowly passed it to Imo, while all the men at the table followed the trajectory with the same rapt expression, as if watching a penalty kick in slow motion that ends up going straight into the net.

An hour later, on a bright morning swept clean by a freezing wind, we were gone.

In the quiet of the early morning we left behind the dense cloud of dust and diesel fumes that hovered over Kabul like a deadly pall. Imo had insisted that I borrow a thick long coat from her and one of her Indian scarves instead of wearing my green parka, "for a better camouflage effect." It felt good to be inside her expensive wools on such a cold day.

After we passed the last checkpoint, everything suddenly spread out like a fan opening with a flick of the wrist. The air was crystal clear, sharp like the point of a diamond, and I could smell snow on the mountains that edged the horizon like lace. The beauty of the mountains loomed before me all at once, taking my breath away. Imo took my hand and squeezed it at exactly the same moment.

"Look at that," she murmured. I was grateful that she would allow me to participate in her surprise, for choosing not to take such beauty for granted.

That morning Hanif had showed up in the hall of Babur's Lodge in a *shalwar kameez* and pattu. I gathered that this attire was the sensible choice for a trip to a traditional village. He looked wretched and puffy-eyed, as if he hadn't had the time to wash his face properly.

"My wife was ill all night. She has pains and some bleeding. I took her to the hospital and the doctor said it's better to keep her there for a day or two."

"Oh. I'm so sorry. Does she also have a cell phone so you can be in touch with her?" Imo said and pointed at his Nokia.

"There's no more signal beyond that hill," said Hanif disconsolately.

"But we've got the satellite phone for emergencies, haven't we?" I whispered to Imo.

"Ah, right, the satellite phone," she said cautiously. And then she sighed.

"You know, I forgot to recharge it. Actually, I left it at Babur's Lodge."

In Keith's lesson on "personal safety," rule number one was to travel with all the important numbers, like hospitals, emergency air rescue and embassy, memorized on the speed dial of your cell phone. If you were traveling where there was no signal, rule number two was to take a satellite phone with you at all times.

"And the flak jackets?" I asked.

"What?"

"Did you leave those behind as well?"

"Yeah. It completely slipped my mind. The first-aid kit too, by the way."

"Ah, I see."

She shrugged. "In any case, if anything happens to us, it won't be bandages that'll save our lives."

I would have liked to tell her that, after my repeated exposures to Obelix's body, I felt I had a couple of tricks up my sleeve, but I let it slide.

After all those classes, notes, slides and practical exercises, which had earned me a Training in Hostile Environments diploma, I was traveling in a battered Ford with no suspension, with a one-liter bottle of water for three people, no torch and no means of communicating with anyone. The only thing that I had remembered to bring along was a roll of toilet paper and some Advil.

The tarmac ended a few kilometers outside of Kabul. We had been traveling for an hour on a narrow gravel track, which then gave way to dirt and finally turned into just a faint trace on the plain. I'd begun to notice green specks fluttering all over the open, inexorably brown space we were crossing.

"They are flags," Hanif explained, "for the mujahideen, you know."

I wasn't sure I understood. I looked at Imo.

"They mark the spot where they've fallen in combat," she said. "Every flag a dead warrior."

I shivered. Cruising amid the flailing of hundreds and hundreds of flags, we were, in actual fact, crossing an endless graveyard.

Children sitting on mud-brick walls enclosing the houses waved at us with the tips of their rifles. Old men, their heads wrapped in rags, urging mules along the path, waved, rifles slung over their shoulders. Young men reclining under straw awnings waved, raising their guns at us, smiling. Turbaned men in the distance were praying on shawls laid out across the bare earth, next to their guns. The guns seemed just an extension of the arm, an everyday object—a cane, a broomstick—that had lost its meaning. And yet for some reason this constant presence of death—whether flapping in the wind or flourishing in the greetings—didn't feel menacing, or even all that sad somehow.

Or maybe it was just me, getting used to seeing it.

I saw a small hill. It would be easy to climb and from its top I could shoot the hundreds of flickering flags which drew the map of the dead. The morning light was still good. It could be the first really meaningful picture of the trip. I felt a surge of excitement.

When I asked Hanif to stop, he pointed at the stones marked in red on the side of the road. I remembered what the red paint stood for—we had been given a lengthy lesson with slides by the Defenders. Red paint marked mined fields. It was a reminder that there was no getting used to anything, that there was no lowering one's guard.

Back in the car I took my worn-out chamois out of the bag and started painstakingly wiping each lens. Touching my equipment eased my frustration—at least it gave me a sense that I was going to do something with all this equipment sooner or later. I took each camera body out and blew the dust off the sensor, the eyepiece, the mirror, then methodically put each piece back.

"Don't worry," I heard Imo say. I'd thought she was asleep, but she had been watching me.

"About what?"

"You'll take your pictures." Her large brown eyes were intent on me.

"Oh, that. I know. It's just that—"

"It's not easy, here. One doesn't have the freedom to move. But when we get to the village you'll have all the time in the world."

I felt grateful that she would act so relaxed just when I was about to get into a frenzy. She leaned with her head on the window, looking out, and remained silent for a while.

Then she said, "Pierre said it would be hard to persuade you to accept this assignment. That you had decided you didn't want to do reportage anymore. Why is that?"

"Oh . . . I've had a sort of, how should I say . . . I think it was a kind of a . . ."

I stumbled. I couldn't find a word that wouldn't embarrass me.

"Yes, Pierre did mention something like a nervous breakdown," Imo said idly, still looking out of the window.

It surprised me that Pierre would actually phrase it like that. That he would talk about it to people who didn't know me.

"Oh. Did he?"

"Yes. But he wants you very much to get back into photo-journalism. He thinks very highly of you. Your work, I mean."

"Yeah, well . . . I wouldn't call it a breakdown. The thing is, I'm just no longer sure that photojournalism agrees with my personality."

"But *why*? I don't understand," she insisted.

"I don't know, really." I paused. Imo scanned me with those big eyes of hers. She was prodding me and wasn't going to let go. I decided to be honest about it.

"I think what happened to me was more like depression. I also went through a very bad breakup. That too, I think."

I was aware of how pathetic it sounded. In that particular moment, in that car, in that country.

"I couldn't handle the pressure, the people. You know, the writers, the editors, the deadlines. I only wanted to shut myself off. Needed a comfort zone. That's why I do what I do now. I got into the details."

"Food stuff, right?" Imo asked a bit icily.

"Yes. Big close-ups. Gastro-porn shots," I said, trying to make it sound light and self-deprecating.

"How long ago was that?"

"Two years? Two and a half now, actually."

"I see. But one has to get over that, don't you think? As they say in those American new age books, 'It's time you reclaimed your power.' "

I looked at the awesome vista before us. I could still make out the green specks, the red dots in the distance. The indelible marks that the history of violence in this country had inflicted on the terrain.

"Besides"—Imo turned to the big view out the window and sighed—"God may very well be in the details, but don't we still need to look at the bigger picture to make sense of what's going on? Isn't this what our job is about?"

. . .

Something had happened to Hanif.

I could tell from the silent, brooding way he was driving; he appeared melancholic and distracted. I knew it must be because of his wife's being in hospital. Imo, who was sitting next to him, probably felt this might be the right time to find out more details about her, to help him cheer up but also to extract some truths about relationships between the sexes. Half an hour of silence had gone by in the car before she launched into an interview.

When did they meet? Three years earlier. Was it an arranged marriage? Yes, she was the daughter of a neighbor in Peshawar. Did his wife work? Yes, she'd worked as a secretary for a few months, but she'd left the job as soon as she learned she was pregnant. Would he let his wife work again once the baby was born? Why not, if she wanted to he'd be happy to let her. I watched Hanif slowly brighten, as if just talking about his wife was enough to buck him up.

Imo insisted we stop at the bottom of the hill, before we lost the signal, so Hanif could make his last call and get news from the hospital. We got out of the car while Hanif paced back and forth, hunched over his cell, screaming against the biting wind, his index finger closing the other ear, in that familiar pose any-one, anywhere in the world, assumes when the reception comes and goes.

Kabul was already a faded, dense cloud behind us. Ahead lay only empty space, mountain peaks cutting white into the lapis sky.

"I'm sorry to make him spend the night away from home when his wife's so unwell, but what else could we do? All we have is this week," said Imo, quickly applying a dab of lip balm, which she had gotten out of a small makeup pouch. She pondered.

"It doesn't sound good, does it? Bleeding in the seventh month?"

"Perhaps we could try and get back tonight," I suggested. "Maybe we don't need to spend the night in the village. Besides, everyone has warned us not to."

I didn't want my voice to sound overeager; by now I knew that was the worst way to convince Imo of anything.

"We'll see. Want some?" Imo offered me the lip balm. "I doubt very much we can make it to the village and back in one day."

Hanif motioned that he was done and we could go on.

"Well?" asked Imo.

"It's all right. My wife's neighbor is there. She says there's fever and pain, but the doctor's coming soon and then we'll see."

"The hemorrhage?"

"Yes, it's still there," he admitted.

"Ah."

"But the doctor is coming," he added quickly.

I detected an uneasiness in his eyes, which I could see in the rearview mirror. I began to sense that he didn't feel comfortable discussing his wife's condition with the two of us. Almost as if the question of his wife's being unwell was too private a matter, too personal and too intimate to be shared so openly with foreigners. Western women, on top of it, who obviously hadn't grasped fundamental nuances of his culture.

"That's good," I said.

"Yes, that's good." He paused and then turned the ignition key. "Let's get going."

Absolutely nothing had been resolved, but the phone call had had the power of calming all three of us. As we pushed farther into this landscape strewn with shells and rusty tank carcasses, where signals, telecommunications, electric generators ceased and the tribal lands began, the idea that Hanif's wife lay in a hospital bed where at any moment a doctor was going to show up perhaps seemed in comparison a condition of great security.

· · ·

The road was magnificent. It cut a straight line through a never-ending plateau, surrounded by three-thousand-meter-high peaks glittering with snow. Along the roadsides we passed the remains of numerous half-destroyed villages, built with the same packed earth they were standing on.

The mud houses looked more like an archaeological find, as if their ruin had occurred through a slow crumbling away rather than from mortar shells. Through the cracks, behind the half-collapsed walls of seemingly abandoned houses, we caught glimpses of skinny children, goats, the bright colors of the washing hung out to dry. We'd see smoke coming from the chimneys, flatbreads piled in baskets resting on the adobe walls, water spurting from wells. Hanif stopped the car and bought a couple of naan, the elongated flatbreads, from an old man resting against a wall. They were wrapped in newspaper, and when I touched them they still felt warm from the clay oven.

Even the vestiges of the Soviet tanks slumbering in the sun like unused tractors had come to be part of the landscape. They looked like cyclopean animals whose fangs had been removed. Rusty pieces stripped from these carcasses had been reutilized here as a dam to divert the flow of a river, there as a beam over the entrance to a house. All this destruction lacked a sense of violence or, at any rate, I couldn't read it. What I saw was life that had obstinately resprouted over the ruins like a climbing plant clinging to a wall. This was not the arrested life of a mortally wounded country.

I looked for the red marks. There were none.

"Pull over," I said to Hanif.

I got out of the car and felt the dry gravel crunch under my shoes. The effervescent air, as light as a wisp, caressed my neck. I looked around. Three hundred and sixty degrees of azure and earth, mountains and valleys, blue morphing into purple, then strips of green, yellow and ocher. I started taking pictures, it didn't matter really where I pointed my camera. On the hori-

zon, a little child running towards us over the frozen ground in
bare feet. A stain of pink in a field, perhaps a woman. Everything worked itself out in the lens, the images were composing
themselves.

It was only a moment, a sweeping breath. The instant when
everything rises by an octave and you feel a shiver come up the
spine.

Imo got out of the car too and came towards me in the stunning light. She smiled and struck a pose, hands on hips. I aimed
at her, pushed the button and knew that this too was a perfect
shot. We grinned at each other.

This was sheer happiness and we knew it.


After about an hour, the landscape suddenly closed in. Without
any warning we entered a narrow gorge cut between high walls,
as if the mountain had been sliced in half with a knife to let us
through. The dazzling morning light suddenly gave way to the
gloom of dark rock. There were men working in the middle
of the gorge, at the narrowest point. They were cutting rocks,
seemingly to build an embankment to shore up the watercourse
that ran through the bottom of the canyon. The Ford jolted
over the stones at a snail's pace. The men lowered their heads to
check who was in the car. Their heads were wrapped in rags
and turbans, their faces darkened by too much sun and their
bodies muscular and strong. Their eyes rummaged inside the
car. It wasn't just—or perhaps it wasn't all—a lascivious look.
It was a heavily charged gaze that left its mark and couldn't get
enough. I instinctively pulled the scarf over my head. The insis-
tence of those eyes disturbed me.

Women. Uncovered. Foreign. Was this the sequence that
flashed through their minds as we moved past them?

We held our breath in unison: me, Imo, Hanif, the sweaty
men who'd laid their stones and pickaxes, all of us joined in the
same moment of suspension.

I felt a molecular change in the atmosphere, as if the scene in front of my eyes had frozen, its contours hardened. It was fear. Nothing had happened but suddenly everything was different. My heart was beating wildly, my hands had turned cold and clammy. I recalled one of the lessons on in-vehicle safety measures the Defenders had given us back in Hampshire. Dangerous routes one should avoid—routes that make the perfect place for an ambush, like a gorge where a car can't go faster than ten kilometers an hour, with no way out. Two Western women and a TV presenter with one bottle of water between them and no phone. How could we have been so stupid? I felt a surge of hostility towards Imo and her arrogant ways of snubbing danger. Nobody made a sound. Not even afterwards, when we'd passed the men and their stares, when everything opened out again and the mountain peaks reappeared, gleaming in the sunlight, the valleys strewn with poplars lining riverbanks. The orchards and the women bent over in the fields, dressed in pink, green and purple, and it was as if the gorge had never happened.

I glanced at Imo, hoping for a look of complicity, but she was leaning her head on the window, gazing out, and didn't turn around. I looked at Hanif's shoulders—they had seemed contracted only a minute earlier—but he didn't say anything. I thought perhaps I had imagined it, that rustle in the air, the feeling of danger and its smell; after all, we'd only driven through a gorge at crawling speed, arousing the curiosity of men who never see anyone go by. Or maybe that ripple of fear had been real—the three of us had actually been holding our breath—but we'd decided not to talk about it because we'd come through it and we still had a long way to go.

The woman we were going to visit in the hospital had set herself on fire to get out of marrying a man four times her age. It appeared that we might be able to talk to the women of her family living in the nearby village if the head of the village would grant permission. Hanif had managed to establish contact with him through God knows which of his many channels and he'd assured us that we would be received.

"When we get there, we'll sit and speak, and little by little explain to him what you want to do," he said.

Imo stiffened.

"What do you mean exactly by 'little by little'?"

"We bring gifts, we drink tea, then we explain that you want to talk to the women. But it's best not to say straightaway that you want to know about suicide," said Hanif, waggling his head and smiling.

"No?"

"No, best not to say it straightaway."

"Right. Not a problem if you want to interview a drug lord who sells tons of heroin, or a terrorist who wants to blow up an American base," Imo said, "but just in case you want to talk to a woman who'd prefer not to marry a toothless old man who's going to beat her up, it mushrooms into a diplomatic incident."

Imo shook her head as she went over her notes in her Moleskine book.

We had been driving through the open plain for at least an hour, in what seemed a completely deserted area. The afternoon light was painting the mountains in an increasingly warm, golden hue. Hanif pointed at the only visible building in the distance. It stood alone, on top of a rise, in the middle of a rocky expanse. He said the building was the district dispensary, where the woman who'd attempted to burn herself had been admitted.

A certain Shirin—another one of Hanif's finds—was supposed to meet us there. She was going to be our translator both in the hospital and in the village, given that Hanif wouldn't be allowed inside the women's quarters.

As we got closer the clinic turned out to be a concrete block

that seemed on the verge of disintegration. Its walls were pep-
pered by bullets, a few of the windowpanes smashed. We found
Shirin waiting for us, sitting on a wooden bench outside reading
an airport thriller in English. Hanif had told us that, like him,
Shirin's parents were Afghan refugees in Peshawar. She had
grown up there, and was able to finish her studies, learn English
and lead a freer life than girls her age back in Afghanistan.

When she stood up to greet us I saw that she was barely in
her twenties and had the slanting eyes and high cheekbones of
the Hazaras. She was wearing a scarf on her head and a pair of
oval glasses, a brown wool jacket and gray flannel trousers. She
looked strangely contemporary in this setting; she shook hands
with us with her eyes cast down. She seemed apprehensive.

"It's the first time she has worked as a translator," Hanif told
us in a protective tone. "She is afraid of making a mistake, but I
told her that you are very kind ladies and that she need not
worry."

The woman who had tried to kill herself was called Zuleya
and must have been barely seventeen. She was lying on an iron
cot with her arms and legs completely bandaged. I had lost a
few minutes setting up the cameras and the lenses outside the
building, and when I went into the small ward, I found Shirin
bending over Zuleya, explaining something to her in a soft
voice. Imo was kneeling in front of the bed and holding her tape
recorder with her arm stretched out in the attempt to record
Shirin's whispers.

There were about ten women in the other beds and they all
looked in pretty bad shape. There was a little girl who had a
blank stare and cropped hair and a blood-soaked bandage on
her arm: her hand was missing. Zuleya had her face to the wall
and would neither turn around nor answer Shirin. All we could
hear coming from her were harrowing, guttural sounds. The
women were disturbed and frightened by our intrusion. Many
had covered their faces with their sheets, others stared at us, but

with a gaze so distant it seemed to be coming from another world. I gingerly approached Zuleya's bed, trying to be as inconspicuous as possible, but the slightest movement in that contained space felt like an avalanche. Imo was asking questions and urging Shirin to translate them. But Zuleya's only reply was that moaning, her face pressed against the wall.

"Please, ask her if she'd ever seen this man she was supposed to marry."

Shirin repeated the question in a hushed, soothing tone. Then, as Zuleya didn't answer, she looked back at Imo. It was a timid look, but I could tell Shirin felt it was a violation to insist.

"Can you ask her what will happen to her once she gets out of here?"

Shirin leaned in to Zuleya again, her voice increasingly tenuous. But Zuleya didn't utter a sound. She lay with her face to the wall, perfectly still, as if she were dead.

"Then ask her if—"

"She can't, she's too sick." Shirin cut Imo short in her thin, grave voice.

Imo lowered the arm brandishing the recorder. She didn't say anything for a moment, as she weighed the situation and looked around. The women were watching her. No one said a word.

"Is she so sick she can't talk?"

"She is suffering," replied Shirin.

Imo heaved herself up with a sigh. For a moment she didn't know what to do. She tied her hair in a knot and looked around. The women were still staring at her, waiting for her next move.

"All right, what can I say? We'll have to leave it, then."

There was a foul smell pervading the room. Someone had thrown soiled bandages in a corner on the floor. Perhaps the putrid smell was coming from there.

"Maria, you try and shoot something. See if you can get her to turn around. I'm going outside. The fewer of us in here, the better."

I drew closer to Zuleya's bed. She was small and thin. Her little feet emerged from the bandages; the tiny toenails were painted dark red. The varnish was chipped; her heels were dirty. Who knows what was under those bandages, how many sores. Who knows how much medication they had to stave off infection in this clinic in the middle of nowhere. Maybe she had burned her face too, I couldn't tell. Who knows whether she had been beautiful and whether she still could be. All I could see of Zuleya was her head covered by a veil, a few wayward locks of chestnut hair and her bony shoulders. She shuddered violently. Shirin and I exchanged a look. She eyed me sternly as I removed the lens cap.

I saw Zuleya's image through the lens: her jutting shoulder blades, her bandaged arms, as she pressed her face against the wall. An oblique ray of light picked out the pale blue of her veil, the flaking, faded moss green of the wall, the russet blanket. They were velvety, powdery hues, already discolored like the pigments of frescoes of the trecento. Even though you couldn't see her face, it would be a magnificent photo. A dying Madonna, shot from the back.

As the image came into focus, its contours now sharp and my finger still barely touching the shutter, I knew this was wrong. I'd known it the minute I'd walked into the room, but now, as I leaned over Zuleya, the feeling had become so clear I couldn't pretend to ignore it. That feeling of shame and rage for what I was about to do had surfaced again.

A voice piped up behind me and was immediately joined by others. Suddenly they were all shouting. Shirin tugged my arm.

"Put it down, put it down, please."

"What's wrong?"

"They don't want you to. Please, put the camera away. Don't take the picture," she pleaded.

An older woman barged into the room; she must have been a nurse or a doctor and she was shouting at me, waving her arms around. She grabbed me and bundled me out the door. As I skirted the beds of the women, some shrieked at me, shaking their fists, while others hid their faces with their sheets.

All the while, the little girl who'd lost her hand stared at me wide-eyed and blank, motionless, as if she were drugged and I were merely a hallucination. Zuleya never turned around.

"You could have shot something."

Imo was sitting next to Hanif on the wooden bench outside the dispensary. She took a long, deep drag off her cigarette and blew it out, looking upwards.

"Did you just lose your nerve—or what?"

"There was no way, Imo. No way. They literally threw me out. Everyone started yelling at me. It was mayhem in there."

"I know, but you could have shot anyway, it didn't matter if it wasn't perfectly framed or focused. At least we'd have something."

"I don't do out-of-focus shots just to *have something,*" I snapped back at her.

I was angry at her, besides being mad at myself. If from a strictly professional point of view I knew I had already failed her at the very onset of the job—and it hurt—on the other hand I was furious that she would pretend not to see how predatory the act of taking Zuleya's photo would've been.

In my earlier days as a photographer I had been in similar situations while on assignment with different writers. I had had to elbow my way into painful situations—hospitals, housing projects, slums—and shoot, despite the anger of the subjects. If being the one holding the camera had made me feel like I was pointing a gun then, this time I couldn't bear to be the hit man again.

Imo sprang to her feet and crushed the cigarette butt under her boot.

"All right, all right. Let's not get all wound up. Maybe we just need to wait a bit and familiarize with them."

She turned to Shirin.

"Tell me something, dear. What were those women saying exactly?"

"They said that you do not enter a hospital like thieves to steal a photograph without asking permission," Shirin said carefully.

"Really?"

"Yes."

"And what else?"

"That you foreigners have no respect. You do not know what honor means to an Afghan woman."

There was moment of silence.

"They also said I should be ashamed to bring you here to help you to steal a photograph of a woman who is suffering," Shirin admitted, her eyes on the ground, her cheeks flushed.

Hanif had started to speak to Shirin in Dari. They went on for a bit; evidently Hanif was concerned about what had happened in the ward and wanted to hear it in his language. Shirin gave her account in her even-tempered voice and Hanif nodded with an increasingly worried expression.

"Okay, I'll tell you what." Imo offered me a sip of water from a bottle she kept in her bag. "Let's relax for a moment and wait for things to calm down in there. Is there anything to eat in the car, by the way? Any of that delicious bread Hanif bought? In a minute I will talk to that woman doctor and explain what we're doing, okay?"

I was still sulking.

"Yes, we better do that. Shirin is right. I can't walk into a room and start taking pictures just like that. It's like armed robbery," I said. "Besides, I think that poor girl was really in pain. To me she looked like she was about to—"

"I know, I know. But we've only got two days, Maria. Today and we have tomorrow. That's forty-eight hours, since it's not a good idea to sleep in the middle of nowhere as far as security is concerned. Our insurance won't even cover it. Hanif advises against it and the paper categorically forbids it."

"But what about that French photographer who spent four years—"

"I don't give a toss what the French woman did. I don't *operate* like the French woman, all right? If I did, I'd still be squatting in a hut in southern Sudan drinking rancid milk curdled with cow piss with some Dinka family in order to write an in-depth story about the war. I just can't afford to work like that. I can't morally, financially."

There was another silence. Hanif shuffled uneasily on his feet. Shirin was looking blankly into space. Imo sighed. She walked away a couple of steps, then turned around and continued.

"And guess what? The world can't afford it either. I wrote my story about Darfur in a week and, yes, people spend years. They write books, they devote their lives to one cause. But my piece—think what you will about how I did it, how I work—my little piece was effective, and that's all I care about."

"Hey, you don't need to explain," I said and raised my hand as one would a white flag. "I didn't mean to say that the way you work is superficial."

The minute I said it I wondered if in fact that was exactly what I meant.

Hanif tapped his finger on his watch face. It was getting late. He said we had no time left if we wanted to get to the village before nightfall. So Imo and I looked at one another and, without saying anything, got in the car.

Halfway to the village a new passenger was supposed to come aboard, a guy called Abdur Raman, whom Hanif had arranged to meet via another one of his many connections. Abdur was either a cousin or a nephew of the head of the village, and he was going to do the introductions and show us the way.

"Very important to show up with Abdur Raman," Hanif said. "If we go in with him, we are under the chief's protection and nothing can happen to us. We won't have any problems, do you understand?"

Imo nodded distractedly, as if these details didn't interest her. Shirin kept silent, as if she wasn't even following the conversation. But I pricked up my ears.

"Why, what problems could we have if we weren't with Abdur Raman?"

"I don't know. There could be some people with strange ideas," said Hanif with that cautious tone he used when he didn't want to alarm us.

Imo had roused herself from her torpor and was energetically brushing her hair in long strokes with what looked like a Japanese wooden brush.

"Hanif means that it won't occur to anyone to kidnap us as long as we're under the protection of the head of the village. That's what you mean, isn't it, Hanif?"

Hanif looked at her, caught momentarily off guard; he wasn't always able to decipher Imo's irony. Then he decided to nod and smile.

"Yes, of course, no one can kidnap you if you are the chief's guests. If anything happened to you, then it would be the chief's duty to revenge you. We call it *melmastia*. It's our tradition."

"Excellent," said Imo and turned to me. I was gripping the back of Hanif's seat, as stiff as if I'd swallowed a broom.

"See? It's the tradition. C'mon, Maria. Relax."

Abdur was waiting for us outside a little walled mud-brick house stuck out at a crossroad in the middle of the plain. He was sitting on an earthen stoop doodling in the dust with a twig, seemingly bored, as if he'd been waiting too long. He was a pale, unobtrusive-looking youth with a fake-leather jacket and cheap sneakers. I would never have guessed that such an unprepossessing and unadventurous-looking kid was going to be a key to our safety. Imo and I got out of the car to stretch our legs while Abdur and Hanif went into the usual lengthy repertory of greetings and pleasantries.

"Remember not to shake his hand," Imo muttered quickly as Abdur at last came towards us. I froze, my arm in midair.

"Women don't touch men's hands here," she whispered as she bowed her head, smiling and touching her collarbone. Abdur greeted us without interest, got in the car next to Hanif, in Imo's seat, without giving it a second thought. Imo got in the back with me and Shirin.

"And thus, it begins," she announced to an imaginary audience. "From here on, all notion of hierarchy will be redesigned."

Hanif had perked up considerably, and was chatting away with Abdur in Dari as if they were picking up a conversation that had been interrupted a moment ago. His movements and the timbre of his voice acquired newfound confidence. He laughed, shook his head and even took to smoking the stinky cigarettes that Abdur had taken out of his pocket. For the first time I saw the male in Hanif, the man who goes home and orders his wife to bring his dinner. Imo seemed quite happy to be sitting in the back with the girls and to have quit being the boss for a change. She proceeded to interview Shirin about her life as a student in Peshawar. She found out Shirin was a fan of American movies and they launched themselves on a lengthy review of *Ocean's Twelve*. Shirin admitted, despite Imo's opinion to the contrary, that she would pick Brad Pitt a million times over George Clooney.

The village clung to a steep wall in the valley. The houses

were made of the same earth they stood on, like natural off-
shoots of the rock. They had the softened edges and irregular,
squiggly contours of the sand castles that children make at the
beach by letting wet sand drip through their fingers. A river ran
along the valley floor, skirting cultivated fields, fruit trees, rows
of poplars. Some children had seen the cloud of dust raised by
the Ford and were already running towards us yelling at the top
of their lungs.

The head of the village—he was introduced to us as Malik—
had been notified and was waiting for us at the entrance of the
village. He was a short but sturdy man in his forties, wearing a
brown pattu over his sweater. He had a fine, open face with
green eyes lined by very fine wrinkles, sunburned skin, a short,
well-groomed beard and a gun slung across his back. We greeted
each other—Abdur and Hanif held shoulders and went through
the motions of embracing. Shirin simply bowed her head without looking him in the eye. Imo imitated her perfectly, as if there
were no other possible way in the world to introduce herself.
She stepped out of the car, at once haughty and modest, and I
was surprised to see her scarf sitting on the tip of her head, partially covering the cascade of black hair she had so carefully
brushed. As for me, I felt awkward and stiff and mumbled my
name, unable to utter an appropriate greeting.

The first thing Malik did was ask Hanif to check if by any
chance he could get a signal on his cell. The three men, Hanif,
Abdur and Malik, walked up a slope and stood there, holding
their cells.

Imo pointed at the trio.

"I bet American intelligence didn't take this into account
when they first went looking for Osama. This Roshan company
is a really good story I should write."

"What is there to write?" I asked, baffled. I often felt Imo's
brain raced miles ahead of mine.

"How introducing mobile communication was going to change the face of war tactics. When they were fighting the Russians or during the civil war, the mujahideen were just a bunch of guys hiding in caves. Now look: everyone can exchange all kinds of information that can't be controlled. Just think of the amount of texting, messaging back and forth, that goes on in this country since Roshan moved in. No wonder they have more mobile phones than running water in these mountains."

We gazed at the men facing one another—dark silhouettes against the clear sky, swathed in flapping cloaks—each hunched over his mobile, plying the keys like three little boys pointing toy pistols at each other.

"Besides, it'd be such a fun story to research," Imo continued. "I bet Paul knows a lot of interesting stuff about this."

I looked sharply at her. She had dropped his name once too often.

"How are you going to get in touch with him?" I asked.

"He'll be at the lodge when we get back. And I got his mobile, anyway. His number is worth gold, believe me."

I watched the men some more; they persisted for a while, reluctant to surrender to the lack of reception, then finally gave up.


Malik led the way through the village and we walked behind him, along narrow alleys winding past the houses. Carved wooden doors opened onto courtyards, offering glimpses of mats and brightly colored quilts spread out on the ground, freshly rinsed aluminum bowls propped up next to cisterns. The sun was beginning to go down, soon it would set beyond the valley; the air was growing chilly, smoky, redolent of firewood and spices.

The rumor that foreigners had arrived must have spread right away. The children scampered towards us from all directions, the smallest giggling with excitement, pretending to run away terrified only to come back again and flit away once more as soon as we took a step towards them. I wondered whether the little ones had ever seen Western women before. This village seemed so remote, we could easily have been the first ones to show up in a long time. The older children lowered their eyes and pretended not to be interested, but we heard them whisper and chuckle behind us the minute we had passed them. Some were bent double under great bulging sacks of firewood. They scrutinized us from below and burst out laughing among themselves, unable to stop.

Young men sat cross-legged in the fading sun in small groups or leaned on the low stone walls; as soon as they saw the camera they asked to be photographed. They huddled together, keeping Malik in the center, next to Hanif, parading their guns menacingly towards the camera. They froze in the same gloomy expression as all the other men I had photographed in Kabul, only to regain their childish nature a second later, as they saw themselves on the digital screen.

Women appeared fleetingly around corners, in the windows, behind the courtyard doors. Unlike in the city, there were no burqas here, Hanif explained, the village being a kind of extended family and the chance of meeting perfect strangers remote; the women wore just a headscarf, but as soon as they saw men coming they would turn away, giving us their profiles, which they swiftly concealed with the corner of their veil as if they were pulling a curtain. It was an economical, graceful gesture; they probably performed it every day, every time they encountered a man. They must have grown up doing this, I thought; it seemed to come to them as naturally as breathing.

A stove was burning in the small room in Malik's house. We were sitting on red cushions on the floor. The room was painted in bright pink and was bare except for a metal cot with peeling blue paint, a stack of folded quilts and rugs in the corner and a

page from the Quran nailed to the wall. Garish red cotton curtains hung over the windows. A boy brought in a tray with an
aluminum teapot and some glasses. Malik smiled at us, sitting
straight-backed and cross-legged. He slowly poured the tea into
the glasses and offered them to us. He cradled his hands in his
lap, waiting for us to tell him what we had come for, what we
wanted from him.

Imo had brought out her notebook, put on her glasses and
was neatly laying out articles downloaded from the Internet, as
if she were at her own desk. Hanif was nervous, fidgeting on the
cushions. He sensed the moment had come and he didn't know
quite how to broach the subject of why we were there.

"So, Hanif," urged Imo as she polished her glasses with the
edge of her shawl, "can you please tell Malik that tomorrow
morning we would like to speak to the women and, in particular, to Zuleya's mother and sisters. That we want to ask them
about the suicides."

Hanif didn't move a muscle.

"Is that a problem?"

Hanif shook his head.

"Come on, then, translate, please."

Hanif shuffled on the cushions, then launched into a long
"discourse, five times the length of the question Imo had asked.
Malik was nodding at first, then suddenly frowned; he appeared
to take umbrage. There was silence. Then Malik began to speak,
very calmly, his fingers laced in his lap. His general attitude
"was indecipherable to me. He spoke at length. Shirin followed him with rapt attention. Hanif nodded nonstop. Then he
translated.

"Malik says first let's eat and then we will talk."

"Is that it?" Imo asked in disbelief. She turned to Shirin, but
the girl looked away, begging off.

"Yes, that's all," Hanif said. "You can wash your hands with
this."

He offered us a basin and filled it with hot water from a brass jug.

The food was a treat for the eyes and delicious. A mound of saffron rice topped with raisins and almonds, studded with gleaming pomegranate seeds. Bowls of freshly made yogurt to accompany pieces of spicy meat and fragrant corn bread just out of the oven. Everything was presented with grace, gathered into little pyramids on aluminum plates, enhanced with spices and perfumed leaves. I asked for permission to photograph it and Malik laughed, making a sweeping gesture as if to say, "Go ahead."

We ate from shared plates in silence, gathering up the food with bits of naan. The men exchanged rapid comments, deftly plucking up the food in their fingers. Malik waited till last to serve himself, letting the guests take the choicest morsels.

Every so often Malik said something to Hanif and then beckoned him to translate to the guests. Hanif proudly explained that Malik had fought alongside General Massoud against the Russians for ten years and then against the Taliban during the civil war. Malik recounted the hard winters spent with his group way up in the mountains.

Abdur Raman and Hanif especially approved Malik's tales of prowess and eagerly translated for us in turn—whether Malik was recounting how he had launched a mortar shell on the target or executed a Russian prisoner who'd refused to convert— as if there were no difference between a cutthroat and a soldier. The impression one got from Malik's tales was that war was not something that had wrenched him and his men from their tranquil village life; it wasn't even tragic or exceptional. War had been like life itself: the guns propped against the wall had become household objects just like cooking utensils and no Afghan man could conceive of living without them.

Imo was interested in the details. Where did they sleep, what did they eat, how did they survive the bitter cold?

"Malik says often they had to walk for days," Hanif translated. "They slept on the ground, sometimes in a cave for warmth. They'd only have a little bread with tea for food."

Imo and I expressed our admiration at their sturdiness with brief moans of wonder.

"Very strong men, the mujahideen." Hanif chuckled.

Malik nodded and encouraged Hanif to translate more.

"He says no American soldier is strong enough to do what the mujahideen did. Americans can only fight a war sitting inside a plane drinking Coca-Cola. And besides, they don't even know how to aim right!"

We all dutifully laughed at his joke and conceded.

Malik stopped laughing. His eyes hardened, as if the joke no longer amused him. He spoke to Hanif at length, raising his voice, moving his hands with fervor. When he was done talking he shook his head a couple of times, making a spiteful sound with his tongue. He seemed bitter.

Hanif translated in a hushed tone.

"Two months ago the people in the Helmand Province had to bury one hundred and seventy bodies because of a NATO air raid. Malik says the Americans bomb without bothering to look who they are killing. They say they have come here to protect the Afghan people, but they keep killing them like flies. It is time they go away."

Imo said Malik was right, that it was a shame and she couldn't agree with him more. She went on for a while, explaining how in the West many people were just as angry and wanted the troops out of Afghanistan, but Malik seemed to be only half listening to her. Maybe he didn't care much for a woman's opinion on the subject of war.

Abdur Raman took away the plates, bundling them in the oilcloth we'd eaten on. He disappeared into the next room, probably the kitchen, where the women of the household had cooked that sumptuous dinner and of whom, so far, we hadn't had a glimpse. He came back with another basin of hot water for us to wash our hands, another sign of their presence next door. It struck me how the women had been looking so carefully after our banquet without making the slightest sound. I had noticed every detail of what had been coming from across the mud wall: the fragrance of their beautifully arranged plates, the way they had scattered flowers in the water basin. I envisioned them as magical, supernatural creatures invisible to human eyes.

Malik rinsed his fingers, still sitting in the same position. There was another silence that no one dared break. Abdur Raman came back in with two kerosene lamps and set them down on the floor. Outside, night had fallen and the stars were flickering through the icy air like bright gems pinned to the sky.

Now Malik spoke, looking Imo straight in the eye. He spoke with composure as before, in a quiet, neutral tone, moving his hands only to bring his cigarette to his lips. He then turned his palm to Hanif to translate.

"Malik says that you foreigners think that we treat our women as if we were living in the Middle Ages and that this is of great concern in the West and you always write about it in your newspapers."

Imo said nothing, merely gesturing as if to say, "Go on." She had adopted a placid, Buddhist demeanor, as though nothing could ruffle her. She had obviously devised a different strategy than the more aggressive one she had used with Roshana.

"He says that now women can study and learn to read and write. Even here in the village there is a school for women who had not been able to learn during the Taliban time and Malik is very happy that now they can go there."

Imo nodded, showing how much that pleased her.

"He says that now women can walk in the streets, play music, laugh and dance at ceremonies, and that even here, not far from the village, there are women who are doctors and they are very good. He also says he himself fought for their freedom when he defended our country from the Taliban together with Massoud."

Imo nodded again, with the same beatific smile.

"And he wishes that in your newspaper article you will say that Afghan women have reclaimed their freedom."

"Of course," Imo agreed in a whisper and bowed her head for a second, closing her eyes. Then she turned to Hanif.

"But tell him, please, that we would like to speak to the women of the village and hear from them about this—"

Malik raised his hand to interrupt her. He probably understood a little English and he must have grasped the sense of Imo's objection. Hanif hastened to translate.

"Tomorrow you may go to the school and speak to the women who are learning, but Malik says you are not to distract them from their work."

"Right. And?"

"And you may speak to them only for one hour, from seven till eight."

After this disposition, which to me felt quasi-militaristic, Malik dismissed us. We were shown to a small room on the other side of the courtyard, where a stove had been lit and mattresses had been prepared with bedding rolled at their feet.

"Oh, look at that," Imo said. "Isn't this cozy?"

I wasn't particularly happy with our sleeping arrangement. It was cold and very dark, and I was afraid there might be mice scurrying across the floor.

"I bet all the men we've met till now have killed someone," I said to Imo.

We were sitting on our mattresses, with blankets wrapped around our shoulders.

Shirin had laid her glasses and neatly folded headscarf at the foot of her bed and had gone to sleep straightaway; we could hear her regular breathing on the other side of the room. It was freezing. Imo had wrapped her precious shahtoosh around her head like a turban and now looked dashing and fairy-tale-like in the oblique light of the lantern. A little earlier a woman had glided into the room with a kerosene lamp. She had whispered the same word a couple of times, patting her hand repeatedly on the bed and then left as rapidly and silently as a ghost.

"You can bet on it," agreed Imo. "I'd say all the clients at Babur's Lodge, and a good eighty percent of the Afghans we passed on the road."

"Not Hanif, though," I added.

She thought about it for moment, tilting her head to one side.

"Yeah. I think you're probably right."

"No, I bet you anything. Hanif's never killed anyone. You can tell."

I knew it not only because it was inconceivable to imagine Hanif with a gun in his hand, but because he still seemed whole and unbroken.


"Are you asleep?" Imo's voice whispered in the utter darkness.

"No."

I couldn't make myself go to sleep. I figured that by now it must be way past midnight.

"I was wondering . . ." Imo began almost absentmindedly. "Did you and Pierre ever have an affair?"

"Pierre and I? Oh, God, no. Why?" I wasn't going to admit to Imo my pathetic fantasy.

"Just wondering. He's such a *tombeur de femme*. I thought he'd be attracted to you. You're very much his type."

"Well, no, never. Did you?"

"Yeah. Ages ago," she said offhandedly.

I waited for her to offer more details. I was hoping she would.

"Were you married to that man you broke up with?" she asked instead, after a brief silence.

"No."

"I thought he was your husband for some reason."

"Why?"

"I don't know. It sounded like marriage."

"What made it sound like we were married?"

Now I was wide-awake. I felt nervous that Imo would be mulling over these bits and pieces of my bio like a detective collecting the tiniest shred of evidence. Perhaps, I thought, under the scrutiny of her magnifying lens my life compared to hers was going to look hopelessly flat.

"I don't know . . . it was just a feeling. Maybe because you look like the kind of person who would get married."

"And is that good or bad?" I laughed.

"Hmm." She paused. "It's good . . . I guess."

"Well, we did talk about it," I confessed. "We had actually even set a date."

There was a silence. Nothing came from her bundle for a few seconds. I thought she might have fallen asleep again.

"Were you ever married?" I tried.

"No. To vow to be forever and ever with one person sounds like an impossible task. I doubt I'd be good at it."

"At the time I believed that was what I wanted the most," I said, somehow forcefully. But I realized it was someone else I was talking about. Someone who had firmly believed that to have Carlo was all she wanted in order to be happy forever and ever. Someone who felt so sorry for herself when this happiness was denied to her that she crumpled to the floor. It felt like such a terrible waste of time, of opportunities. I'd given up so much for so little.

"Do you . . . are you in some kind of relationship at the moment?" I felt strangely embarrassed to ask. Imo was one of those people who have no problem asking others about their intimate lives but manage to keep theirs a secret. There was an invisible barrier whose boundaries she must have ingeniously set up when I wasn't looking.

I heard her toss under the blankets.

"Yeah, I'm seeing someone. But I wouldn't call it a relationship. He's younger than me and very handsome and very spoiled." She sighed. "It's more like physical exercise. I know I sound horribly superficial, but . . . hey, I figure I'll burn in hell later on."

"You won't burn in hell for seeing a beautiful young man," I offered.

There was another long silence. I thought it might be a hint that it was time to go back to sleep. In fact, Imo was only eager to shift the conversation onto me again.

"So, do you despise your ex and wish him dead now?" she asked in a lighter tone.

"No. Not anymore. I just don't think about him anymore. The whole idea of him bores me now."

To be able to pronounce those words and for the first time realize they were true was exhilarating.

"Excellent. Being bored is a true sign of victory."

"Then I must be victorious."

We laughed.

"I've got to pee," Imo said.

"Me too. But where?"

"Right outside. Come on, no one's around at this time."

I heard her moving, then the door creaked on its hinges.

"Wow, it's fucking freezing out here. Maria, bring your blanket with you or you'll die on the spot."

"I don't want to, it's too cold."

"Don't be silly, come on, it's amazing out here."

I grudgingly pulled on my boots and swaddled myself with everything I had. The moon was high; I could make out the mountain peaks shimmering in the silvery light.

Outside in the courtyard the air smelled sweet. After breathing all that dust and the kerosene fumes of millions of stoves hovering over Kabul, to me this felt like the purest, freshest scent imaginable. All I could hear was my own quick breath and the sound of my boots creaking on the frozen ground. I pushed the thick door that closed the compound and peeked outside on the alley. The flicker of oil lamps sitting on the windowsills lit the rest of the village randomly. Imo pointed in the distance, towards the opposite side of the valley. There was another village, perched on the ridge, facing us. Its lights were distant and tiny but in the total darkness they glittered with piercing clarity. We stood there, leaning against the crumbling mud-brick wall, in that absolute quietness that was like a blanket, like the regular breathing of husbands, wives and children sleeping next to each other.

I imagined seeing myself from above, from a satellite roaming through space, and homing in on the exact spot where I was at that moment on the map of the world. As soon as I tried to envision the distance between the village courtyard and my renovated one-bedroom in Milan, it seemed impossible that my apartment actually existed somewhere on the planet. I tried to visualize it: steeped in the quiet hum of appliances, its shutters closed, the clean sheets folded in the closet, the chocolate cookies I had bought just before I left sitting in the cupboard, the frozen food in the fridge. In a breakneck rewind I retraced the journey that would take me from that courtyard looking out on the valley back home. I reversed from the village, through the gorge with the fierce-eyed men, over the endless graveyard and its fluttering flags, over to Kabul along the Jalalabad road and then soaring over Pakistan, Iran, Turkey, Greece, all the way to Italy. There was way too much space and too many unknowns between me and my front door—to which I still held the key in my purse—for me to believe that I could re-cover all that ground and succeed in putting my key in that lock. I felt a shock, as if I had just discovered where I was—dangling in the void, way too high, and I'd never be able to come down again.

The idea that there is only one route out of a thousand that leads one back to the assigned seat on the plane that will take one home—and that it needs to be followed to the letter without any detours, delays or accidents in order not to miss it—is terrifying. That's why I'd been carrying all around Afghanistan a key ring in the shape of a rubber frog wearing a crown that held my house keys. Despite its absurdity, the frog and those thick long keys reassured me. Their presence in that particular moment seemed the only incontrovertible proof that I did have another life.

I heard a subdued gurgling. Imo had crouched down next to me: she was actually peeing at ten below zero. I saw the steam rise from the ground.

"Ohhh, how lovely," she lilted. "You know what, darling? This is so perfect, so magical. I wouldn't want to be anywhere else in the world. Would you?"

The first morning prayer woke me before dawn.

A deep, powerful voice was singing without the aid of a microphone not far from us. Almost immediately the voice of the muezzin from the village across the canyon traveled from the opposite direction and their different modulations of Allah Akhbar echoed in ripples throughout the valley. It was still pitch-dark, but I could feel the village begin to stir. I listened to the sequence of noises from underneath my blankets, not daring yet to move away from the warmth I had managed to create during the night. Rustles and hushed voices at first, water being poured from a jug, a baby crying in the distance. A rooster. The shrill voice of a woman calling another, the deep raucous cough of men clearing their throats, their sleepy voices blurting out quick, commanding phrases. The door to our room creaked and a barefoot woman slipped inside holding a kerosene lamp and a bucket of steaming hot water, followed by a little girl. The woman gently shook Imo's and Shirin's shoulders, and when she touched mine I could smell firewood and soap on her skin. The girl put down a tray with teapot and glasses.

"Good morning, girls!" sang Imo in her cheerful tone as she stepped out of her blankets, her head still wrapped in her scarf.

An hour later we shared breakfast with Malik and Hanif in the same room where we'd had dinner. Malik offered us green tea and warm flatbread with honey. It was delicious and I ate ravenously. An unexpected feeling of calm and well-being had finally descended upon me. We ate in silence, then Malik stood up and gestured for us to follow him. We walked a little way, then he pointed out the door to a small mud-brick house and he and Hanif turned their backs on us. This is the school, they said. The fact that men could not enter, or even look inside, electrified me.

The morning sun slanted in from the small windows, slashing light into the room. We were sitting on the floor covered in mats and carpets in the middle of a bare room, Imo, Shirin and me, surrounded by about twenty women staring at us as if they were in front of an otherworldly apparition.

The colors the women wore were faded but magnificent: pink and emerald-green veils, purple and orange draping. With the exception of a few withered, toothless ones, who looked worn more by fatigue than by time, most of the women were startlingly beautiful. They had fair skin and light eyes, some of them as green as grass, with dark, thick braided hair. Others had full pink lips and thick eyebrows, straight noses. After all those days spent in male company, striving to interpret their gestures, their expressions, to weigh the danger, it was a relief to be alone with women at last. And yet, now that I finally had them in front of me, these women seemed more indecipherable than the men. I had seen men drive cars, talk on cell phones and somehow or other I felt they belonged to the world I lived in, but these women seemed to have been cast out of a time machine. Everything about them was archaic; the smell of mud, flour, sweat and livestock, the feral energy they emanated. I couldn't begin to imagine them undressed (what would they be wearing underneath? did they have panties and bras?) or as they had sex with their husbands (were they modest, experienced? did they enjoy different positions?). In other words I couldn't find any indication that suggested our parallel existence on the planet.

They were staring at us, hardly stirring—I could even hear the sound of their breathing—and we were watching them with equal astonishment. In terms of our reciprocal curiosity we were equal, but I felt their gazes were impudent and unsettling, just like those of the men working on the dam, revealing a morbid, almost sexual curiosity.

I felt the urge to photograph them there and then, capture those hungry eyes, those bent knees, the way their elbows were resting on them, their chins on their hands, the small blue tattoos between the eyebrows that some of the older women had, the henna red tresses spilling down their backs, the cheap earrings made of tin and colored glass, as they listened to what Shirin was explaining to them. That is, that we had come from a long way away to talk to them about what had happened to Zuleya.

"Many countries in the rest of the world are concerned about the plight of Afghan women and want their suffering to stop," Imo said and gestured to Shirin to translate, "so we're here to listen to your stories, and hear what you have to say. Women among women."

A worried silence ensued. The women exchanged wary glances. Shirin plowed on in a courteous tone but received only monosyllabic grunts. A tall woman, a Julia Roberts look-alike, with the same thick mouth, perfectly arched eyebrows, long silky lashes framing eyes the color of moss, jerked her chin to indicate a younger woman with fair hair and a straight nose who looked like the bas-relief of a goddess from the Parthenon frieze. The bas-relief nodded, looking down at her bare, cracked feet.

"That one is Zuleya's sister," Shirin said. Then she pointed to an older woman huddled at the back of the room. "And that's her mother."

The mother made an abrupt gesture with her hand, then covered her face with her veil. She drew herself in even tighter, like a spider hiding in a crack in the wall.

"Would any of you like to tell us what happened, why did Zuleya want to kill herself?" Imo asked gently and smiled around the room.

Another lengthy silence followed. Then, as if they had been given an invisible clue, the women all began talking at once, the tone growing louder and louder, increasingly excited. Shirin directed them, interrupting them, translating what she could, getting worked up herself.

It was the same old story, the women said: Zuleya was unhappy, she didn't want to marry a man who was too old and who would have taken her away from her village and her family. She was afraid he'd beat her, that he wouldn't allow her to come back and visit her mother and her sisters. That's why she thought it better to kill herself, rather than dishonoring the family with a refusal.

Imo pondered. "Right. So, if a woman refused to get married, what would actually happen? Her family would disown her?"

The women shook their heads vigorously: impossible. There's nothing you can do when a marriage has been decided. Nobody can refuse.

"I see. Okay. Then let's say a girl and a boy from the same village are in love with one another, right? But the girl has been promised to someone else. Ask them what would happen," Imo whispered to Shirin.

Shirin swallowed hard and nodded. She seemed wary, as if the word "love" had some dangerous possibility attached to it. She translated the question slowly, neutrally, as if she were handling explosives. Again, the women started speaking one on top of the other, more and more excitedly. Everyone seemed to have a strong opinion about this. Julia Roberts stood up—she was very tall and statuesque—silencing the others, and drew her index finger across her neck. The women burst out laughing.

"What did she say?"

"She says love doesn't make a difference. That either you do what the father decides or you end up like that," said Shirin, mortified.

"Like what?" Imo had put on her red glasses and was taking notes.

"Like that, with your throat cut."

"Ha? With your throat cut?"

Shirin nodded. Imo eyed me with a triumphant look. This was just the kind of quote she'd been hoping for.

"So why do you think they're laughing?"

Shirin shrugged.

"I don't know."

"No, I'm sorry, I'm interested. What's the joke?"

"Nothing. They're laughing because they think it's funny," Shirin replied, her words tinged with a nuance of sarcasm, which Imo didn't seem to notice. "They too have a sense of humor."

"A pretty dark one, it seems." Imo made a face. "Ask them if that's ever happened in this village. You know, whether a father has killed his daughter who disobeyed."

The women nodded vigorously, without any hesitation, as if it were a silly question that only a foreigner would ask, then carried on a lengthy discussion among themselves, completely oblivious to our presence.

"See? Probably our friend Malik would too," Imo whispered to me as she scribbled it all down. "Isn't that just insane?"

She turned back to Shirin.

"Please ask them whether they know that in the West a woman's life is worth the same as a man's and if a father kills his daughter, he's sent to prison for life."

Shirin dutifully delivered the translation and the women stared back at us, in a sort of impenetrable way.

"Do they know that?" Imo asked.

A little discussion ensued among Shirin and a couple of older women.

"Yes, they do," Shirin said. "But they say that according to Islam you can't, that it's not possible, that you have to obey your father and then your husband. These are the rules, the tradition."

There seemed to be no way out of it. All that mattered was the rules. Their volition didn't seem to exist anywhere in between.

"Yes, I understand that, but then why are so many women committing suicide? It must mean they don't want to follow the rule, right? Or do you think these women are afraid to speak?"

Shirin adjusted her glasses on her nose. Then she nodded and looked down at the floor.

"Yes, maybe they are a bit afraid to speak," she admitted.

I had a sense that Shirin's feelings were becoming more and more ambivalent as the day in our company progressed. I couldn't tell what was making her more uneasy, having to translate what she felt was her compatriots' backwardness to us or having to translate our lack of tact to them. The Parthenon Frieze, Zuleya's sister, took the floor and suddenly there was silence. The girl spoke for some time. Her stretched arm was resting on her knee, and the cheap bracelets around her wrist kept tinkling as she moved her hand.

"She said that if she could turn back time, she would have

killed herself too," Shirin translated impassively. "Now she can't, because she has children. She says she had to marry a man three times older than her who has always beaten her, since the very first day. She says that the life of a woman is a very sad life; in truth she says that it's not a life at all."

Imo leaned slightly towards me.

"What a fabulous profile this one has, try and shoot her while she's talking. Can you work with this light?"

"Yeah, sure . . . but first shouldn't we . . . I mean, I'm afraid that if I start shooting without asking permission they're going to go crazy again like those—"

"Just give it a go and let's see what happens."

I took out one of my cameras and held it for a second so they could get used to its presence. Every woman looked in my direction and stared at the object in my hand. I acted like I was not aware of their attention and started to fiddle distractedly with the lenses. But just then a wan, sickly-looking woman, older than the others, shouted something. She was pointing to the camera and instantly I felt the same hostility wind through the room that I had encountered the day before in the hospital.

"You cannot take their picture," Shirin warned me with her usual stern gaze. "Malik told you yesterday that you are not allowed."

"Did he, really? Sorry, I didn't hear."

It was true. I hadn't heard, or perhaps understood, so I looked at Imo, who nodded imperceptibly so as to suggest that somehow yes, that had been the message. Slowly I lowered my camera and slung the strap around my shoulder, so it hung unobtrusively by my side. "I thought that—"

Imo interrupted me with a gesture and turned to Shirin. "Please explain to them that the pictures we are taking will never be shown in this country. I give them my word of honor."

Shirin complied. The women were listening, some of them nodded.

"But tell them also that in order to bring about change in their lives it's important that the rest of the world sees their faces and knows who they are."

The women shook their heads vigorously in protest. Some started to cover their heads with their veils, getting ready to conceal their faces.

"No," Shirin said, firm. "They say you can't, that it's not permitted."

"Okay." Imo tried to conceal her disappointment. She knew she couldn't rush it this time. We looked at one another. I felt my camera resting against my side.

She glanced at her notes, scribbled something and then gazed around the room with a sympathetic expression. Then she turned to Shirin.

"Well. You should tell them that there are many organizations in Kabul that help girls like Zuleya and that soon, if they change the laws here, a father will no longer be allowed to kill his daughter if she dishonors him."

While Shirin was translating, Imo tried quickly to elaborate the rest of her argument. She still had to come up with an explanation as to why they—out of millions of Afghan women—had been designated to be the ones to show their faces to the rest of the world. But somehow I knew her rhetorical skills wouldn't fail her, not even in this predicament. She paused and sighed, casting a glance around the room. The women were waiting. She leaned over to Shirin and said, "Tell them this, that we've come all this way because we want to take not just your voices, but your faces as well back to our country." Imo continued, "So you won't be ghosts but real people. If Afghan women keep hiding their faces behind burqas, they will always be only ghosts, and ghosts don't exist."

She'd taken a short run-up, pleased with the efficacy of the image she had conjured.

"Yes, exactly. Tell them that. You know, that ghosts don't exist."

Imo smiled at her small audience, but the women seemed unswayed.

"I do not think it will be possible, I am sorry," Shirin said quietly. "It is very difficult to make them understand what you're saying."

I noticed Shirin was beginning to act restless. I had a feeling that the way Imo sounded so pleased with her imaginative metaphors, heedless of the fact that they didn't even translate, was clearly beginning to irritate her.

"They're very simple, very ignorant and are all afraid of what their husbands will do to them if they let you," Shirin added, somehow severely.

Imo sighed. I think by now she had realized it was a lost battle and that none of her seductive skills or the force of her personality was going to make these women change their minds. They would have had to take an enormous risk in exchange for—most probably—nothing at all.

If the photos of the women were going to bring advantages to anyone's life, it was more likely that the beneficiaries would be Imo and me. Pierre had suggested it when he had first offered me the job: more World Press Photo award material.

And even so, I could still imagine the outcome. The *Sunday Times Magazine* spread open on the table of some elegantly furnished kitchen in London. A couple (certainly in favor of the emancipation of Afghan women) distractedly flicking the pages while sipping a foamy cappuccino made with an expensive espresso machine. The supplement being tossed in the recycling bin by Monday morning.

But then, something happened.

Julia Roberts stood up again, Junoesque and commanding as a queen. She harangued the room, raising her voice if anyone tried to interrupt her. A subdued grumbling rose from the back of the room. It was Zuleya's sister, who had come to the aid of Julia Roberts's arguments, and who quickly raised her tone a couple of octaves until the two of them were rebutting and countering the others, and the room went finally quiet.

The Parthenon Frieze pointed to me many times, speaking in a huddle with Shirin. Julia Roberts came forward, rearranging her veil on her head. They stood next to each other and fixed their eyes on me, stock-still, rigid as a couple posing in an old-time family portrait.

"They say you can take their picture, if you like," said Shirin.

"Really?"

"Yes. This woman, the taller one, says that nothing has changed since the new government is in power. Women are still slaves, and the world must know about this," Shirin said forcefully, with sudden excitement.

The Frieze stepped forward, her voice shrill and on the verge of breaking, as she rubbed her teary eyes with the back of her hand. The room had plunged into a deep silence, everyone was holding their breath.

"She says all women in our country live in fear, but fear is like a prison. She says you are very much welcome here and wants to thank you for coming all this way to talk about Zuleya and her sufferings."

Imo joined her hands together and bowed her head gracefully.

"That's wonderful. Well, for us it is an honor to have been able to listen to them. Please," she said, looking straight at Shirin for the first time since we had been sitting in that room. "Please tell them this."

Julia Roberts interjected, the Frieze nodded in agreement. They readjusted their veils again and went back into their pose.

"The other lady also welcomes you and she hopes this photo can help all women to have a better life," Shirin added briskly, yet somehow also communicating her personal disbelief about this particular hope. I had a feeling that by now she had developed some doubts about the sincerity of our mission.

She wasn't alone in that. A few of the other women exchanged dubious looks. And yet, slowly, a couple of them, followed by a few more, moved and sat behind Julia Roberts and the Frieze. They shuffled, rearranged their clothes, primped their hair, tied it back or let it loose. Some of them laughed, embarrassed; others withdrew to the back of the room, to keep out of the shot. A solemn silence fell.

"Hurry up, Maria," hissed Imo, "before they change their minds."

They stood, straight-faced, looking the other way, intimidated by my gesture. I peered through the lens. The women were holding their breath, their eyes wide open and devoid of any expression, looking more like they were made of wax than of flesh. There was no way they were going to relax. I had to find a key to shoot them and I had to think fast: maybe I could use the awkwardness, show their passiveness through those petrified expressions. Through that unnatural pose, perhaps I could convey the idea of an even deeper coercion.

I was sweating. I had to work with what I had, so I framed the shot and focused. The colors were amazing—just now a shaft of light had painted a golden stripe on the wall. I felt every eye in the room on me and my clumsy movements. This time I couldn't afford to get it wrong.

And yet, I knew there was a remote possibility. One in a thousand.

If, let's say, an Afghan cabbie who had emigrated to London— say someone like Hanif's cousin, there were hundreds of thousands of them living in England—bought the paper. What if he recognized those faces? What if he called a relative in Kabul? What if he e-mailed him the pictures? What if the relative went to the village and showed the pictures to Malik? They all had cells, and soon—if not already—someone like Malik would be able to receive photos straight on the screen of his mobile.

How would these women be punished? Would they be disowned, beaten? Would they lose their honor? And what exactly did that mean or imply?

It was one in a thousand, yet nothing was impossible now that there was no longer a village, a stone, a hut that had been forgotten, left unturned, overlooked by the satellite.

Just then, at the back of the room, Zuleya's mother—the old woman who had flattened herself against the wall until we'd forgotten about her—got to her feet. Now she was moving forward, all bones and sagging flesh. She was screeching like a banshee. I saw her come at me with outstretched arms, hooked fingers.

I took the camera down from my eye and held it close to my chest, fearing she might smash it. I caught a glimpse of her livid, harsh eyes, as the rest of the women were quickly moving out of her way, silenced. I heard the rustle of their dresses, the thud of their bare feet on the mud floor. Then, all of a sudden, everyone was gone, they'd all disappeared. The room now was empty, as if a hand had brushed away a cluster of flies swarming over food.

Not even an hour later we were giving our good-bye to Malik, who had walked us to the car followed by a large group of villagers. He had had our car loaded with baskets of apples, almonds, freshly baked bread and sun-dried apricots. There had been handshakes and hugs between the men and Hanif, a request for yet another group photo, which I had dutifully taken. The umpteenth picture of stiff men holding guns looking like suspects in a police mug shot. The women had disappeared, swallowed behind the mud walls of their compounds as if they had never existed. As Imo had said—like ghosts.

Either Malik had decided to ignore what had happened

inside the school or he hadn't found out yet. Either way, he didn't make any reference to the fact that we had attempted to take pictures despite his restrictions. However, he had decided he had a thing or two to unload on us before he let us go.

Shirin was standing next to the car translating what Malik had to say. She kept her eyes to the ground, careful not to meet his gaze.

"Malik says that Westerners feel their culture is superior to ours because women don't have to wear the veil. He says what you Westerners never understand is that Muslim women cover themselves out of choice, because in our society, the physical aspect of a woman shouldn't interfere with her place in society." Shirin's voice was barely audible, with no trace of emotion or intonation, as if she wished to make herself invisible. "In our culture, the more a woman ages, the more wisdom she acquires, the more authority and power she has in the family. In the West, instead, a woman who has lost her looks is worthless and has no place in society."

She fiddled with her headscarf as she waited for Malik to say more, then she continued.

"He says that whereas for you the value of a woman is only in her appearance, for us it lies in her soul and in her heart. According to the Quran a woman's beauty belongs only to her husband and it is a gift reserved for his eyes only, whereas in the West it is like, how do you say—merchandise?—something to trade and put on show, like at the market."

Shirin was done talking and swallowed. Her cheeks were flushed.

Imo was standing perfectly still with that smile plastered on her face that she had decided to wear as a countermeasure to any offensive.

"Well, firstly, tell him it's not true that in the West a woman's worth lies only in her beauty," she replied graciously. "Our women have a place in the government, teach in universities, they are judges, prosecutors. And"—here she lowered her gaze, affecting modesty—"they are reporters, like Maria and me. In other words, women help determine the fate of the country."

Malik nodded gravely and pondered. He scratched his beard. Then he added some more.

"Malik wants to know if it's true that women in your country sometimes have operations to stay young."

"Yes, it's true," Imo admitted with a hint of impatience, "but tell him that it doesn't mean that—"

Malik stopped her with his hand open, then spoke in a tone that had no polemic or hostile tinge but sounded cautionary.

"Malik wants to know what you are going to write in your article after this trip." Shirin maintained her neutral tone. She hadn't lifted her eyes off the ground yet. "Whether you're going to say the Muslims are backward or barbaric because their women choose to cover themselves in order to preserve their dignity, or whether it is the Westerners who are savages, since they allow their women to cut themselves to pieces when they lose their youth and their looks."

Imo nodded pensively, then gave me a look. I saw a sparkle flash through her eyes.

"Just wait till he finds out about *Nip/Tuck*," she said quickly under her breath, trying not to smile, then turned to Shirin.

"It's such a complex issue, this one. First of all it's a big mistake to generalize. Not all the women in the West do this, you know." Imo checked the time on her cell. We had to get going if we wanted to reach Kabul before nightfall. She sighed.

"Oh, God, we'd need a whole day to discuss this at length. Please tell Malik I'd be very honored if one day he would allow me to sit and explain to him my point of view."

She then pulled out her card and handed it to him. Malik studied it carefully, then passed it to a couple of men behind him.

We left, laden with gifts, after a send-off befitting high-ranking dignitaries, invited to come back soon and showered with blessings for our journey, escorted to the village gates by a clamoring host of children and men waving their guns. I turned back before the track curved around the hill and the last image I had was of a small crowd of men bent over Imo's card.

"It's a total waste of time getting into an argument on women's rights with men. It's the women one has to educate, in this country," Imo said once our hosts had disappeared from the rearview mirror.

"Choice. What choice is he talking about?" she said after a while. "What is choice to a woman who grows up believing that baring her face is a crime? Whose parents, community, teachers inculcate in her that her body is a piece of meat that only induces lust?"

Shirin didn't answer and adjusted her scarf once more, looking out of the window. Hanif seemed concentrated on the driving and lost in his thoughts.

"But what he said about plastic surgery was quite . . ." I began. "I mean, how for us it has become culturally acceptable to fill your boobs with silicone, go under the knife in order to look younger and sexier and—"

"But we have a choice, Maria. Come on. We don't have an imam or an Islamic court who made this a law."

"I know," I said. "But isn't it interesting to look at it from their point of view for once? Something mustn't be healthy in a society where one woman out of three refuses to age and let go of her sexual power. The balance must lie somewhere in the middle between Zuleya and Pamela Anderson, no?"

We left Shirin near the clinic where we had picked her up. Imo hugged her and promised to send her some DVDs and film magazines. I promised that I would slip in a few good shots I had taken of her. Shirin was surprised by our sudden affection towards her and especially by our kisses on both cheeks. We left her flushed, sweaty despite the cold, a big smile on her face.

We had been driving for some time and Imo was immersed in the biography of Catherine the Great. I don't know how she could read on such a bumpy drive without getting sick. She had torn out the chunk she had read already, and was holding only the last fifty pages. I would never have the heart to mangle a book like that; according to my family religion it would have been sacrilege.

My frustration had been gnawing at me, especially now that we had left the village behind and I was beginning to gauge the scope of my failure.

"I'm feeling really bad that I did not shoot the women." I had finally pried the words out of my mouth and looked at Imo expectantly.

She lifted her eyes slowly from her book and stared at me for a second, almost surprised, as if she had forgotten I too was riding in the car next to her.

"I know. I feel bad too," she said slowly. "Those women looked incredible. What a shame, really."

"I should've been . . . I don't know, more surgical about the whole situation. It was a split-second decision. I choked . . ."

"It's not your fault. You would have never had the time and the peace of mind to shoot them the way you intended to shoot them." Imo sighed and went back to Catherine the Great.

"We do have plenty of other good shots," I tried to offer.

"We do, we do. We have lots of wonderful shots," she agreed, lifting her eyes again and looking out the window, but I couldn't ascertain whether she really meant it. She seemed detached. Bored, almost, as if her energy level had suddenly plummeted.

"In any case, when I get back to London I'm going to have

my editor track down that French girl," she said after a pause, "the one who's spent her life in hospitals, and see if she's got any decent shots we can use."

For a minute no one said anything. It gutted me that the editor would have to buy photos from that woman.

"Although, guess what I'm thinking?" Imo shoved the book inside her bag. "I'm actually tempted not to publish any photos of the village women. You know, I could write the story precisely about that; about the fact that it's impossible to shoot a picture of a woman and how we weren't able to get any one of them to lift the veil off her face. About this idea that women have become ghosts, that they don't actually have a face, or a voice. In that case you'd actually be part of the story, Maria. A character in it. I think it'd be interesting." She seemed amused by the idea and smiled. "In that case I'd have to take a picture of *you* for the piece. That would be fun, no?"

I mumbled something. Imo seemed increasingly taken with the idea.

"In fact, you know what, I could build the whole piece around it. It's truer and, above all, more forceful. And besides, people love reading stories where writers fail to get what they had set out to do. I think it's a very cool idea."

It was true, Imo could always give facts a slightly different reading and turn them to her own advantage. For me it was much harder; with my work there was very little space for interpretation. Either you had the photo or you didn't.

"In any case," she went on, "I want to talk to what's-his-face, that Paul guy, about the licenses to produce legal opium. Now, that's an absolutely sensational story and I'm going to pitch it to my editor the minute I get back. And the mobile phone company story as well. I think they'd jump at it. Don't you think?"

"Yeah. It's possible."

Typical, I thought. How reporters move forward to the next

story without ever looking back. Each piece like a passionate one-night stand that fades and loses appeal the minute it's been consummated.

"You know what? I'll pitch both ideas. Besides, they would be all-male stories, at least that way we won't have to walk on eggshells the whole time. In fact, these guys just love being photographed. They just love posing, don't they; such a bunch of narcissists, all natural-born actors. It would be such a walk in the park."

I wondered whether the "we" she had used included me or was supposed to define a generic figure of discourse, a *royal we,* which would have been very much her style, given the book she was reading.

We drove back through the gorge. The men were still there, with the same dark rags rolled around their heads, breaking and moving rocks in the gloomy early-morning shade. I felt their gaze again, as we crept through the canyon with the Ford's exhaust pipe clunking ominously over the stones.

Then, from the corner of my eye, I saw something move. Two crouching figures stood up simultaneously and ambled toward the middle of the passage. They had guns. The one on the left slowly waved his, grinning, and seemed to say something. Hanif stopped and rolled down the window. The man pushed the tip of his Kalashnikov inside the car and blurted out an order. He was in his thirties, no beard, wearing military pants. The other one suddenly opened the passenger's door. He looked younger, his clothes were filthy, I noticed he had a bandaged hand. They didn't look like the rest of the men working at the dam. These guys were no stonecutters.

Hanif spoke warily, but the man shouted his order again, silencing him.

"He says you have to get out," Hanif said to Imo and me.

"What do they want?" Imo asked. She was pale. The man

who had opened the door grabbed her by the shoulder and pulled at her. Hanif looked at me pleadingly.

"Please do as they say."

He then lowered his gaze as if he couldn't bear to watch me as I got out of the car.

The younger of the two said something to us in Dari in a harsh tone, and motioned us to walk ahead of him, as he followed with his gun. The men cutting stones had stopped their work and were all staring at us. Just our footsteps on the gravel were breaking the silence. A swallow darted above our heads, the only swift movement in the absolute stillness. As we reached the steep wall of the canyon, I felt the man's hand press on my shoulder, motioning me to stop and sit down. It was rough; the feeling made me sick.

Imo and I sat on a boulder. The man remained standing, a couple of steps away from us. We had walked a couple of hundred meters and we could see Hanif speak to the other man in the distance. He was showing him some papers, he kept nodding, keeping his gaze down. My heart sank. It felt like a terrible mistake to have let them separate us from him and the car.

"What the fuck is going on?" Imo asked me. "Is it money they want?"

"Please be quiet," I said. "The less you speak now, the better it is."

I had reached a point where I wasn't going to take any more lessons from Imo Glass.

The man with the bandaged hand looked at me and mimicked holding a cigarette between his fingers. I didn't answer and lowered my gaze to the ground.

"I think he just wants a cigarette," Imo whispered. She had sensed something had shifted between us. I could tell from the way her warm shoulder was leaning into mine.

"I know. But don't let him know you smoke."

I don't know why I said this, but it felt like the right thing to say in that moment, like a sensible rule. I didn't think it'd be helpful to show that we carried cigarettes and confirm their idea that all Western women smoked in public.

I looked towards the other man. He was still interrogating Hanif and, judging from his body language, he seemed angry.

All it had taken was one instant. The moment two men with two guns had stepped in and we had been pulled out of the safety of the Ford, our tiny world had shattered all at once. If we couldn't figure out what had just happened—were we actually being kidnapped? were these men military or bandits, were they Taliban?—how could we possibly foresee what could happen next?

I heard Imo sniffing. I turned to look at her. Tears were rolling down her cheeks. I was shocked: I had never expected that she would be the first to break down. But maybe this predicament was too much even for someone like Imo Glass. I took her hand and she immediately grabbed mine.

"This is horrible. It's fucking freaking me out," she said and gave me a crazed look. Her fear was tangible, wild like the fear of an animal trying to escape, wiggling through the holes of a fence. Whatever had been holding her mask together till this moment, now it had broken loose and she wasn't going to be able to control herself anymore. Somehow I sensed it was the first time this had happened to her.

"No, don't panic. I don't think it's that bad," I said. My heart was beating like a drum in my lungs, but it made me calmer to say that.

"How do you know?"

"I don't think this is a kidnapping."

It was amazing: my mind kept racing back to the Defenders' classes, in an attempt to select and replay any instruction that could help me rationalize. I had actually been able to think. Like a rock climber, I was trying to hold on to any tiny hook, any cranny I could find.

If they had been right, I thought, then the phase they had called initial takeover hadn't played out. Yet the minute I tried to hold on to the thought, I felt pathetic. As if the world would play by the rules the Defenders had printed in their booklet. As if one could interpret the intricate reality of this country by checking off the boxes of the safety tips I had learned in the English countryside.

"No, this *is* bad. Really bad," Imo retorted, still crying.

"Stop it," I snapped. "That isn't going to help."

I didn't want her fear to infect me. I knew I needed to stay away from that kind of panic if I wanted to function.

I heard the young man's footsteps move closer to us. I kept my eyes low on the ground and saw his boots slide into my peripheral vision. They were worn out, covered in dust. I had seen similar ones piled up in the stalls around the market in Kabul. I felt the slow-motion close-up of a dream, yet the boots seemed so tangible, probably made in China, so ordinary and so cheap, they had the power to anchor me to some kind of reality.

The man was very close to me now and I could smell his sweat, and something acrid, like rancid milk, on his skin. I also smelled metal. But that, I knew, must be the barrel of the gun.

The other man and Hanif were coming towards us. Hanif looked exhausted, drenched in sweat, as if he had been beaten up.

"He wants your passports, please," Hanif said, a guilty look in his eyes.

Giving away our only piece of ID didn't feel right. I wanted to say something but realized we had no choice but to follow to the letter absolutely everything the man wanted from us. He scanned both passports and photographs, then he pointed at me. Again, whatever he said sounded harsh and accusatory. Hanif replied, the man rebutted, his fingers still pointing at me.

"What is he saying?" I asked Hanif.

"He says you look American. Because of your colors."

I shook my head violently.

"No, no America. *Italiana,*" I said firmly, looking the man in the eye.

I watched the man flip through the pages of my passport shaking his head. Then he handed it back to me. He withheld Imo's passport for another minute, haranguing Hanif, who kept nodding.

"He says your prime minister is a dog, a slave of Bush," Hanif translated.

"Yes, I know," Imo murmured under her breath. She wiped her tears and bowed her head, as the man returned the passport with the royal crown stamped on the cover.

There was a pause. Then the two men turned their backs on us and walked away.

"We can go now," Hanif said.

We got back in the car and none of us uttered a word until we came out of the gorge. Imo sat in the back next to me and gripped my wrist. She wouldn't let it go. I felt her nails digging into my skin.

"Pheeewww!" I hissed as soon as we drove out into the sun and the plain. I was drenched in sweat. I rolled down the window. My hair got in my eyes and I felt a rush of cold air on my face; I breathed deeply, filling my lungs with it.

Imo finally let go of my arm and hugged me.

"I swear I thought we were done in!" She was nearly screaming over the sound of the car rambling along the stony terrain "It really scared the shit out of me, man!"

I tapped on Hanif's shoulder. "Who were they? What did they want?"

"They were just checking. Just control." Hanif looked at me in the rearview mirror and grinned. "These people, they always think foreigners are spies."

"What did you tell them we were?"

"Doctors from an NGO," he said in an unexpected tone of

jubilation. "I was sure that those people working with the stones knew we would be coming back this way and they would spread the rumor. I lost sleep over it last night. So I had my story ready. You know, they always let doctors go through because NGO people help the people from every side."

"You're so clever. So you knew," I said.

"I had a feeling. But we were lucky nothing happened this time."

"And what about the permits we had from the ministry? Couldn't you show them those as well?" Imo asked.

Hanif smiled and waved his hand dismissively.

"These people, some of them don't even know how to read. And those who read, if they learn you are journalists they may think you are a spy even more."

"Jeeez. And we're not even that far from Kabul. Imagine what it must be like in the south."

Imo closed her eyes and let out a deep sigh.

I felt dizzy. Only moments before, the universe had shrunk into a hard ball dense with danger and threat, with no space left for anything else. Only menace and terror and thoughts of imminent death. It was difficult now to stretch the ball again, let the light of day, the feeling of the ordinary, seep through once more, allow my muscles to relax. My mouth felt dry, the fear had sucked all the fluids from my body. I drank from a water bottle and handed it to Imo. The water was cold. It tasted wonderful.

Imo sighed and fell back on the seat. She looked at me.

"Sorry I totally lost it. But you were very cool, Maria."

I smiled.

"Have a piece of bread. It's really good." I tore off a piece and offered it to her.

"Thank you," she said, then grabbed my hand and squeezed it hard. We looked at one another.

"Never again, Imo," I said.

"What?"

"Going off like this without precautions. It's—"

"I know, I know. Oh, God, please don't make me think about it, I beg of you. I feel I've acted like such an idiot, I don't—"

"You *are* an idiot," I said calmly, looking out the window, her hand still in mine, basking in the sun that was warming up my shoulder.

I checked Hanif in the rearview mirror and met his eyes. I saw how he creased his lips into a smile.

Beep-beep. Beep-beep. Beep-beep.

It was as if all our cells had simultaneously gone nuts. They came out of hibernation as soon as they caught the signal on the hill outside Kabul and were now like machine guns firing off notification of messages received.

I had five texts, all from the same sender.

ALL IT TOOK WAS 2 C YR NAME ON THE DISPLAY. CAN'T BELIEVE WE'VE STAYED APART 4 SO LONG. ALL I THINK OF IS US.

The language sounded ridiculous. I felt nothing.

Hanif was reading his texts holding his Nokia over the steering wheel with a worried expression. Imo was jabbering away to someone, as if nothing had happened, keeping her left finger pressed on her ear.

"Remember, they need five days to process the visa. . . . Yes, yes, I know that. . . . Please try and book me into the Sofitel but remember to ask them whether there is broadband in the room, it's very important. . . ."

WHY DON'T U ANSWER ME? SHOULD I WORRY?

It was amazing how he thought he had taken command again. He was already talking to me as if I was his property. How could I dare rebel?

There were another three, all with his name. I didn't bother to read them.

The car swerved lightly on a curve, as a big truck appeared in the opposite direction.

"Hey! Watch it!" I yelled.

"Sorry, sorry." Hanif reluctantly put the mobile in his pocket. Imo didn't even notice, she was so taken by her conversation.

There was another text, this one from my father.

I WON 1,500 EUROS AT BINGO PLAYING YR BIRTH DATE AND LEO'S. WILL TAKE BOTH OF U OUT FOR GRAND DINNER ON MONDAY 2 CELEBRATE YR RETURN AND MY LUCK. WE'LL SPLURGE.

Only then did I realize how much I'd missed him. I felt a sudden impulse to hear his voice, to recount to him what had just happened. But I knew the story, told over the phone, was going to sound too frightening, that my voice would break if I heard his and I didn't want to scare him. Besides, 1,500 euros was an astronomical sum in the life of a retired professor, and I felt I had no right to spoil the day of a winner. I texted him my congratulations and that I loved him.

We arrived at the lodge after ten. The dining room was deserted, so was the bar. The staff greeted us with big smiles as if we had been away for ages. It was odd, because it did feel that way, but what was even stranger was that stepping inside Babur's Lodge made me feel as if I had finally reached home.

The next day we woke up to discover that the city had been shrouded in snow during the night. Everyone at the lodge— the waiter, the guards in the sentry box, even the unfriendly guests—seemed more cheerful than usual, as if the snow had brought back childhood memories for everyone.

It was our last day in Kabul. Imo did an interview in the morning with an Afghan journalist who hosted a radio program on women's issues and gathered more information and data talking to people on the phone. She was done by lunchtime and we managed to dash to Chicken Street—our last chance for a quick fix of shopping before leaving. The street was lined with carpet sellers, antiques shops crammed with leftover goods from the seventies, which the hippies had bought for nothing at the time: piles of wonderful tapestries, Uzbek hangings, shawls, silver jewelry covered in dust.

I didn't like the idea of meandering on Chicken Street for too long—the incident at the gorge had made me extra wary. But Imo seemed to have forgotten about that already. She insisted on sitting down in the shop on a pile of carpets as if she had all the time in the world; she drank the tea the shopkeeper offered her and chatted him up as if they were old friends. She looked carefully at each shawl of the twenty he showed her, testing the softness of the wool between her fingertips. She even burned a strand of the fringe with her lighter to make sure there was no synthetic mixed in the weave. This was her next mission and she was taking it very seriously: she was determined to leave with the best shawl in the whole of Afghanistan. In the end she picked an orange one—a warm, vibrant color that suited her dark hair—and managed to pay only ten bucks for it, a bargain considering the delicate hand-stitched embroidery. I'd forgotten what a pro Imo could be when it came to haggling with the locals.

# Three

THE AIRPORT LOUNGE WAS FURNISHED with heavy salmon velvet drapes on the windows and had dusty plastic carnations on the tables like a congealed interior from the sixties.

It felt colder in there than outside in the snow, but Imo had asked the waiter—a little man in a worn-out suit and tie—if he could bring an electric heater and had been instantly obliged. She studied the menu as if she were lunching at the Plaza and ordered a plate of Kabuli rice pilau with raisins and pine nuts. It had seemed highly unlikely that in this deserted mausoleum there would be a stove, let alone someone prepared to cook a pilau, but what seemed miraculous was that there would be raisins and pine nuts in a jar somewhere. However, like many other things in this country, what you asked for was at one point or another magically produced. Even in the midst of ruins and utter desolation, heat, food and life materialized when you least expected it.

Imo was wolfing down her pilau while chatting in Russian to the waiter. She must have been saying something quite witty, because he kept on laughing—in other words, she was actually being *funny* in Russian, which says a lot about her mastery of the language. She insisted on a particular joke, which got the man to laugh even louder. She went back to her pilau shaking her head and chuckling to herself, feeling no need to translate the joke to me and Hanif and share the humor.

Hanif was busy too, texting away on his mobile. He caught my inquisitive gaze and for some reason he seemed embarrassed and quickly justified himself.

"I'm sending a message to my sister-in-law. She's about to go and check on my wife at the hospital."

"Sure. You go ahead," I said, trying to communicate to him that he didn't have to explain if he didn't feel like it. Again I felt his uneasiness.

"How is she doing? Any better?" Imo asked, peremptorily.

"A bit better maybe. The doctor saw her last night," Hanif said and then paused, discouraged. "But she still has pain."

"Have they found out what exactly is wrong with her? She's been in the hospital for three days now, hasn't she?"

"They took some new tests. The doctors are very good," he said.

"Oh, okay. Well, then I'm sure she'll be all right," I said, hoping this comment might suffice to appease him. I caught Imo's expression out of the corner of my eye. She looked at me—impatiently—as if I had said precisely the wrong thing.

"Hanif, you know the German hospital?" she said. "You should take her there. Really. I'd do that if I were you."

Hanif nodded. I wondered how much they would charge him at the German hospital. His cell beeped twice, announcing a text. He scanned the display, then put the phone back in his pocket.

"I wouldn't wait another day. It sounds like they have no clue what's wrong with her, wherever she is now," Imo added with a touch of gloom.

Hanif nodded again uneasily, as if he wished Imo would stop telling him what to do. Not to mention the fact that we had been in Kabul only a few days and here we were, already lecturing him on which hospital would take better care of his wife.

We'd been in the airport restaurant for an hour, with the electric heater under the table warming our feet, when the other passengers—the ones who had been left outside to brave the elements—had finally been granted permission to enter the building and prepare for check-in.

Some of them came up to the restaurant to warm themselves with a cup of tea and looked at our table with overt antipathy. They were almost all Westerners: aid workers, soldiers, UN personnel. There was a lot of pulling out cell phones, lighting cigarettes, screeching of chairs being moved across the cement floor.

There were a few young women—NGO workers most probably—wearing *shalwar kameezes* under their coats. Most of them had their heads covered.

Imo was in the midst of settling up accounts with Hanif. He had signed a receipt and was flipping through a wad of dollars with the nimble thumb of a bank teller. Imo pointed out a couple of veiled German women addressing the waiter in Dari.

"Ha, ha. The Saint Teresas of Kabul are here."

She grinned at me and Hanif. The way she had a clever nickname for everything was beginning to feel a bit stale by now.

"How much longer before your flight leaves?" she asked me.

"An hour and a half."

"Good, then you don't have to wait too long."

She rubbed her freezing hands, blowing on them.

"I'm dreaming already of the bottle of red and the filet mignon *au poivre vert* I'll be having tonight."


I realized the moment had come.

Hanif, the village women, Malik and I were already fading in Imo's memory; we were about to turn into nothing more than mere extras in another one of her many adventures. She had just given away her clothes to the Tajik cleaning woman and she was ready to put on new ones and go for another spin.

From her cell phone conversations, I'd gathered that she and Demian—the young, very handsome and very spoiled man, I had assumed—were going to meet in London in less than four-teen hours, at the end of the Kabul–Dubai, Dubai–London flight. He would be waiting at Heathrow and they would go to dinner at some tiny, dimly lit French restaurant. She was about to move on to the next exhilarating banquet where she would pluck and sample new interesting morsels of delicious food. It was pathetic, but I couldn't help feeling a pang of jealousy.

I thought of how, back at the gorge, our relationship had dra-matically shifted. Ironically, the first time I had been able to react and shut her up had also been the first time I managed to feel something akin to true affection for her. When Imo had come undone I had finally caught a glimmer of who she really was. I had seen Lupita Jaramillo surface beneath the tears, the fright-ened child whose chromosomes Imo still carried within her.

But now, as we were about to part, she had swiftly put her mask back on and reactivated her former self. I was disap-pointed that it was this version of Imo—her glamorous persona rather than little Lupita—that I had to say good-bye to. Yet part of me felt grateful: down at the gorge Imo had bestowed something upon me without her being aware of it.

I had found her gift hidden in the folds of my own fear, while we were under the muzzle of the gun, smelling metal mixed with the man's sweat. It was there and then I had realized I'd be able to face my deepest fear, that I would not have to suc-cumb to it.


I peered out through the dusty salmon drapes of the Kabul air-port restaurant, looking down at the final passengers dragging their luggage over the tarmac under the thickening snow.

Suddenly a prolonged screech issued from the loudspeakers, followed by more crackling sounds, then by a voice that first spoke in Dari and then in equally unfathomable English.

"That's the last call for my flight," said Imo, smiling and

checking the time on the display of the minuscule cell she had been holding for hours like the hand of a child.

"Good, it looks like it's actually on time. Amazing, isn't it?"

Almost all the passengers crowding the tables in the restaurant got up simultaneously. The urge, the anxiety, was tangible: there was a rush, a general eagerness to accelerate, like a flock pushed towards the gate. Everyone rushed except for Imo. She picked up her hand luggage, wrapped herself in her shawl, left a more than generous tip on the table and hugged me. I took in her musky exhalation, the smell of her hair.

"Maria, promise you'll call me as soon you land in Milan."

She kissed me, cupping the back of my head with her hand.

"Oh, this is so sad," I managed to say. "I can't bear to see you go."

It was true and I wanted to let her know I felt that way.

Imo looked at me, blinked. I think she was surprised. She stroked my hair.

"Maria, *carina mia.* Isn't this terrible? Didn't we have just the best time together?"

"Yes, we did." I wanted to say more, but I didn't know how to phrase it in a way that wouldn't sound clichéd, and besides I could tell she was gone already, her energy focused elsewhere, her body still here, her mind at her destination.

"You must come to London. Soon, promise. There's so much more we need to do together!" she said. Then she turned to Hanif, who had sprung to his feet, bringing his hand to his breast.

"Hanif, you have been simply the greatest," she said, although with just a touch of formality. "I beg you, please, if there's anything I can do at my end. You know, about your wife. You let me know if you need any help for the German hospital. You have my e-mail and my phone number. Anything I can do, really."

Imo took hold of Hanif's hand and gave it a squeeze for her final supplication.

"Will you do me a favor and stay here with Maria until they call her flight? Here, have something to eat, tea, coffee, cake, whatever you want."

She left more notes on the table and gave me a look, to check out how I was faring. She knew I'd be nervous to be left alone without her.

"Shall I leave you some more money, Maria? I've still got some dollars, if you like."

"No, what for? I don't need anything."

"Are you sure? Then I'll leave you in Hanif's capable hands. He'll see to it you get checked in okay, and then in an hour you'll be on the plane. Everything cool?"

"Sure, don't worry, I'll be fine." I smiled at her.

"Good. Call me tonight or tomorrow," she said. "Actually tomorrow would be better."

She winked at me, alluding, perhaps, to her evening ahead.

*"Ciao, bellissima,"* she said. "I'll miss you."

So she left, waving her hand until the last moment, until she disappeared behind the salmon drapes. She exited the stage just like that, letting the fabric fall back behind her like the drop of a curtain.

Hanif and I sat down again in the lounge that was empty once more. He was furtively checking his watch. He had just pocketed his fee in cash and was probably itching to get away from me and rush to his wife. I doubted he was going to miss either one of us; this had just been a hundred-and-eighty-dollar-a-day gig for him. His obligation was going to end in less than an hour, as soon as they called the Kabul–Istanbul–Milan flight, the one I was going to take. Once on the other side of the gate, I wouldn't be Hanif's responsibility any longer. At the passport control we would say good-bye, exchange business cards and the usual promises of keeping in touch. Then, with a sigh of relief, he would bolt to his car with the sole thought of getting to the hospital as fast as he could, and Imo and Maria would disappear from his mind as if we'd never existed.

We didn't say anything to each other for a few minutes. I realized that Imo's absence had redesigned the way we related to one another; we were unsure whether we were supposed to feel more intimate or more estranged now that she was gone. Of the three of us, he and I had been the shy ones. Without Imo's constant chatter, we no longer knew how to interact.

I drummed my fingers on the tabletop and sighed. He and I were the only two left in the room, the waiter was wiping the tables down with a rag, the early-afternoon light waned on the snow-whitened tarmac. I asked Hanif if he'd like some tea, a plate of rice, a drink. He shook his head at each offer and closed his eyes, pressing his hand on his tie. Now that only a handful of minutes still tied him to me, he had withdrawn into himself even more. His English had deteriorated; he didn't seem to speak it anymore. It was as if his clockwork mechanism had wound down and these were his final movements, increasingly inexpressive and insincere.

"Hanif, go. There's no need for you to stay."

"No, no, no," he said, shaking his head, solicitous and diligent. "No problem."

"No," I cut him off, raising my voice slightly. "Go. You go and check on your wife, please. I'll be absolutely fine on my own."

He looked at me questioningly. He couldn't suppress his hopefulness.

I nodded emphatically. After all, I only had to wait for them to call my flight, go downstairs and check in.

Enough already with the babysitter, I told myself. Show some dignity.

"Go, Hanif. I mean it."

· · ·

A sign with "Turkish Airlines" written in felt-tip pen had suddenly appeared over a desk in the departures hall. A corpulent woman with a headscarf presided over it, broadly gesticulating to the passengers to put their luggage on the ancient scales.

There weren't many of us traveling to Istanbul, just a scant group of tired-looking Turkish men in tattered clothes with dusty hair. I figured they must be construction workers who had come to Afghanistan to make some money building roads, dams, who knows what, for a big reconstruction project.

Imo's fellow passengers had definitely been more cosmopolitan: an assortment of do-gooders and consultants with whom she was bound to be arguing about international strategies, exchanging cards and finding mutual acquaintances. My travel companions, on the other hand, didn't speak English, had calloused hands, cheap quilted jackets, plastic shoes ill-suited to the snow. They looked weary and exhaled the acrid smell of cheap cigarettes. Once my luggage was on the scale, the woman with the headscarf at the counter gave me a handwritten card that I presumed was my boarding pass. Someone pushed me towards the long line for passport control. I was the only woman on this flight. Apart from the workers with that forlorn look of returning emigrants, there was no other Westerner as such and not a single Afghan.

Once we were through security and passport control, we were herded by soldiers up some steep, narrow steps that looked more like the stairs of an apartment building, but in fact they led to the departure lounge. There were no signs anywhere in the airport, or indications of any kind; I felt I was being constantly prodded, directed, driven on by orders, gun barrels suddenly pointed, showing the way.

When we got to the gate—a large room, empty except for two rows of plastic chairs and a window where a man was selling biscuits and tea in plastic cups—I slipped into that reassuring limbo that awaits every traveler after he's been checked, stamped and scanned. We had finally entered the space that was no longer the country we were coming from, or the one we were on our way to, but the gap in between, the non-place of supreme suspension that would lead straight to the desired direction like a needle pointing steadfastly north on a compass.

The minute I had entered the gate I had felt a completely new state of mind envelop me. It was the smug gratification of the traveler who has finished making allowances, participating, who no longer needs to understand or share. Here I was at last, the passenger who thinks only of what awaits ahead: my first real espresso, my own bed with crisp, clean sheets.

I had at least an hour before they'd start boarding. I could close my eyes and take a nap at last.

I awoke with a jolt.

The alarm set in my subconscious had gone off, alerting me I had been asleep on my plastic chair way too long; by now we should have already boarded the flight.

Out of the corner of my eye I noticed a crowd gathering at the back of the room. But something wasn't quite right: instead of going through the last check and boarding the plane, my fellow passengers were heading in the opposite direction, the one we had come in from. And, although they had their backs to me, I sensed that their posture bore nothing of the usual excitement that people about to board a plane show. There was no buoyancy in that crowd. Something was off, I could smell it.

At the back of the room I saw—another worrying signal— a soldier waving the barrel of his gun, funneling the passengers into an orderly line.

"I don't believe this," I groaned to myself.

They were turning back.

Yes, they were leaving the departure lounge and were being herded by the guard towards the same narrow stairway we had trudged up in single file earlier on.

"What's going on here? Why is everybody leaving?" I started asking haphazardly of no one in particular. I felt a terrible sense of foreboding.

"Where are you going?" I almost yelled to one of the Turkish workers, who shrugged and flung his hands heavenward.

"No English. No English."

But his companion, a man with a gray moustache who looked like a mangy old wolf, waved his hand with the typical gesture that erased everything and banished all hope.

"Flight cancel, flight cancel."

"What do you mean, *canceled*? Why?"

Now the soldier was signaling directly at me, indicating that I too was supposed to follow the others. By now the entire lounge had emptied out. The only ones left were me and the cleaning woman with a blue headscarf, trailing a bucket and an old broom behind her. I looked at the spectral deserted space, the empty black plastic chairs, the crumpled chips packets on the floor, the ashtrays brimming with butts.

"Flight cancel," the soldier repeated. "No fly today." And he signaled to me that I had to leave too.

Outside, the snow had picked up more heavily than before.

"Why have they canceled the flight?" I asked the soldier. "Is it because of the snow?"

He just made an imperious gesture with the muzzle of his machine gun, indicating that I was to move on, period. The cleaning woman had started to mop a rag over the floor of the empty room.

Down in departures, it was chaos. The passengers were swarming around the desk where only a couple of hours earlier we'd been issued our handwritten boarding passes by the heavy woman with the headscarf. Now the same woman was screeching in Dari, and she held a wad of boarding passes in her hand. This time, though, she wasn't handing them out but taking them back. I watched the passengers return the strip of paper

that had conferred upon us the status of almost-in-flight, of no-
longer-subject-to-the-laws-of-this-country. I leaned across the
counter close to her.

"When is the next flight? I absolutely have to leave today!" I
said haughtily, as if I were the only one among the crowd who
had this pressing need.

But the woman didn't bother to give me any kind of
indication.

"No flight, go home," she repeated, reaching for my boarding
pass. I readily withdrew it, as if this piece of paper with the
Turkish Airlines logo on it were the last hope I had of ever getting on a plane. I knew that handing it in would amount to losing my citizenship as an almost-in-flight, and I would have to go
back to being just another still-grounded.

The woman pointed to a pile of suitcases stacked near the
conveyor belt. They too had been spat out from the belly of the
plane and had now snuck back to us. I watched the Turkish
workers as they retrieved their luggage from the mound. None
of them had the desperate look that I had. This seemed to
be merely the umpteenth hindrance, yet another of the many
setbacks they must be used to enduring. None of them wasted
time arguing, trying to get their point across, none of them
demanded to speak to the airport manager. They all submitted
and headed outside again, disgruntled, lugging their baggage.
They knew perfectly well that there was no one in charge, no
supervisor, no airport manager; that, in short, there was no hope.

The room had rapidly emptied. There were only two bags
left. Mine.

The woman had managed to snatch the boarding pass from
my hand at last. A man in overalls was tapping on my metal
case. He gestured for me to take it.

"When is the next flight out? What am I supposed to do?"

They both shook their heads, "No flight, no flight, cancel."

"Yes, all right, but when? WHEN?"

They shrugged and started locking up. The woman detached the handwritten sign with our flight number and reached for a fake-leather purse with a zipper from underneath the counter. She grabbed her coat. It was time to go home. Both she and the man in the overalls began to walk away.

By now it had become clear to me that this was not an airport like any other, where stranded passengers could sleep on the floor while waiting for the next flight. This was more like a military zone where civilians had to obey orders and shut up.

I quickly took stock of the situation: all I had was a fifty-euro note and some change in local currency. Imo was going to be in the air for the next fourteen hours. I tried Pierre's cell and it was off. It was Friday night, and I knew he went to the country for the weekend; I also remembered him saying proudly that he always turned his mobile off on weekends, to de-stress. I didn't have Hanif's number either: Imo had always been the one in charge and I'd never thought I would need to have it. I didn't even remember the address of Babur's Lodge. I knew that as soon as I found myself out in the parking lot with my suitcases, I'd be lost.

Suddenly I saw him from behind. He was still wearing his *pakol,* his green cargo pants, a heavy sweater. A tuft of blond hair stuck out from under his cap. He carried only a canvas bag flung over his shoulder, as if he were going away for the weekend. I saw him head for the exit too, but more slowly than the others because he was engrossed in the display of his cell, either checking or sending a text.

"Hey! Hey, wait!"

I leapt at him.

"What happened? Why did they cancel the flight? Did they tell you when the next plane is?"

The Blond slowly lifted his eyes from the display. He didn't seem surprised to see me, maybe he pretended not to recognize me, or maybe he really didn't have a clue who I was because he'd never bothered to look me in the face before.

"I don't know," he said listlessly. "Could be the weather. Or maybe a bomb."

"A bomb? Where?"

"I don't know, I heard something."

The Blond shrugged and kept walking toward the exit. I followed him, struggling with my two suitcases. He didn't offer to help me.

Outside, the parking lot was nearly empty. The Turkish workers had almost all dispersed. There were only a few parked cars left.

"But what happens now? When's the next flight? Were you going to Istanbul too?" I babbled in a torrent, tailing him. The Blond was my last hope. If I let him go, I knew I'd be left in the snow together with a handful of soldiers with moustaches and machine guns.

"Nobody knows. They cancel flights every second day here. You have to keep going back to the airport every day until you manage to get on a plane."

He was heading for his car. I was right behind him. I realized I was in such a panic I might just burst into tears in front of him.

"No, listen, hey, excuse me . . . wait." I made a gesture of trying to stop him as he turned his back on me. He was already fiddling with the car keys, considering our exchange over and that I'd be off about my business.

"Listen, can you just wait a minute? I . . . I can't stay here, I don't even know where to go . . . I haven't . . ."

The Blond looked at me, not exactly alarmed, but he was beginning to realize that getting rid of me was going to be more complicated than he had bargained for. I moved closer and put my hand on the car door that he had just opened.

". . . I don't know where my driver is, the journalist I was

with has left, I have no money for a taxi . . . I . . ." As I listed all
the certainties that I had lost, I actually did start to cry.

A few seconds went by. In the meantime, the Blond was staring over the roof of the car, his gaze unfocused, like someone
trying to look away from an embarrassing scene. He patted his
pocket, searching for a packet of cigarettes. He pulled one out
with his teeth.

"Don't you remember me? My colleague and I were staying
at Babur's Lodge too last week. I was in the room opposite . . ."

But the Blond jerked his chin, a sort of assent that, however,
also seemed to mean "Move it, get in and shut up." Which I
instantly did.

The Blond's car reeked of dirty socks and cigarettes. It was
full of stuff—boxes, muddy boots, electrical gear, a car battery,
pages ripped from old magazines thrown on the floor. I spotted
an ad for a hunting rifle on one of them. I wiped my nose on my
coat sleeve. The Blond put the car into first gear and drove
through the checkpoint, with a quick salute to the guard as if
they were old acquaintances. He kept his gaze straight ahead;
he wasn't thrilled to have me on board.

The traffic was infernal. It was a different frenzy from the
usual one, as if the level of tension had risen exponentially.
American soldiers were flailing their arms with frantic, hysterical gestures in front of the many roadblocks we encountered.
Sirens wailed in the distance. The Blond braked and got out of
the car. I watched him cross the road, stop in front of the soldiers and show them something, some sort of ID, I supposed.
He showed it with the same rapid gesture that plainclothes cops
use in movies when they pull out their badge to get into an off-
limits area. They talked for a bit. The soldiers gesticulated,
pointing in a certain direction. The Blond scratched his chin
and then shambled, slow and gangly, back to the car. I didn't
expect any explanation, but I gave it a moment. Then, after he
reversed, once we were back on the road, I cleared my throat.

"What did they say? Is there a problem?"

"A bomb. They blew up sixteen people."

"Where?"

"On the way to the Canadian base, by the Darulaman Palace."

"The one with all those holes, on the hill?"

The Blond nodded, slowly lowering his eyelids.

"Oh, my God. We were right in front of it just a few days ago. The journalist and I with our fixer," I said, as if the fact that I had narrowly avoided that explosion could shake him, rouse in him the desire to look me in the face—this person restored to life, escaped from death—and perhaps be a little nicer to me. But instead, the Blond kept his eyes on the road and scowled.

"They plant them on purpose, the bastards, where everybody goes past."

The Blond pulled up at the sentry box outside Babur's Lodge. He waved at the armed guard, the other responded and opened the gate.

"There," he said.

"You're not getting out?"

"No, I'm not staying here anymore."

"Ah," I said, not even bothering to conceal my disappointment.

At this point even the Blond had turned into a familiar figure, one whom I didn't want to leave.

"All right, then. Well, thanks for the ride, it was very kind of you."

He didn't reply. He waited for the guard to take my suitcases out and screeched away in reverse as if the bomb about to explode was me.

Babur's Lodge looked like it had been evacuated.

I crossed the deserted lobby and went into the dining room.

There was no one there either. I did, however, hear a voice coming through the closed door of the bar.

They were all in there, watching the news, propped up on the bar in front of their drinks, their eyes glued to the TV on the wall. There was the South African and the German, drunk and heavy-lidded, in his worn-out Tyrolean outfit, General Dynamics nervously chewing gum, his hair damp from the shower, in his perfectly ironed multipocketed vest. There was Paul, the King of Questions, the sleeves on his military jacket rolled up, the khaki shirt and the boots, vodka and tonic in hand, unmindful of the thread of smoke from a cigarette forgotten in the ashtray. Next to him, the Dark One in a Springsteen concert T-shirt sipping a Coke, stroking his short beard. The lodge staff were in there too: the cooks, the waiters, the dishwashers, but they were standing in a second row and not drinking anything, their aprons still on.

On the screen I took in what must have been CNN footage of the bombing, with a voice-over in Dari commenting on the incident.

I saw debris, the remains of a military vehicle, injured Afghans being carried on a stretcher. The body of an ISAF soldier halfway emerged from the stones. He was covered in blood; someone had laid a sheet over his face. A solitary man in civilian clothes was standing holding his head between his hands, looking at the ground.

In the background, I recognized the shape of the palace I had photographed only a few days back, the battered wedding cake that now stood as a backdrop to death and destruction.

I had been standing right there, on the left-hand side of the frame to be precise, right next to the barrier that said "No Entry." I had taken pictures of the guards from that very spot, carefully framing out the barbed wire. Could it be they were all dead? I tried to remember their faces, their smiles while they puffed up their chests next to Hanif.

Just as when I watched the video of my kidnapping with the Defenders, I could analyze the scene of my potential death on live TV, picture the position my body would have been in under the rubble, how the shot would have depicted my demise.

Then the vision stopped; they returned to the studio.

And then Hanif appeared.

He was still wearing the same clothes he'd had on when he left me at the airport. I recognized the tufts of hair coming out of his ears, the length of his moustache, the slight double chin that spilled over the collar of the striped shirt that I knew for a fact to be polyester and not cotton. The familiar sight of his face shocked me precisely because I couldn't put any distance between me, him, the location of the bombing and the news he was reading. What had happened wasn't somewhere else, it was here and now, the death on the screen had spilled too close to me.

Someone switched off the TV and only then did the men of Babur's Lodge turn and notice my presence. They merely tossed the odd opaque glance; none of them smiled. Only Paul grinned and raised his glass. But it didn't feel like a greeting as much as a sort of obscure threat.

"Ah, here you are. So, you couldn't bear to leave, huh?"

I ordered a gin and tonic, then I tried to explain first to the South African, then to General Dynamics, that I had been grounded and I needed to get hold of my friend Hanif, the newscaster, but they just shrugged and ordered another beer. The Dark One and the German had heard what I said perfectly well but decided to ignore me just as the others had done. I asked the staff, but no one had any idea how they could find the number of the TV station in Kabul, as there were no "Yellow Pages" or phone books in the hotel and no one seemed in any way moved by my request for help.

The owner of Babur's Lodge, tracked down on the phone by

the cook, was not coming to the hotel that night. The city was in gridlock because of security and anyway he said he didn't have any rooms available.

"I told you when you came last week that I had a booking. Paul took your room. When he comes to town he stays with us for two or three months, he's an old client," he said.

"But what am I supposed to do?" I was standing in the deserted reception area holding the receiver. I heard my voice boom in the empty room. "The city is at a standstill, I don't even know if I can find a taxi to go looking for another hotel."

"You can sleep on the other bed in my room."

I swung around. It was Paul, who had silently approached.

"Give me that," he said and snatched the phone from my hand.

"It's cool, Ahmed, I'll put her up for tonight."

He hung up and bared his teeth. He had pointy canines, or perhaps that was just the way he looked to me then.

"No, absolutely not." I tried to object, politely, but then in a crescendo. "It's no problem, really. I'm going to look for a hotel right now. I'm sure there must be a room somewhere."

"Where do you think you're going now? There's a curfew. You can't go anywhere."

He touched my arm, indicating that I should follow him to the bar.

"Let's go in there and have a drink. Come on, Maria. It's Maria, isn't it?"

"No, listen, what I really need is to get in touch with our fixer, that guy who reads the news on TV, Hanif. Do you know him? He came to get us this morning, he's quite well—"

"Hey, chill out. I'm not going to eat you. I said you can sleep in the other bed. We can look for your friend tomorrow. Relax now, let's go in there and have a drink."

He put his hand on my shoulder and pushed me lightly but

firmly towards the bar door. His touch felt like handcuffs snapping shut.

Paul insisted on ordering me a second gin and tonic. All within the space of three minutes—as soon as he had offered me his spare bed, leaving me no option—he was treating me as if I were his property and he had made this clear to the others. It was strange, but I had already given in. Maybe it was the weariness, but I felt exhausted, like I had actually been to Europe and back; I even felt a sort of hysterical jet lag and slipped into being a hostage without any resistance. Passive, careful to attract as little attention as possible, just like the Defenders had recommended.

Paul, on his third vodka since I had arrived, was now in the process of explaining to no one in particular why this country was going straight to hell. The South African, the Dark One and the German nodded in turn, but each one was thinking about his own stuff.

". . . No one from NATO, none of the diplomats, none of the guys working for intelligence, not a single one of them speaks a word of Dari. They don't know the people, the topography, the history, the culture. They come here for three months max, get astronomical salaries and then go back home again. None of them have a fucking clue how an Afghan's head works. And do you know what that means?"

The others nodded for him to go on, just to keep the background noise of his voice on and be left in peace.

"The helicopters, the cars, the armored vehicles are all crawling with interpreters. And do you know what these interpreters do?"

The others shook their heads. No, they didn't.

"They get paid twice. Once by us, and once by the Taliban, who pay for the information. We're paying spies who are paid again to translate all our information, you see what I mean?"

General Dynamics shook his head, urgently needing to add his bit, to reestablish the authority that Paul was endangering. Perhaps General Dynamics was one of those who came for three months, took the money and ran without understanding a thing.

"It's nothing to do with spies, in the end it's just a question of money," he rebutted. "The Taliban pay double what the Afghan army does. In the Helmand Province, the men get up to twenty bucks a day to fight us and for twenty bucks a family can live for at least two months."

But Paul wasn't listening. He kept haranguing to the wall.

"You want to win the war on terror? You want to eradicate Al Qaeda? Then you've got to hire the guys who can sit with their legs crossed for hours, drink green tea and chew tobacco with every village elder, listen to every bit of local gossip, learn every track, road, name of the tribal leaders. Forget defense specialists, technology, expensive weapons. Hire the anthropologists, the linguists, the mad historians, any genius kid with a Ph.D. in Islamic culture "

I let my eyes drift out of focus. Right at this time of the night my body would have been flying over Iran toward Turkey. And yet here I was, in the company of men I had nothing in common with, one of whom I now was supposed to share a room with. I knew that room, I had slept in it for a week and I knew perfectly well that it did not have twin beds.

The conversation was slackening, had taken a drunken, nasty, end-of-the-night turn: *god-crazed cutthroats . . . blood-thirsty fanatics . . . with an IQ of fifty . . .*

Paul knocked back the last of his vodka and shot me a look. He ran his hand distractedly between his legs, rubbing his dick. He looked at his watch. I remembered what I had felt when Imo and I had first sat among those women in the village school. How they had seemed—compared to Hanif, to his cousin, even to Malik—like characters spat out from another era. But in this particular moment—as hopelessly impotent and frustrated as I was—I felt that the distance between my world and theirs had vanished and we were almost on equal footing. In fact, my nationality, education, race, profession counted zero as far as Paul or the rest of them were concerned. When the money and the guns are in the hands of the men and there's a war outside, a woman who has neither can't do much except what she's told. I sat with my glass of gin and tonic and let this bewildering thought sink in.

Given that what was outside this room terrified me and what was inside it horrified me, I was obliged to choose the lesser evil. I slipped out of the room.

"Where are you going?" Paul asked, suddenly alert.

"To the bathroom, why?"

He nodded. In other words, *he was giving me permission.*

I climbed the stairs to the second floor and sat on a freezing marble step. I trawled the names in the phone book of my cell looking for Imo's number. As soon as she landed in London and got my text, she could send me Hanif's number and it would all be over. It was a question of killing time for a few hours, no mean feat.

Suddenly next to the "I" of "Imo" I read the name of someone I didn't remember meeting.

Jeremy.

Even before I could answer the question "Who is this Jeremy?" I knew—my survival instinct had told me already, a charge of pure adrenaline had made me vigilant, clairvoyant, ready for anything—that his name held my salvation.

Jeremy What's-His-Name. I had stored his number on my phone because Imo's battery was flat. The one who had said, "Come to dinner whenever you want, I'll give you a plate of pasta." Pasta!

"There you are."

Paul was coming up the stairs.

"What are you doing out here?"

He pulled me up. His breath smelled of peanuts and vodka.

He grinned, then touched my hair, my neck. I shook my head.

"Stop it," I said and tried to slide past him. He grabbed my wrist.

"Hey."

I felt his body press on mine, then push me against the wall. The stiffness of his prick beneath the fabric of his pants.

"Don't you want to lie down a bit now?" he slurred.

His hand was already fumbling under my sweater. I pushed him away.

"No. I don't want to. You leave me alone."

"Hey, what's wrong now? What's your problem?"

"Fuck you," I snarled. "Get your hands off me, you filthy motherfucking bastard."

I caught a glitch of surprise in Paul's glassy stare. I gained momentum and pushed him harder. I felt a supernatural force shoot from my shoulder into my fingertips, as if my arm was an extension of the laser-beam sword in *Star Wars*. For a split second I thought I would actually be able to kill him with my bare hands.

He stumbled and nearly tripped on the step of the stairway.

"You'll be so fuckin' sorry if you try and fuck with me," I hissed.

He raised a hand.

"Hey," he said, like a drunk to no one in particular down an alley, and stumbled away.

KABUL'S STREETS WERE deserted and cloaked in snow. The city had sunk into an unearthly calm, more like a suspension than peace. Jeremy's Land Cruiser was the only car on the road.

"I don't get it. Is there a curfew or not?" I asked, alarmed.

"No. This is not an official curfew. There's just nobody around."

"Are you sure? Won't they shoot us on sight?"

"What? No, 'they' won't. It's okay, I told you," he said as he checked the rearview mirror again. "I'm not completely out of my mind yet, you know."

"Sorry. Do I sound paranoid?" I asked.

"Yes."

We smiled at one another. I broke into nervous laughter. I liked him.

He had recognized me at once when I had called him. He remembered both Imo and me perfectly.

I had inundated him with my torrential list of problems. I was stranded, I had no money, I was in the hands of weird guys who—

"Okay, okay, calm down," he had said, stemming the flow of excuses. "I'll be there in ten minutes. Tomorrow we'll call Hanif and tonight you can stay at my place. I've got plenty of room."

Chet Baker's nocturnal trumpet was spreading softly from the CD player. The darkness in Kabul at night was thick as petrol—more like a bottomless pit than an absence of light. Every so often there would be a flicker on the side of the road— it felt like just a quick flutter of wings—but it invariably turned out to be what seemed to always be the same man: the same dark silhouette on every street, walking with the same stride, the same cloak wrapped around his shoulders, the same turban on his head.

As he drove confidently through the pitch-black streets and alleys, Jeremy tried to explain to me what it had been like to be living there for the last two years; how the situation had been getting worse since he had first arrived, it crept along so slowly that it was hard to register; how he felt hope, excitement at first, but then things had gradually worsened, like a fever rising half a degree every day, until one day it was clear to everyone that the country was on its knees again.

"Kamikaze attacks are increasing, security is decreasing, the government is corrupt and the country is in the hands of drug dealers. And this is only the beginning of the bad news. Everyone knows the Taliban are coming back, stronger and stronger. They'll launch their attacks again as soon as the snow melts on the passes."

He seemed permeated by a deep exhaustion, as if he had lost his reserves of good faith.

"My family, my friends back home, even my boss, everyone tells me I should get out. But from here it's hard to imagine that London does really exist somewhere. Even Islamabad seems like a mirage. I'm happily stranded, I guess. Or maybe unhappily, I can't tell which at this point. It must be the Kabul syndrome."

He sounded like someone who had been holding the rearguard to keep watch over a place that had been forgotten by everybody and was slowly falling apart, someone who was going to hold out till the end—for purely sentimental reasons, in any case certainly not for the money—until the day the roof would collapse. Perhaps only then would he give in and pack his suitcase.

"These days, there are fewer and fewer people prepared to work in Muslim countries. You know, there are no more American journalists living full-time in Kabul," he said. "And certainly nobody with wives and kids, that's a given. We're a thinning tribe."

He said this with a mixture of sorrow and pride and looked at me to gauge my reaction. I smiled at him. I wondered whether he wanted me to know he didn't have a girlfriend or a wife.

"Well, maybe that's a good thing. We *should* all leave, proba-bly, and let them decide for themselves," he added, patting his breast pocket in search of his pack of cigarettes. He lit one with-out asking if I minded the smoke, and exhaled deeply, like a long, forced sigh one would perform in front of a doctor.

There were some friends at his house, he said.

"We were having dinner when you called. I hope they left us something to eat."

"I'm sorry you had to get up from the table for me."

"Don't mention it. I'm glad I could help. No, I just said that because maybe some of them will stay over tonight. You know, not everyone likes driving at night, especially after a bombing, so we'll just have to make do the best we can."

"No problem. Listen, I can sleep on the floor."

Jeremy stopped in front of the armored sentry box at his compound.

"You don't have to sleep on the floor. There's a spare guest room. I don't know how comfortable the bed is, though, that's all I meant."

He leaned out the window and greeted the guard—an older man wrapped in a thick coat and a shawl tightened around his head—who opened the gate. It was still very cold, but it had stopped snowing. As I got out of the car my lungs filled with the icy air mingled with the scent of coal and for some reason I felt utterly safe. It was only for a second, but my heart leapt with a sudden bout of intense happiness.

The remains of dinner were left on the table, the ashtrays crammed with butts. At that time of night the generators had been turned off, so the room was lit only by candles dripping onto the lid of a paint tin and a couple of kerosene lamps. There were four people sitting at the table smoking and slowly work-ing their way through a bottle of whiskey.

"This is Maria, a friend of mine, who—surprise, surprise—

has been grounded," said Jeremy, who in the meantime had taken off his boots. I noticed everyone in the room was barefoot except for me and I was smearing the rug with snow and mud.

I made them out by the dim light of the candles. One of the two guys had a thick handmade scarf around his neck and a woolen vest; the other looked bookish, with round glasses, a keffiyeh, an old tweed jacket patched at the sleeves. The two women were both wearing *shalwar kameezes* under thick woolen sweaters. One of them was heavy, with a square jaw, thick wrists and the rosy complexion of a country maiden. The other one was wafer thin; she wore her curly hair piled up on her head like a girl in an Egon Schiele drawing and had long, nervous hands. Jeremy quickly did the introductions. The stocky girl and the man in the vest, Ylva and Fabian, were Swedish, UN staffers; the guy with the keffiyeh, Reuben, was a Spanish journalist; and the blonde, Florence, was a photographer.

I took a closer look at her and realized I had seen her before. It took me a few seconds and then it clicked. It was the French woman Imo and I had briefly met that day with Roshana, the one who had the pictures to go with Imo's story. She looked at me; there was a flicker, but she didn't say anything. Maybe I was one of the many faces she hadn't memorized, or perhaps she had just decided to ignore me.

The house was bare, there were thick rugs on the floor, a brown couch with tattered upholstery, a few pieces of ugly office furniture, probably inherited with the house; a kitschy poster of General Massoud with the inscription "The Lion of Panjshir" on the wall, shelves full of books, a wildly eclectic CD collection. There were bars on the windows, padlocks and chains everywhere. It was a sad house—more like a box designed to contain transient foreigners than a home to anybody. I doubted it had ever had a family living in it or children growing up in it; it had no soul and seemed to possess no memories.

Jeremy made me up a plate of leftovers. Cold spaghetti with congealed tomato sauce.

"Would you like me to heat it up for you?"

"No, please. Really, it's fine like this."

I looked around as the others topped off their glasses with what was left of the whiskey and picked up the thread of their interrupted conversation, a rosary of shocking stories and rumors. This was the drill, by now I had come to know it. As I listened to them recite, I was struck yet again by how little all of us foreigners—including the ones who had lived here for years— seemed to actually know about what was really going on in this country. Their sources were never quoted, their tales sounded more like guesswork, or hearsay. The round of hypotheses must have been a mantra that got repeated every day to keep the worst at bay—another form of exorcism.

The interpreter of a colleague who lived in Herat had his throat cut in broad daylight as an act of retaliation. It seemed that insurgents opened fire on an English convoy in Helmand Province, that their Pakistani friend who worked for a children's aid organization in Bamyan had received a death threat, that the UN personnel were going to be repatriated any day. That today's incident was nothing, just a warning. The big one was coming tomorrow.

There was neither apprehension nor fear in what they said, only weariness. Actually, now that I was able to take a better look at them, they all seemed to have become like their clothes: rumpled, washed out from too much laundering. They had lost shape and luster. Perhaps this progressive discoloration was taking place precisely because they were lacking in the necessary dose of madness and cynicism that the men at Babur's Lodge had, with their automatic weapons on their bedside tables and their stratospheric salaries.

I looked at Florence.

"We've met before, perhaps you don't remember. I came to speak to Roshana with Imogen Glass, the English journalist."

Florence gave me an inquisitive look. Her sweater had slackened around the wrists, the sleeves were too long and covered half of her long, thin hands. She seemed in need of calories and warmer clothes, but was quite beautiful despite her somehow tragic appearance.

"Yes, now I remember. You're the photographer, right?"

"Yes."

She didn't say anything more and started rummaging in the bag hanging off her chair, looking for her cigarettes. I was toying with some breadcrumbs on the table; I could feel Florence's gaze still lingering.

"Did you succeed in photographing the women who attempted suicide?" she asked, and I detected a note of apprehension or suspicion.

"No, of course I didn't."

I didn't offer any explanations. There was a pause. We both pretended to be following the conversation going on around the table. My desire was to ignore her for the rest of the evening. But I swallowed my pride.

"It's likely my colleague will be getting touch with you if she needs any photos," I added. "Roshana told us you've done great work around Herat on the women in the hospital."

She nodded, sucked on her cigarette.

"It depends. I'm trying to do a book with those photos. I don't really want them published beforehand. But if they pay well, maybe it can be arranged. It depends what kind of magazine wants them. I'm not going to sell them just to anybody."

Despite my friendly tone, she was defensive.

"It's the *Observer.* I think it could be worth your while," I said, trying to still sound forthcoming.

Florence shrugged and did the sort of pouting sigh that only the French dare to do. That unbearable emission of breath through pursed lips that sometimes stands for irritation, sometimes for scorn and sometimes simply for tedium.

I didn't let it get to me, although I did find it difficult to warm up to her.

"It was good to see you again," I said as I got up from the table, "but now I'm off to sleep. I'm absolutely exhausted."

I slept on a monastic bed in a small room on the second floor. A *Da Vinci Code* probably left by another passing guest was sitting on the bedside table, a gas stove burning in the corner.

Jeremy had taken me upstairs, showed me the bathroom, taught me how to avoid flooding the shower. He seemed rather drunk when we said good night and I saw him wobble a bit on the stairs as he returned to his guests.

Distant thuds woke me at dawn.

I leapt out of bed like a jack-in-the-box and looked out the window, heart in my throat. The world appeared like the inside of an empty fridge, everything white, the sky opaque like milk. I heard the cars plowing over the asphalt: the ominous thuds were not bombs in the distance but rickety suspensions on the potholes.

There was no one down in the kitchen, but someone had already tidied up. Clean plates were dripping in a rack by the sink, the table had been cleared, the ashtrays emptied. I put on some coffee and sat waiting for it to brew.

The silence of the kitchen was broken only by the ticking of an old-fashioned alarm clock. I realized this was the first time I had been able to sit all by myself and be still since I had left Milan. It was good to feel the quiet. I needed it.

As the smell of coffee filled the room, something slowly insinuated its way under my sternum and gradually spread out lightly, inoffensively, like ink in water. A longing, a sudden burst of nostalgia I didn't even know I had in me.

· · ·

It was almost ten years ago. My mother was in the hospital in the early days of her illness. It was morning; my brother and I had been looking for the doctor all over the ward, desperate to hear what he had to say. Finally, we collapsed in silence outside the nurses' station. There was nothing more we could say to one another. At last, we saw the doctor coming: a surprisingly young man with a pleasant face. For some reason, I thought he might be kinder than an older doctor, friendlier. But as it turned out, he had no time for niceties. "I've seen the scan," he said, but he didn't look at either of us. He was very quick, saying that what he'd seen left no doubt. Leo and I stared at him as he named the thing that was going to kill our mother. It was a difficult word—neither of us was able to retain it to repeat later to our father. The doctor said he was sorry, but I could tell he was impatient to get rid of us. There were other patients, other families, other bad news he had to give.

Later that evening, I painstakingly covered moldings and fixtures in duct tape and repainted the walls of my kitchen in pistachio green, possessed by a relentless determination. I painted all night, cold, till I felt as if someone had thrown a knife between my shoulder blades. As I was cleaning the brushes and the sky was beginning to lighten, I was already planning how I could do the living room and the bedroom in a different color. I checked the hours of the paint store, contemplated going back there as soon as it opened. It seemed very important at the time that I finish right away.

I know what it's like, that new feeling that arises in the proximity of pain. A need for numbness, for a personal anesthetic. When I saw my mother again at the hospital the next day, something had shifted. I was ashamed to admit it at the time, but I had removed myself already, even if by just a fraction.

I had hardened, just when I should have softened.

And now the scene had come to me the way dreams do, unbidden, with staggering clarity.

· · ·

Jeremy was standing in the kitchen doorway watching me cry. He touched my shoulder as he went to turn the coffee off.

"Has something happened?"

"No, nothing. I'm just . . . I don't know . . ." I quickly wiped my nose with my sleeve.

"It's okay. Sugar?"

"No, thanks. Have your friends left?"

"Not all of them. Some are still sleeping."

He sat down, facing me. There was only the sound of the teaspoons stirring the coffee in the cups. I sniffed.

"I'm sorry, it's just that . . ."

"Don't be sorry. You have no idea how many people I've seen burst into tears in this kitchen first thing in the morning. Men lose it too, you'd be surprised, and are much harder to console."

"I bet."

"Normal people are supposed to break down under this kind of pressure. Getting used to it is the first sign of insanity."

"Funny you should say that. I remember you seemed so casual about, you know, the whole security issue when we first came to see you," I said, dabbing my eyes with a paper napkin.

Jeremy laughed. "There are days when I like to act a bit more macho than I am."

I smiled and sipped my coffee.

"This is good espresso."

"Italian. Would you like a chocolate chip cookie? Reuben brought some from Madrid."

He opened a packet of chocolate biscuits and ate one carefully, savoring it. I wondered if Florence was still there. And in which room.

Reuben—the Spanish journalist with the keffiyeh—stumbled into the kitchen in a worn-out T-shirt and an Indonesian sarong tied around his hips, barefoot. He cleared his throat and greeted me with a friendly smile, then started opening and closing the kitchen cabinets.

"That red wine last night. Oh, man . . . or maybe it was the scotch," he said in his nearly perfect American English.

Jeremy stood up and touched him lightly on the shoulder.

"Hey, sit down, let me put on some more coffee."

Reuben smiled.

"Thanks. That would really help."

I watched them move around the kitchen, with ease, as if they both were equally familiar with its space; I detected a slight, almost imperceptible stir of excitement in the room, as if a different type of energy was generated by their bodies. Suddenly it struck me that they could be the couple of the house and that I had gotten it all wrong.

After he had put the coffee back on the burner Jeremy looked at his watch.

"I have to dash. Today is going to be crazy at work, because of yesterday's attack. I don't think I can meet you and Mark for lunch," he said to Reuben.

"Don't worry, it was just a thought."

Jeremy pulled a business card out of his wallet and handed it to me.

"Here's Hanif's number. You'll see, he'll get you on some flight or other. The best thing, usually, is to get on a flight to Islamabad, those are more likely to leave. And in any case everything there is simpler, as you know. Islamabad has a normal airport, I mean, not a madhouse like this one. Let me know if you need any help. Anyway, you've got my number."

"Thanks. You've been so . . ." I couldn't think of a good enough adjective. "I don't know what I would've done without—"

"Yes, yes, yes." He waved a hand to stop me and grinned. "In case you still can't get out, call me at the office. This evening, if there isn't another blast like yesterday, we could go out to dinner, or we could watch a DVD back here. If you like."

When I rang Hanif, he actually sounded frightened, as if it were his fault that I was still in Kabul. He kept repeating that he was sorry, that he should never have left me on my own, that he should have waited until the plane took off.

But I was so happy to hear his voice at last that I kept laughing—I felt like I had been fortuitously reunited with a long-lost brother after many adventures—and I kept reassuring him that it didn't matter, not to worry, it wasn't at all his fault. All I wanted was for him to help me get on a flight, any flight; I absolutely had to get out by that evening at the latest. Could he help?

"Yes, yes, yes, not a problem. I'll be there as soon as I can," he said breathlessly. "There's very much traffic. It will take me a while because I am on the other side of Kabul."

When he showed up at Jeremy's house two hours later—in the meantime I had hungrily read an old "Style" issue of *The New Yorker* cover to cover lying on the couch next to my packed bags—Hanif looked more disheveled than I had ever seen him; even his usually impeccable Inspector Clouseau uniform was crumpled. He smiled at me with such warmth that it moved me.

"Today is red alarm," he announced as if this were a piece of good news while he pushed my luggage into the trunk.

"How come?"

"They say that perhaps the big attack will be today. They said it on Al Jazeera too."

"I heard it. Do you think that's possible?"

Hanif shrugged and jingled the keys to the Ford, eager to get in the car and start the day. Obviously this type of news had long since ceased to affect Kabulis. The rumor of another explosion probably sounded to them like a snowstorm announced on the weather forecast.

"Who knows. And anyway, what can we do?"

The snow was reduced to a dirty brown sludge and there was a stench of kerosene in the air from all the burning stoves in the city, black fumes, car horns blaring.

We moved slowly forward, Hanif speaking on his cell.

I watched him, impressed as ever by how resourceful he was—and, judging by how crumpled his clothes were, I had a feeling he might have slept in them. His hair too needed a wash.

He nodded, thanked someone and shut the phone. Maybe, he said, a friend of his at a travel agency could help us. We drove in silence for a while.

"How is your wife?" I asked him.

Hanif's expression changed, as if my question had finally given him permission to talk about what was really on his mind.

"She's not well. She has a high fever."

"Where? Is she still in the hospital?"

"Yes." He ran his hand over his moustache. "Yes. There is an infection. She is rather ill."

"But what is it? Why does she have an infection?"

"I don't know. Another doctor is coming today to see her."

"But when I called you this morning, were you at the hospital with her?"

He nodded, as if it were normal to just leave her there and rush to pick me up. And now I felt too guilty to ask just how bad she was; I didn't dare ask whether there was a risk she'd lose the baby. All I said was that I was sorry I'd had to bother him, that I would have much rather left him in peace. But Hanif smiled and swore it wasn't a problem at all, that it was his duty to see to my safety until the end and that I mustn't worry.

We both knew this wasn't true, but we both pretended that it was and crawled on through the traffic in silence.

· · ·

At the travel agency, there was a crowd of people who had been waiting in a disorderly queue for a long time. I recognized some of the passengers from my supposed flight the day before. The same cloud of heavy malcontent had followed them and now hovered over their heads here too.

A big man with gray hair and the weathered, Scandinavian looks of a ski instructor (aid worker? diplomat? medical personnel?) looked up from the five-hundred-page book he had brought with him—some kind of narrative history, or so it seemed from the golden lettering on the jacket—as he noticed Hanif jump the queue. He watched him extricate himself from the crowd with insouciance, lean on the counter and call to one of the employees. Now the man was glaring at me with open hostility to demonstrate that he knew perfectly well that I was the one who had unleashed my fixer like that, in blatant disregard of precedence. Others noticed too, but they were Afghans and therefore used to the shortcuts that Westerners thought they deserved.

Out of the corner of my eye I followed Hanif's negotiations, the dubious face the clerk pulled as he looked at my Turkish Airlines ticket. The man rubbed his chin. Hanif interrogated him repeatedly. The man kept staring at the ticket, then the screen, without replying.

Hanif came over and handed me my ticket. He told me the airport was still closed and might reopen only tomorrow. He also informed me that if I wanted to leave on the next flight, they'd have to issue a new ticket to Dubai with PIA and then on to Europe. Apparently my best bet was to leave the money with his friend behind the counter, so that as soon as the flights resumed, he could immediately reserve me a seat.

"All these people are waiting to get on the first flight out of Kabul, you see. He is my friend, if you leave him the money he can do us a favor and buy the ticket straightaway."

"Of course. How much is it?"

"Seven hundred dollars."

I held out my credit card. Hanif scratched his head dubiously.

"No cash?" he asked.

"No. No cash." I waved my Visa card. "But this is like cash."

Hanif showed his friend behind the counter the card, but the man shook his head.

"Only cash," Hanif reported back dejectedly, as if to excuse a country that had not yet entered the world of plastic money.

"But I *have* to leave tomorrow," I insisted with a new, harsh edge to my voice.

Hanif nodded and stared gravely at the toes of his shoes.

"What can we do?" I prodded.

We looked at each other. We both knew that there was only one solution to the problem.

Hanif put his hand in his pocket.

"I can lend you the money," he said with only the slightest hesitation. He took out the wad of dollars, his pay for a week's work. It was a fat roll of fifties.

"Hanif. You don't have to do this," I said weakly.

"Yes. It's the only way. We must pay right now."

I knew it too. Yet I couldn't believe the swift certainty of his offer.

"Hanif, I swear, I'll get it back to you straightaway. I give you my word of honor. I'll send it to you through Jeremy. Next week at the latest, you'll have it back."

He smiled politely.

"Sure. Not a problem," he said and went over to the counter. I watched him as he slid the rubber band off the roll and, with the same experienced movement of the thumb, counted out fourteen bills.

There was nothing else we could do but wait. Once we got

back into the car I suggested that we go to the hospital and check on his wife. I was tired of being only a nuisance.

"We'll wait for the doctor, so you can talk to him," I said.

"No, the hospital is a long way away," Hanif said, "and besides, it's not a very nice place. I'll take you to Jeremy's office. It's better."

"No, no, please don't worry about me now. Let's go and see how your wife is. I'll sit somewhere and read a book. Look, I have a book in my purse."

Hanif glanced at his watch. He got in the driver's seat and turned the key in the ignition. Then he smiled uneasily.

"All right, then. Let's go."

We crossed the city again in the opposite direction. The sky had lowered and was looming heavily over us like a comforter filled with snow.

"Tell me about your wife," I said to him. "Tell me how you two met."

I was suddenly aware I had started speaking to him in the same tone Imo would have used, a cross between affectionate and condescending. I was also aware that I was beginning to feel rather at ease in Imo's shoes.

"She was the daughter of one of my neighbors in Peshawar. Her mother is a schoolteacher and her father is a printer. They are good family, very well educated. They used to live here in Kabul, but they fled to Pakistan when the Taliban first started. I used to always see her coming home from college. She was always loaded down with books. She was reading even on the auto rickshaw."

Hanif paused, looked straight ahead, waiting for the traffic to untangle.

"I liked that."

"What?"

"That she read. I didn't want a wife from a village. I wanted someone I could talk to. About anything. About the world."

"Of course. Absolutely. That's important." I encouraged him: "And then?"

"After I spoke to her father, you know, about marrying her, she said to him, 'All right, but I'll only marry him on the condition that he does not bring me back to Kabul.' Because at the time Kabul was under strict Taliban rule and she did not want to live in a place where she couldn't work. When we first met she said, 'If I have a daughter, I want her to be educated.' I promised her I would. We only came back to Kabul when the Taliban were forced out. And now look. We might have to flee again." He sighed.

I thought it might be a good idea to steer the conversation away from gloomy political predictions.

"Can I ask you a personal question?"

"Yes, of course."

"Why did you choose her precisely? How did you know you'd get on for the rest of your lives?"

Hanif thought this over. Something in him loosened, warmed up.

"I don't know, but the first time I saw her, I felt something here." He placed his open palm on his chest and flailed it.

"Ah, yes, I see. We say *farfalle nello stomaco.*"

"Pardon?" Hanif frowned.

"Butterflies in the stomach. See?" I made a flapping movement with my hand. "They move their wings like this."

"Yes, of course, butterflies. Quite right." Hanif nodded energetically and laughed. "And when I saw her eyes," he added.

"Her eyes?"

"Yes. Green. Like those of a cat."

"Was that all it took?"

He nodded.

"We say, if a man feels, then a man *knows.*"

. . .

At the entrance to the Rabia Balkhi Hospital was a sign with a drawing of what looked like a toy gun crossed out and the warning "No Arms Inside."

I followed Hanif along the corridors and we quickly went through the maternity unit, which smelled of Lysol. Voices and noises boomed with a strange echo, like eerie submarine sounds.

I saw a shoeless woman in an apron hosing what looked like sheets stuffed inside aluminum tubs. The water that spilled onto the floor was stained with blood.

Hanif motioned for me to take a seat on a bench in the corridor together with some other women.

"Please sit down. I'll be right back," he said.

The women's heads were covered and only some of them had coats and closed shoes in that freezing temperature. For the most part, they were wearing plastic slippers on their bare feet and thin cotton clothing. Their children at their necks, they clutched plastic thermoses and parcels of home-cooked food they had brought for their relatives. They squeezed in to make room for me, startled by my presence. I smelled spices, kitchen smoke and sweat on their skin and felt their eyes boring through me, checking my clothes, my heavy boots, my bare head. I felt it was too late to pull up my scarf, I would've felt awkward doing it then, but I wished I'd thought about doing it earlier. I took the book out of my bag so they could spy on me in peace.

I could feel them pushing gently in on both sides, very gradually regaining possession of the space they had given up to me. They all looked at me, some of them pointing and whispering to one another. Obviously they wanted me to be part of the group and were disappointed to see me read. One of them patted me on the shoulder and offered me a cup of steaming green tea she had poured from a thermos. Now they all stared at me, encouraging me to drink. I smiled and said, *"Tashakor,"* thank you. They nodded, some laughed, covering their blackened teeth with their hands. I drank a few sips then returned the glass, signaling that I'd had enough. This seemed to make them happy.

An elderly nurse in a white coat opened the glass door to the ward. She gestured towards us with her hand—it was visiting hour at last—and the women gathered their things, rearranged the babies in the blankets, huddled together with their tiffins, children, baskets and thermoses. They turned to look at me, waiting for me to follow, but I waved, as if to say that I was fine where I was, not to worry about me. They waited for a few seconds, then, seeing that I kept shaking my head, they moved off, disappointed, perhaps, to be losing their new object of interest so soon.

"There's a big problem now."

Hanif slumped onto the bench next to me. There was a new heaviness about him. I quickly put my book away.

"My wife needs a transfusion, but in this hospital they do not have her blood type."

"They don't?"

"No. She has Rh-negative"

Hanif looked at his watch.

"What can we do? Unfortunately, I'm not Rh-negative, otherwise I'd . . ." I wanted to have a brilliant idea, suggest something that would save the day, but I couldn't think what.

"Oh, no, please. That is not necessary, but thank you. I have to go and look for it at the other hospital because they don't have a blood bank here. The doctor told me I might find it there."

"Okay, then let's go."

I stood up, gathered my things.

Hanif hesitated for a moment, scratched his head.

"What's wrong?"

"Nothing. Perhaps is best I go. And pehaps you can . . . well, maybe you could stay with my wife so that, if something happens . . . I don't know, in case there's an emergency, at least you can call me. You know, men are not allowed into the wards."

"What do you mean they aren't?"

"No. Out of respect for the other women. Only in critical situation men are allowed to be with them. In the final moments the doctors will let them. And they can enter to collect the remains, of course."

He said this with a strange detachment, as if this were just another custom of the country that he was explaining to a foreigner.

"Of course, absolutely. I'll stay, it's not a problem."

"Her mother and her sister are on their way by bus from Peshawar. My sister is at the doctor's today and our neighbor will come later. So right now there's no woman from the family who can stay here. I'll be as quick as I can, I'll go and come straight back."

"It's fine, really, don't worry."

I switched on my mobile and turned it towards him, miming a connection between our two phones. Hanif nodded, and smiled back.

"All set. Now if anything happens, we're in touch," I said, holding up my phone.

As I sat outside her room, keeping watch over her, it struck me as inexcusable that I'd never asked him her name before.

Hanif had led me through the stairs on the second floor into another ward, where his wife was. I had peeked behind the plastic curtains that shielded the overcrowded rooms, stealing glimpses of rusty iron furniture, chipped tiles on walls, bodies bundled in sheets. There were two women to a bed, with their heads at opposite ends, dozing.

"That's Leyla."

She had a room all to herself. Hanif had pointed her out to me from the corridor. It looked as if it was some kind of emergency room, outfitted with obsolete equipment.

I had taken a seat on a bench in the corridor, right outside her room. The door was ajar and I could see her perfectly from where I was. She had an IV tube in her arm with a bluish liquid flowing into it. Behind her, hanging on the wall, was a chipped oxygen tank. I had a feeling the machinery and the equipment didn't work but just sat there gathering dust. The room, like the rest of the hospital, was freezing.

I'd been sitting there for almost an hour when my cell rang. Imo's number appeared on the display.

"Maria! I just read your text! This is unbelievable. Can you get on the next flight out? I just rang Pierre, he's going to take care of it from his end, tell me if there's anything I—"

"Don't worry, I'm fine. Really. It's okay."

I told her where I was and about Leyla. I tried to sound calm and unaffected by what was happening.

"Darling, I'm going to make sure you get on that plane. They will fly you back on business. Whatever it takes. Don't worry, I'm right on top of this, everyone is."

"Okay, okay, don't worry. I'm fine. I really am."

"You're such a trouper."

I laughed.

"I'm not, actually. You should see this hospital. I'm sitting across from this sign that says 'Laura Bush Maternity Ward.' Next to it there's a sink clogged with filthy water, the window has a shattered pane, pipes are leaking onto the floor, it's just appalling."

"Great. Take a picture."

"I already did. Did you have that bottle of red wine and all the rest?"

"Yes." I heard a chuckle. "Lots of all the rest."

"Okay, then," I said conclusively. I didn't want her to spend a fortune on this call, even though her phone bill probably counted as expenses.

"Wait. Don't rush off," she said. "Guess what? I'm going to pitch a couple of stories out of Afghanistan to my editor at the *Times* magazine. If they like the Roshan idea we may have to go back in right away."

I smiled. Despite the fact that all I wanted at that moment was to board a plane and be homebound, the idea that she was serious about us working together soon cheered me up.

"Maria? Can you hear me?"

"Yes. Yes, I can. Yes, you were saying about the *Times* magazine."

"I'm going to pitch that and the one about opium licenses. I'm going later today."

"You're mad."

"No, I'm not. Just manic. Are you game?"

I paused. She was serious.

"Yeah. Sure. Why not?"

"Wonderful. I just wanted to make sure I could count on you."

It felt good to be listening to her voice again. It reminded me how the atmosphere Imo created wherever she went, that always surrounded her like a room spray, had a much lighter, safer quality than the world I inhabited, especially at that moment. I realized I didn't want to end the phone call because I needed a bit more of that precious scent.

Visiting hours were over, but no one had come to tell me I had to leave, so I didn't move from the bench outside Leyla's room. I kept waiting for Hanif to return from the other hospital and tried to go back to reading my book. Yet it was hard to concentrate on a story, a voice, sitting there, with the thought of Leyla lying in that bed right across from me. She seemed so much weaker and sicker than I had expected her to be. In the time that I had been sitting out there, no one had come to check on her. I couldn't figure out whether she had been forgotten—I wouldn't even know whom to ask—so I lifted my eyes from the book and tiptoed over to her bed.

I leaned over and looked at her closely.

Hanif hadn't exaggerated: she was exquisite. She had very white skin, smooth, almost translucent. Her mouth pale, fleshy; a shadow of down over her top lip. Beneath the closed eyes, two dark, almost purple crescents that underscored the pallor of her face. Some auburn locks had strayed from her headscarf and covered her cheekbones and I delicately pushed them aside with the tip of my finger. She didn't stir. Her body seemed very small, almost bony, save for her round, full, pregnant belly.

I was hoping she'd open her eyes so I could see them too, those cat-green eyes Hanif had described. I would've liked her to see me, so that I could smile, squeeze her hand, tell her that everything was okay, her husband was coming back soon. That everything was going to be all right with the baby.

At first I wasn't quite sure why I did this, but I took my digital Leica out of my bag. As I pointed it at her I realized what an aggressive gesture it was in this situation. And yet I couldn't help myself; I had this urgent need—at last alone, nobody stopping me, no fear of offending her—to see her up close through my lens.

Now her skin was perfectly in focus; I could make out the tiny pores. What I saw wasn't just her flawless complexion but a face that was losing heat and color and was becoming more and more remote, otherworldly, because of what was leaving her. Leyla didn't appear to be suffering, or even sleeping, for that matter. She looked as if she had withdrawn into some deep recess, as though this were merely her vacated body, smooth and cold as a beautiful statue lying on a marble bed. Suddenly I felt a new determination, as if this photo was the most important one of all, the one I'd be ready to risk anything for. I don't think I realized it just then, but what pushed me to capture her image was probably my sense that she was slipping away. I wanted to retrieve her somehow.

I pressed the shutter release. She didn't open her eyes. I did it again. And again. I ran my hand over her shoulder. I let it rest on her skin. It felt cold, stiff, so I pulled the covers up. But the feeling of that coldness lingered on my fingers.

I ran out to find someone, hoping they could reassure me, someone who would tell me that everything was under control, that there was nothing to fear. As I walked the deserted corridor, hearing the wailing of newborn babies filtering from the rooms, doors slamming, footsteps quickening, metallic cabinet doors creaking, as I went in the direction of these sounds in search of someone who would reassure me that, really, I needn't worry about her, I was assailed by a frightening thought: while I had been holding the lens so close to Leyla's face I hadn't even checked to see whether she was actually still breathing.

Everything dilated and softened as in a dream. The corridors stretched, they became infinite, just like those in nightmares. I went into the rooms looking for a nurse, an orderly, and yet all I could see was women sleeping, their breath heavy and stale. They all looked abandoned to me, like bodies piled up one on top of the other. As I went in and out, in and out, opening and closing doors, I realized how this situation was deadly serious. How hopeless. How could I have ignored the pallor, the temperature of Leyla's body? Everything had been telling me what I wanted to ignore. Life was rapidly flowing out of her. I couldn't figure out what would be the right thing to do: whether it was more urgent to go on searching for help throughout that frozen labyrinth, or to stay close to her. Suddenly, the fact that I had left her alone seemed terrible. I thought of Obelix. How

I had held his hand till the end. I couldn't bear that I had abandoned her.

I tried to ring Hanif, but a mechanical voice in Dari told me
he was out of range. But even if I had reached him, what else
could he do, other than what he was doing already? As I strode
back to Leyla's room, I came across a woman with bare feet in
a green plastic apron. I pointed to Leyla's door and shouted,
"Doctor, doctor!" The woman nodded and moved away, but I
didn't know whether she had understood that she had to go and
get someone.

And as I entered the room again, I saw her eyes. And a look I
can't forget.

The green eyes were open, wide and staring, as if she had
just woken from a nightmare. I rushed to her and took her hand
in mine. I leaned over her and saw her pupils dilate and shrink.
The dark pupil, encircled by specks of gold navigating in the
moss green of the iris. Yes, they were the eyes of a cat, but now
they were staring at me, alarmed, questioning.

Where am I? Who are you? What's happening? Am I dying?

Her breathing had changed. It was shallow and rasping now.
As if she couldn't get enough oxygen into her lungs.

"Okay, it's okay," I whispered and stroked the back of her hand.
It was cold like stone. "Hanif is coming. Hanif is on his way."

It was dark when Hanif came back. He had managed to get
hold of only one bag of blood for the transfusion. He said that
was all he'd been able to find in the whole city.

"And I went to pick up your ticket," he said, as if it were
quite normal to have stopped off at the agency. "Your flight is
tomorrow at nine a.m."

The envelope with the agency's logo had my name on it,
misspelled.

"Oh, Hanif. Thank you, you shouldn't have. I would have
done it later."

"It's nothing. It was on my way."

In the meantime, a cousin and the neighbor had arrived. They were bony young women with the same unhealthy complexion that comes from spending too much time indoors. At first they had seemed more taken by my presence than by Leyla's pallor and stillness. Now they fretted around the bed, straightening up sheets and pillows.

Hanif was filling them in in Dari. They kept nodding and at the same time checking me out, sneaking sideways glances. Hanif was speaking rapidly, with a more authoritarian tone than I was accustomed to hearing him use. Then he leaned over Leyla and whispered something to her.

"Her breathing is . . ." His voice had tensed up. He brushed her face with his fingertips. He too looked pale, rigid with fear.

"Yes, I know," I said quickly. "We must call someone. Now."

"They're coming. I left the blood bag downstairs and they said they're getting ready to—"

"No. They must come *now*," I said forcefully. "Tell them to run over here fast. We can't wait another minute."

Hanif stared into my eyes for a second, then cleared his throat and looked around.

"You'll stay here, won't you? Just in case . . ."

He didn't finish the sentence, pulled his phone out of his pocket and looked at me. We nodded at each other and he was gone.

I sat on the bench outside the room for what seemed an eternity, while the cousin and the neighbor sat by Leyla's bed in the room. I kept my eyes fixed on them, ready to read any sign that something new was happening, and constantly checked the swinging door at the end of the corridor. The two women had taken out some food from a plastic container and were eating slowly with their fingers, cross-legged on the floor. They seemed quiet, as if they were sitting in their own kitchen. At last I saw Hanif show up, out of breath and in the wake of a tall, portly woman with thick glasses, a mole on her cheek and jet-black hair shot with a streak of white. I figured she must be the doctor. She was wearing a stained white coat and was speaking loudly to a couple of nurses who were following behind.

Now everything happened fast, in a succession of orders, people rushing, the doctor raising her voice, the nurses hurrying in and out of the room. Whereas before everything had been still and silent, suddenly it turned into chaos. A whirl of people, apprehension, adrenaline. Even though I couldn't make out what they were saying, I sensed that we had moved into another realm. I saw Leyla being wheeled out on a gurney. I caught a glimpse of her face, her eyes still closed, the lids so heavy they seemed sewn shut. She was being pushed with such haste, her head flopped from side to side as if her neck were broken. And this was the last I saw of her.

The doctor spoke quickly to Hanif, in an urgent tone. He looked at her with a pleading expression and then, just before she left, he put his hand on his heart and whispered, *"Tashakor, tashakor . . ."*

He looked at me with shiny eyes and mumbled something. I didn't catch what he said. I asked him to repeat it.

"They're giving her a Cesarean. They're going to try and save the baby."

But I couldn't figure out whether this meant it was still possible to save Leyla.

Then I found myself alone once more in the large, empty corridor. The hospital sounds reverberated, cavernous and obscure. I stood at the window for a few minutes, looking out at the snowflakes that had started falling in the deserted courtyard. Only now was I aware of the cold that had seeped into my bones.

I called Jeremy's number. He said, "Yes, I know. The Rabia Balkhi Hospital. I'll be there in forty-five minutes."

• • •

It must have been nearly two in the morning.

We had gone through a whole bottle of corky wine between the two of us and we were now sipping vodka from small coffee cups. The remains of a burnt omelette sat on the table next to the overflowing ashtray. We'd come home from the hospital hours before, but Jeremy hadn't been able to get through to Hanif on his cell until eleven thirty.

There was nothing they could do, he had said. The blood wasn't nearly enough for a transfusion, and then there were other complications. But the baby had survived. A girl.

"She's very small, but the doctor says she will be all right," Hanif had said.

I motioned to Jeremy to hand me the phone, but as soon as I heard Hanif's voice, I knew I couldn't go on.

"Hanif . . . Hanif . . ." I whispered into the phone. "I'm so sorry."

"Thank you, thank you. You're very kind. I appreciate everything you did. Thank you, Maria."

His voice cracked slightly. Like glass.

"No, I'm the one who should be . . . Really, Hanif, anything you . . . I'm so sorry . . . I just wanted you to know that if you need any—"

I stuttered, unable to take that extra step and go beyond the propriety of our exchanges. I ended up sniffing, as Hanif remained politely silent on the other end of the line.

This man who was so kind, so composed, so understated in his grief.

"Please forgive me for tomorrow morning . . ." he said.

"What for?"

"Unfortunately I can't take you to the airport. In the morning I have to . . ."

"Please, Hanif, don't even think about it. You are the one who must forgive me. Because of me and Imo you didn't get to spend those last days with Leyla. I was . . . and Imo too . . . we were so—" Suddenly I remembered Hanif's absorbed expression while driving, the way he'd been constantly struggling to get a signal on his phone, waving and talking in the wind, up and down any hill. "Oh, my God, I am so, so sorry."

But each and every word that came to mind seemed inadequate and too small.

I was leaving Kabul, thanks to a ticket paid for with half of Hanif's salary, a sum I had accepted without hesitation. I had felt, no longer than a few hours ago, that I had every right to do so; at the time it hadn't seemed possible that someone else might be in greater peril than me. If it's true we are all more dignified in the face of death, well, in the face of this death, I'm afraid I wasn't able to feel dignified at all.

Jeremy was smoking, staring at the bottom of the ashtray as he stirred up the butts with the tip of his umpteenth cigarette. Bread crumbs were clinging to the woolly down of his sweater; he brushed them off with the back of his hand.

"I didn't know her, I had never seen her," he said as he spit away a scrap of tobacco stuck to his lip. "You know someone for a long time, you do so many things together, once he even saves your life and then . . . you realize you've never been to his house, you don't even know what his wife looks like. It's depressing."

I asked him whether he was going to the funeral. He shrugged.

"I don't know. I don't think so."

"Why? It would mean a lot to him, I'm sure."

Jeremy sighed.

"It's different here. It's a more closed ceremony. For non-Muslims, I mean. Anyway, I don't know. I'll see."

We sat in silence, trying to deal with our awkwardness and the sense of inadequacy that had followed us all the way to his place from the hospital. We didn't talk about it, but we both shared the knowledge that we—us, the foreigners—didn't know what to do with ourselves at a time like this. When all that was needed was to be able to be close. To Hanif. To one another.

"Never once in these ten days did he say anything that hinted . . ." I began. I felt guilt, shame. I had to justify my carelessness. "I mean, I don't think he had any idea it was this serious, otherwise I'm sure he would have—"

"Of course he didn't know," Jeremy interrupted me. His voice had a bitter strain. "But he needed to work, he needed the money. He couldn't afford to sit by her bed and monitor the situation closely. Which is what he's hating himself for."

There was a pause. I felt sick to my stomach.

"I've borrowed half of his money to pay cash for my ticket," I confessed.

Jeremy looked at me, incredulous. He buried his face in his hands. I rushed to defend myself.

"This was when I had no idea that this was going to happen, I swear I—"

"How much?"

"Seven hundred dollars."

Jeremy stared at me. He shrugged. "Fuck."

"I told him you could advance him the money, that I'd pay you back and—"

"Of course I will."

"If you could let him have it tomorrow. I thought he might need it now for . . ." I paused. "For the funeral."

"Sure, no problem."

"It's really important."

"I know, I know. Don't worry, I won't forget." Jeremy poured more vodka in his cup and gulped it down in one go.

"If Hanif's wife didn't make it in a hospital in the center of Kabul," he said, "just imagine the other women in the rest of the country. In winter, all the roads are blocked with snow. If there's an emergency, nothing can get through, no helicopters, no trucks, nothing. One in seven Afghan women dies in childbirth. Did you know that? It's horrendous."

He exhaled the last of the smoke and ground the butt forcefully in with the others.

I thought of how Imo and I had been mainly concerned with bringing our goods back home and getting out as fast as possible and in one piece.

"What kills me is that we were too busy doing a story on violence against women to pay attention to the fact that one of them was dying of childbirth. If that wasn't shameful I'd say it's ironic."

"It's both." Jeremy was biting his nails, staring at the wall, his eyes going out of focus. "And that's exactly the point. As a Western journalist I have to decide each day which portion of these people's suffering is going to be my theme of the day and which is the portion I'm going to have to ignore so it doesn't get in the way."

I shook my head and we remained silent.

Jeremy got up and slipped a CD into the slot. Now the notes began to fill the room, slowly swelling, spreading like a fog that saturated the void that had come between us. Jeremy stretched out on the couch and held his hand out to me.

"Come here. Get those shoes off."

I slid in next to him and laid my head on his shoulder. His arm squeezed me lightly, with delicate pressure. I adjusted myself to find my position. I listened to his breathing and the music.

"What is it?"

"Some guy from Kentucky. I don't remember his name."

"Where is Reuben?" I asked after a silence.

"He's in bed. He has to get up very early tomorrow."

So I had been right. I knew nothing was going to happen between us and that made me feel better. We just needed to generate some warmth to balance out the cold in the place that has been left empty. I closed my eyes.

"I'll take you to the airport tomorrow," he said.

"Thank you."

The tip of my nose brushed against his neck. I got a whiff of his scent; it was dry, saline, like a shell found in the sand.

"Are you cold?"

"No, I'm fine."

"Then let's stay here."

From so close I could make out his lashes, strangely long for a man, the short bristles of the sandy beard that had started growing on his chin, the whole magnified panorama of his features. It had been a long time since I'd heard the regular breathing of a man so close, his warm breath on my face.

We fell asleep like this, without speaking. At some point during the night I felt Jeremy getting off the couch. He returned with a quilt that he lightly laid over me. He was careful not to wake me and he lay down next to me again. I settled into the same hollow in his shoulder, pretending it was an automatic movement made in the unconsciousness of sleep, for the sheer pleasure of feeling myself welcomed again, as if we were a couple used to sleeping like this every night and this was our usual position.

I got up before dawn, leaving Jeremy fast asleep on the couch.

I wandered through the living room, then walked into his small study. It was cluttered with newspapers, books and thick folders. I sat at his desk and quickly checked my e-mail on his laptop. I was hoping to find a message from my father or from Leo. I needed to hear their voices, to know they'd be expecting me. Instead I found an e-mail from Pierre.

"Maria, Imo has been raving about you, the editor is very excited and she wants to use the feature as a cover story. The problem is that, according to Imo, you didn't succeed in getting the picture of any woman who had attempted suicide, which is what we'll need for the title page. Imo has mentioned you spent the day at the hospital in Kabul because of a problem with your fixer's wife, so I'm writing you in haste, hoping this reaches you before you leave. Please, please, try and shoot that picture in there. We need a strong image of a suffering, beautiful woman. At this point it doesn't even matter if we see the burns or not. Just give it a try, will you? It would be a shame if we had to purchase the photo from someone else. Don't forget you got the Barbie doll pix by a fluke!"

I didn't write back. I couldn't face having to explain.

I made myself a cup of coffee. It was still dark outside. I sat and waited for the sun to come up behind the mountain.

The sky had cleared. My head still hurt from the vodka, but it felt lighter: the bitterness, the despair that I had felt the previous night talking to Jeremy had vanished like vapor dissolving in the first morning light. The light that was going to be so beautiful again.

It was then, as I watched the first ray blink behind the dark silhouette of the mountain, that I knew I was going to miss everything about this place. I had fallen in love again and I hadn't even known it.

I heard the first cart stumble over the potholes, a man's voice singing in the distance. Soon the streets of Kabul would be crowded again with men shrouded in their camel pattus, the market stalls would be loaded with shiny apples and pomegranates.

This was another day, and everyone in this city needed another dose of hope in order to get through it.

I had touched Leyla's cold skin, her tiny body. I had held her hand, whispered in her ear. I had been the last person she'd seen when she had opened her eyes for just a moment. Now I was leaving Kabul with a different heart. I had jumped off the diving board and floated back to the surface. And what I saw now from the window looked beautiful—heartbreaking, sure— but nothing I saw felt so distant or alien anymore. A tiny part of me belonged to it now. In some strange way, I knew it had changed me.

Yes, I was in love again.

And I wasn't running away. I was only going.


THE PLANE ON THE SCREEN is now tracing the route backwards from Asia to Europe. From my seat I follow the icon on the map: I see Dushanbe, Samarkand, Tashkent, Baku, Tehran, and then Budapest and Baden. There's a feeling of tenderness in this backwards journey, I can't explain why.

I recall some images, random fragments.

The way the women I met in the village opened their hands, turning the palms up and running them flat over their faces to wipe away either tears or sweat, in a gesture that was at once feral and graceful. And how Malik, when he spoke, offered his words one by one and every now and again made a particular gesture, bringing his thumb and forefinger together then opening the fingertips again as if he wanted us to receive these particular words one by one, set apart from the rest.

As if he was placing them, gently, on the surface of water. Letting the river take them, like an offering.

The sky is lightening as I'm flying above the Hindu Kush. Imo must be just waking up next to the man she made love to last night; Jeremy is rinsing my coffee cup in the kitchen, wiping away the dark ring I left on the Formica table. Zuleya is probably back in the village from the hospital and is blowing on the fire while the water boils for tea and the bread bakes in the terra-cotta oven. And Hanif.

Hanif is getting ready to bury his wife.

I don't know what it is that holds all these images together, but there's something that threads them one after another like glass beads on a string. And for an instant no one seems distant or separated from the others anymore.

I don't know how to explain this—how to translate the thought—but I feel the excitement, and a sudden hope. I keep feeling it with my hand.

It feels round, its surface cool and smooth, like a shiny pearl that I keep turning and turning between my fingertips.

From: Hanif Massoudi [mailto:h.massoodi@yahoo.com]
To: Maria Galante [mailto:m.galante@fastwebnet.it]
Subject: Greetings

Dear Maria,

I am glad you had a good trip and that you have been reunited with your family. I hope that your father's health is good and that you are all well.

Thanking God I am still alive (every day we thank him for this here in Kabul!) and as you know God Almighty has granted me the gift of a daughter who every day grows more beautiful. Thank you for sending me the seven hundred dollars through Jeremy, I am very grateful to you. I particularly want to thank you for the photograph you sent. It is a truly beautiful portrait and does justice to how I remember my wife and I will always keep it in my heart. The portrait is in a frame next to my bed and it's the first thing I see in the morning when I wake up. Thus, one day little Leyla will also know how beautiful her mother was. For this we will always thank you, Maria, and for your kindness.

Let me know if you ever need anything, I will be always happy to help you.

May peace and God's blessings be upon you.

Hanif

# Acknowledgments

I'm deeply grateful to my editor, Robin Desser, and to my agent, Toby Eady.

I want to thank Angus MacQueen, Joe Oppenheimer and Mark Brickman, without whom this book could not have been written.

I also would like to acknowledge Susan Adler and Filippo di Robilant.

A heartfelt thanks to Hanif Sherzad.

A breakthrough new collection of stories from

# Francesca Marciano

# *The Other Language*

"An astonishing collection written with extraordinary clarity and elegance."
—*Jhumpa Lahiri*

"Worldly, political, funny."
—*Gary Shteyngart*

"Outstanding." —*Tom Rachman*

Coming Spring 2014 in hardcover and eBook from Pantheon.
Please visit PantheonBooks.com

Printed in the United States
by Baker & Taylor Publisher Services